H. C. Clarke

Diary of the War for Separation

A Daily Chronicle of the Principal Events and History of the Present Revolution

H. C. Clarke

Diary of the War for Separation
A Daily Chronicle of the Principal Events and History of the Present Revolution

ISBN/EAN: 9783337033682

Printed in Europe, USA, Canada, Australia, Japan

Cover: Foto ©Andreas Hilbeck / pixelio.de

More available books at **www.hansebooks.com**

DIARY

OF THE

War for Separation,

A DAILY CHRONICLE

OF THE

PRINCIPAL EVENTS AND HISTORY OF THE PRESENT REVOLUTION,

TO WHICH IS ADDED

NOTES AND DESCRIPTIONS OF ALL THE GREAT BATTLES

INCLUDING WALKER'S NARRATIVE OF THE BATTLE OF SHILOH

PREFACE.

~~~~~~~

The following compendium of the principal events in the History of the old Union have been gathered from reliable data. The matter was originally prepared for the "Confederate States Almanac," for 1862, and is now re-published with some corrections, and many additions.

The Diary of the War has been compiled with care and considerable labor, having to search and sift out dates and facts from the often-times contradictory statements of dispatches and correspondence. Great pains have been taken to avoid errors; and we believe that the facts are correct, although in many instances an approximation to correctness is all that can be obtained in a matter like this, made up from the sources at hand. The losses of the Confederates in battle was made from official Reports, whenever such reports have been published, and from reliable correspondence. The Federal losses in battle have been taken from the reports of Confederate officers, as no reliance can be placed in Federal accounts. It is a notorious fact that they are always underrating their losses in every engagement with the Southern forces. Their official Reports are seldom, if ever, published.

The Narrative of the Battle of Shiloh was written by Alexander Walker, of the New Orleans Delta. The sketch was published in parts, in the columns of the Delta, and is now published complete for the first time. It is one of the most graphic descriptions of a battle ever written.

POLITICAL REVIEW OF THE OLD UNION

The movement that threw off the rule of the mother country began in the New England Colonies. These were settled by those Puritans who effected the revolution of 1620, and decapitated Charles I. The Southern colonies were occupied by a more loyal class. To the noble family of Baltimore was granted, by Royal Charter, the province of Maryland. To other staunch adherents of the crown were accorded grants and privileges in Virginia, North and South Carolina, and Georgia.

With antecedents so opposite both North and South joined heartily in the War of Independence, making equal sacrifices and dividing fairly its triumphs. In 1781, the struggling States formed a Confederation, and essayed self-government. The written Charter of 1789 followed the form and usages of the British Constitution. Supreme power was divided between the executive and legislative branches; but all were elective. The executive power was vested in one person for a term of four years, with special duties assigned. The Legislature was divided into two Houses, with separate prerogatives. All power not positively delegated to the Federal Government was reserved to the States.

George Washington was the first Federal magistrate, chosen from a list of twelve candidates.

Up to this period, the politicians of the country had, first, contended in a body against the supremacy of the mother country ; and, next, had united their energies in the structure of a Republican Constitution.

During President Washington's term, they divided into two hostile parties, each striving for office through the profession of opposite principles.' The New England States, led by John Adams, advocated the power of the Federal Government, even to straining the Constitution. This was the Federal party. The Southern States, led by Thomas Jefferson, maintained State rights against Federal encroachment. This was the Democratic party.

In 1797, John Adams, of Massachusetts, was elected President of the Confederacy. During his term the Alien* and Sedition† laws were passed by the Federal Congress. These enactments were opposed by the statesmen of the South, since, in their opinion, they invested the Executive with powers not conferred by the Constitution and inimical to popular rights. The creation of a National bank was also a subject of keen controversy. The public men of the North sustained it with energy, while those of the South opposed it as unconstitutional and of doubtful expediency.

In 1801, Thomas Jefferson, of Virginia, was elected President. During this term, the New England States displayed a bitter animosity to the South, which arose, chiefly, from the South having put a limit to the slave-trade, in which these States were profitably engaged. When, therefore, President Jefferson proposed the purchase of Louisiana from France, the Eastern States violently resisted, because it increased the territory and power of the South. Congress empowered the purchase, April, 1803.

In 1805, Thomas Jefferson was re-elected to the Presidency. His second term was troubled by the war between

---

* By the Alien law, June, 1800, the President might order all such aliens as he deemed dangerous, to quit the country, on pain of three years' imprisonment and civil disability.

† By the Sedition law, any person who should libel the President, or either House of Congress, should be fined $2,000, and be imprisoned for two years.

England and France. The Berlin and Milan decrees of Napoleon, and the Orders in Council of the British Government, equally assailed American interests. Our vessels, bound either to English or French ports, incurred capture and confiscation. This left but one alternative, either to abandon our trade with Europe, or go to war to protect it. To escape the latter, President Jefferson recommended an Embargo Act, to put a temporary stop to all our foreign trade. This was vehemently opposed by the New England States, because their interests, being chiefly commercial, were seriously damaged. The Embargo Act was passed by Congress in December, 1807 ; whereupon the Eastern States threatened to secede from the Union, and form a Northern Confederacy.

In 1809, James Madison, of Virginia, was elected President. Soon after his accession, March, 1809, the Embargo Act was repealed, to appease the New England States ; and a less stringent law, the Non-intercourse Act, was passed by Congress, May, 1809, which prohibited trade with England and France. New England, however, carried on an indirect trade with Europe, through Canada. In spite of all these precautions by the Government, our interests and dignity were incessantly outraged by England. Finally, the indignation of the country compelled Congress to declare war, May, 1812.

In 1813, James Madison was re-elected President. During the war, the Government was supported by direct taxes and requisitions upon the States; but the New England States refused for the most part, to contribute.* The war closed, January, 1815. To rescusitate the Federal treasury, a new financial policy was inaugurated. A tariff of high dut. was passed by Congress, April, 1816. New England advocated this law, because, during the war, she had transferred her capital from commerce to manufactures, for which she desired protection. The South was injured by the tariff, but she supported it from patriotic motives. John C. Cal-

---

* Niles' Register.

horn, of South Carolina, went so far as to introduce a *mini-mum* rate for *ad valorem* duties, that is, a rate below which the duties should not fall. A new National Bank act was also passed, April, 1816; the old one having expired in 1811.*

In 1817, James Monroe, of Virginia, was elected President. During this term, the interests of the country prospered. No struggle occurred between the politicians of New England and the South, till 1820, when Missouri applied for admission into the Union as a slave State. The Eastern States opposed it violently, on the ground of extending slavery. The Union was in danger of dissolution, when, finally, Missouri was admitted by Congress as a Slave State, on the compromise that thereafter no Slave State should be created north of 36° 30' parallel of latitude.

In 1821, James Monroe was re-elected President. During this term, a new conflict arose between the politicians of New England and those of the South, on the subject of the Tariff policy inaugurated at the peace. New England demanded more protection for her manufactures. This the South opposed, on the ground that her manufactures had protection enough, and next, because an increase of the Tariff was seriously detrimental to the interests of the South.

In 1825, John Quincy Adams, of Massachusetts, was elected President.* During this term, a heated contest was carried on between New England and the South, on the Tariff policy. In 1828, a new act was passed by Congress, which raised the duties to an almost prohibitory standard. The average was 40 per cent. on imports. The South designated this act as the "Black Tariff."

In 1829, Andrew Jackson, of Tennessee, became President. During this term, the extreme Tariff policy of New

* The election was made by the House of Representatives, as provided the Constitution, in default of an election by the people.

England led to violent remonstrance in South Carolina, whose interests were seriously injured. She alleged that a policy to enrich one section of the country at the expense of another was unjust and unconstitutional. She threatened to resist this policy by force. A compromise was effected, March, 1833, by which the obnoxious Tariff was modified by Congress.

In 1833, Andrew Jackson was re-elected President. During this term an acrimonious struggle was carried on between the politicians of the North* and South, on the National Bank, created at the peace. The former maintained it was necessary to their trade and commerce; the latter, while denying its constitutionality and expediency, also avowed their fears of its becoming a political machine, that might, in the hands of unscrupulous politicians, do much harm. The charter was allowed to expire in 1836. A policy known under the name of "Internal Improvements," was also discussed in this term. It had the support of the North, but the South opposed it, as favoring one section at the cost of the others.

In 1837, Martin Van Buren, of New York, was elected President. During this term, great financial disorder prevailed in the country. The Northern politicians proposed, as a panacea, a new National Bank, a higher Tariff, and a Bankrupt Law. The South opposed them all, as unnecessary and sectional in their tendency.

In 1841, William Henry Harrison, of Ohio, was elected President. He died soon after his accession to office. The Presidency was then administered by the Vice-President, John Tyler, of Virginia, as provided by the Constitution. During this term, Northern policy mostly prevailed. The Tariff was augmented, September, 1841, and August, 1842. A Bankrupt Law was passed, August, 1841.† A law was

---

* The Northern politicians dropped the title of "Federalist" in 1824, and assumed that of "Whig" in 1828.

†By this act, private debts to the amount of $440,000,000 (£88,000,000) were cancelled.

carried through Congress, July, 1841, dividing the public domain to the respective States, in proportion to their population. The effect of this was favorable to the manufacturing States of New England : for, by cutting off from the Federal Treasury the receipts from the public lands, it made a higher Tariff imperative, to insure a sufficient revenue. The new bank charter failed. At the end of eighteen months, the Bankrupt Act was repealed 1843. A new slave State, Texas, was admitted to the Union, March 3, 1845. The act for dividing the public lands was repealed, January, 1842, as it was found necessary to retain them as security for Federal loans.

In 1845, James K. Polk, of Tennessee, was inaugurated President. During his term, the Tariff, which was pressing heavily on the interests of the South, was modified July, 1846. The President, in a special message to Congress, May, 1846, announced that the Government of Mexico had committed an act of war against the Confederacy. On this occasion, all sections of the country, North and South and West, united in declaring war against Mexico. The war closed February, 1848. The treaty of Guadalupe-Hidalgo, which followed, ceded California and New Mexico to the United States.

In 1849, Zachary Taylor, of Louisiana, became President. During this term, the old issues between the politicians of the North and South were abandoned, to wit : the Tariff policy, a National Bank, a system of Internal Improvements, a Division of the Public Lands. The recent acquisitions of territory, however, afforded the public men of both sections a fertile field of discussion. The North contended against admitting slavery into the new territory. The South declared that its right to joint occupation was incontestible, both in law and equity, and proposed that the compromise of 1820 should be renewed, by extending the Missouri line of 36 30' to the Pacific Ocean. This the politicians of the North refused. The controversy became so violent that a separation of the North and South seemed imminent. A compromise, however, took place in 1850, which stopped the discussion, but did not settle the main point in dispute, namely : the right of the South to joint occupation of all new territory.

In 1853, Franklin Pierce, of New Hampshire, became President. During this term, the discussion on slavery was renewed. A portion of western territory, named Nebraska, was divided into two territories. One of these was called Kansas, and the other Nebraska. The compromise line of 36° 30′ ran to the south of these territories, which would have given Kansas as well as Nebraska, the largest, to the North. On the proposition of the Senator from Illinois, Stephen A Douglas, the compromise* line was repealed by Congress. Emigrant societies were established in Massachusetts and Connecticut, in 1854, to furnish pecuniary aid to settlers in Kansas. In consequence, a hostile population from the North poured into Kansas. Bands of armed men from the North paraded the territory. The Federal Government, whose jurisdiction extended over this distant country, was finally forced to interfere. The leaders of the anti-slavery propaganda, having violated the Federal prerogative· by passing a Constitution† and electing a Governor, were indicted for treason, and obliged to take flight.‡

In 1857, James Buchanan, of Pennsylvania, was inaugurated President. The whole of this term was disturbed by a heated contest between the politicians of the North, on the subject of slavery in the territories. Towards the close of this Presidency, the prolonged strife between the politi-

---

* The Missouri Compromise line.

† Called the Topeka Constitution, after the village where the Convention met.

‡ The Northern politicians, during this term, dropped the appellation of "Whig," and assumed that of "Republican," better known as "Black Republican."

cians, on the topic of slavery, was taken up by the people of the two sections, in an election for a new President, November, 1860. The Northern States, being in the majority, pronounced in favor of Abraham Lincoln, of Illinois, the exponent of their sectional views. Under these circumstances, the Southern States have dissolved their connection with the Union. The civil compact they made with the Northern States, in 1789, guaranteeing equal rights to both, and equal protection to all, had been violated. Being in a minority in the Confederacy, they could oppose no legal barrier to the anti-slavery sentiments of the North, which, carried into legislation, would confiscate their property, and even involve their lives.

RESUME.

This closes the brief retrospect of our Federal history. I trust it is lucid, as I believe it to be unbiassed. It thus appears that, from the first Presidency to the last, the public men of the North and South have differed in their notions of policy.

It also appears that these differences ran so high in the case of the Embargo Act, 1807, that the New England States, whose commercial interests were injured, were on the verge of seceding from the Confederacy.

It likewise appears that the Southern States, to the detriment of their interests, voted for a Tariff and a Bank, 1816, in order to resuscitate the Federal Government and conciliate the Eastern States.

It furthermore appears that the Southern States, finding themselves oppressed by the extreme Tariff policy of the North, threatened, through South Carolina, 1832, to nullify the Federal laws.

It finally appears that the various points of national policy discussed by our public men of the North and South, having been successively disposed of by the popular voice, the politicians of the North, in spite of compromises, thought fit to re-open the abstract question of slavery, in 1854.

HISTORY OF

ABOLITIONISM IN THE NORTHERN STATES.

AGGRESSIONS OF THE ABOLITIONISTS AND FANATICS OF THE NORTH ON THE
RIGHTS AND PROPERTY OF THE SOUTH, SHOWING THE CAUSES
THAT LED TO THE DISSOLUTION OF THE UNION.

Abolitionism, under the guise of philanthropic reform, has pursued its course with energy, boldness and unrelenting bitterness, until it has grown from "a cloud no bigger than a man's hand" into the dimensions of the tempest which is to-day lowering over the land, charged with the elements of destruction. Commencing with a pretended love for the black race, it has arrived at a stage of restless, uncompromising fanaticism, which will be satisfied with nothing short of the consummation of its wildest hopes. It has become the grand question of the day at the North— of politics, of ethics, of expediency, of justice, of conscience, and of law, covering the whole field of human society and divine government.

In this view of the subject, and in view also of the surrounding circumstances of the country, which have their origin in this agitation, we give below a history of abolitionism from the period it commenced to exist, as an active element in the affairs of the nation, down to the present moment.

ABOLITIONISTS AND THEIR OBJECTS.

The real ultra abolitionists, who comprise the larger body of the people of the North—the "reformers," in the language of Henry Clay, are "resolved to persevere at all hazards, and without regard to any consequences, however calamitous they may be. With them, the rights of property are nothing; the deficiency of the powers of the general government is nothing; the acknowledged and incontestable powers of the States are nothing; civil war, a dissolution of the Union, and the overthrow of a government, in which are concentrated the fondest hopes of the civilised world, are nothing. They are for the immediate abolition of slavery, the prohibition of the removal of slaves from State to State, and the refusal to admit any new State comprising within its limits the institution of domestic slaves—all these being but so many means conducive to the accomplishment of the ultimate end at which they avowedly and boldly aim—so many short stages, as it were, in the long and bloody road to the distant goal at which they would ultimately arrive. Their purpose is abolition, 'peaceably if it can, forcibly if it must.'"

Utterly destitute of constitutional, or other rightful power; living in totally distinct communities, as alien to the communities in which the subject on which they would operate resides, as far as concerns political power over that subject, as if they lived in Asia or Africa, they nevertheless promulgate to the world their purpose to immediately convert, without compensation, four millions of profitable and contented slaves into four millions of burdensome and discontented negroes.

This idea, which originated, and still generally prevails, in New England, is the result of that puritanical frenzy which has always characterized that section of the country, and made it the natural breeding-ground of the most absurd "isms" ever concocted. The Puritans of to-day are not less fanatical than were the Puritans of two centuries ago. In fact, they have progressed, rather than retrograded. Their god then was the angry, wrathful, jealous god of the Jews—the Supreme Being, now, is the creation of their own intellects, proportioned in dimensions to the depth and fervor of their individual understandings. Then, the Old Testament was their rule of faith. Now, neither old nor new, except in so far as it accords with their consciences, is worth the paper upon which it is written. Their creeds are begotten of themselves, and their high-priests are those who best represent their peculiar "notions." The same spirit which, in the days of Robespierre and Marat, abolished the Lord's day and worshipped Reason, in the person of a harlot, yet survives to work other horrors. In this age, however, and in a community like the present, a disguise must be worn; but it is the old threadbare advocacy of human rights, which the enlightenment of the age condemns as impracticable. The decree has gone forth which strikes at God, by striking at all subordination and law, and under the specious cry of reform, it is demanded that every pretended evil shall be corrected, or society become a wreck —that the sun must be stricken from the heavens if a spot is found upon his disc.

The abolitionist is a practical atheist. In the language of one of their congregational ministers—Rev. Henry Wright, of Massachusetts:

" The God of humanity is not the God of slavery. If so, shame upon such a God. I scorn him. I will never bow to his shrine; my head shall go off with my hat when I take it off to such a God as that. If the Bible sanctions · slavery, the Bible is a self-evident falsehood. And, if God should declare it to be right, I would fasten the chain upon the heel of such a God, and let the man go free. Such a God is a phantom."

The religion of the people of New England is a peculiar morality, around which the minor matters of society arrange themselves like ferruginous particles around a loadstone. All the elements obey this general law. Accustomed to doing as it pleases, New England "morality" has usually accomplished what it has undertaken. It has attacked the Sunday mails, assaulted Free Masonry, triumphed over the intemperate use of ardent spirits, and finally engaged in an onslaught upon the slavery of the South. Its channels have been societies, meetings, papers, lectures, sermons, resolutions, memorials, protests, legislation, private discussion, public addresses; in a word, every conceivable method whereby appeal may be brought to mind. Its spirit has been agitation!—and its language, fruits, and measures, have partaken throughout of a character that is thoroughly warlike.

"In language no element ever flung out more defiance of authority, contempt of religion, or authority to man. As to agency, no element on earth has broken up more friendships and families, societies and parties, churches and denominations, or ruptured more organizations, political, social, or domestic. And as to measures! What spirit of man ever stood upon earth with bolder front and wielded fiercer weapons? Stirring harrangues! Stern resolutions! Fretful memorials! Angry protests! Incendiary pamphlets at the South! Hostile legislation at the North! Underground railroads at the West! Resistance to the Constitution! Division of the Union! Military contribution! Sharpe's rifles! Higher law! If this is not belligerence enough, Mohammed's work and the old Crusades were an appeal to argument and not to arms."

It is a very common error that the Puritans persecuted themselves for opinion's sake, sought liberty of conscience in the wilderness of America, and there erected its altar. To Sir George Calvert belongs the imperishable glory of first establishing a government of which universal toleration and religious freedom were the chief foundation stones. It is a remarkable fact that the same spot—the shores of Maryland—which was thus embalmed in the affections of freemen, should, after the lapse of a little more than two centuries and a quarter, be the first territory of the great republic desecrated by the foot of the tyrant, and the extinction of political and civil liberty.

It is true that the Puritans fled from England on account of violent opposition, amounting to persecution. In thus expatriating these schismatics, the English of that day, as subsequent developments have demonstrated, exhibited a thorough insight into the nature and tendencies of their principles and character. One of their first acts, after their colony had assumed some form and substance, was the establishment of a spiritual despotism and religious intolerance as cruel and relentless as the Roman Inquisition in Spain. Professing to be themselves religious refugees, they denounced a dreary banishment against all heretics and non-conformists. Every student of American history is familiar with the sad but ever-glorious story of Roger Williams. He was a fugitive from the persecutions of the old world, but, unlike his fellow-sufferers, comprehended the nature and wrong of intolerance, and proposed the true remedy. He taught that "the civil magistrate should restrain crime, but never control opinion ; should punish guilt, but never violate the freedom of the soul." He contended for the abolition of all laws punishing non-conformists, requiring the performance of religious duties, enforcing pecuniary contributions to the support of the church; and that equal protection should be extended to every religious belief—the peace of the State, like the vital fluid we breathe, surrounding and gathering alike over mosque, synagogue, cathedral, and the humble " house of God" of the Protestant, securing to their respective worshippers unmolested sanctity of conscience. For holding and advocating these just and truly sublime doctrines, now fully recognized and enforced by the free Constitution of the Confederate States, this " young minister, godly and zealous, having precious gifts," and whose opinions and teachings we have given in almost the identical language of a Yankee historian, was most cruelly persecuted by the Puritans, and forced to hide himself in the recesses of the howling wilderness "in winter snow and inclement weather, of which he remembered the severity even in his late old age." "Often," says Bancroft, "in the stormy night he had neither fire, nor food, nor company ; often he wandered without a guide, and had no house but a hollow tree." The savage of the forest, more tolerant than these narrow bigots, and who knew not his

2

God at all, kindly rescued him from the dread doom to which he had been consigned, to find a new home, and found a new State, by the undisturbed waters of the Narragansett. Mrs. Hutchinson, a most pure and excellent woman, for the same *crime*, suffered the same miserable persecutions. There is no more infallible criterion of the *tone* of a people than the position occupied by the weaker sex. Gallantry was the guiding-star of returning light in the mediæval ages. Devotion to women makes gentlemen. And where gentlemen inhabit, there woman "rules the court, the camp, the grove;" her refined presence elevates him above his more grovelling nature; and in return he is in every truth her slave, and with life and limb and manly honor devoted to her service. The historical fact which we last mentioned, therefore, truly illustrates Yankee character. Heavens! what a spectacle! A horde of mean-spirited, whining Yankees pelting a shivering, defenceless woman into a rigorous exile, for entertaining a peculiar opinion, or not conforming to some rite of public worship. And with what unutterable indignation does the Southern blood boil at the hanging of Mary Dyer, simply because she was a Quaker. This was her only offence. She died, and died on the gallows, because she held a faith different from ...se people *who had devoted themselves a sacrifice on the altar of religious liberty.* The ferocious and bloody fanaticism of the witchcraft persecutions is too revolting for statement. It is enough to recur to it.

> And what man, seeing this,
> And having human feelings, does not blush,
> And hang his head, to think himself a man."

Glance for a moment at the Puritans in power in the colony of Maryland, in the year 1676. We have already alluded to the fact that the Roman Catholics had there established perfect freedom of conscience, and opened an asylum for the persecuted and proscribed of every faith. Availing themselves of this liberality of religious jurisprudence, many Puritans from New England entered the colony, and in the course of a revolution, in the year we have named, mounted into political power. The earliest exercise of sovereignty by this new and godly *regime* was an edict prohibiting the freedom of public worship to all papists and prelatists. Here we see manifested the same despicable spirit that now animates the Lincoln government. Indeed, the Yankee is the same animal in all ages, and in all situations. He is "universal."

The great fathers of the State were convinced that the heterogeneous peoples, whom they had bound together, would not long dwell in peace. Washington sincerely desired the perpetuation of the Union, but he died in the belief that, in the course of time, his tomb would become the exclusive property of the South. And John Adams, perhaps the next man to Alexander Hamilton, among the Northern patriots, had a clear and unclouded vision of the great rupture, though he was somewhat deceived as to its proximity to his own day. The following passage from Mr. Jefferson's diary, presents the views of Mr. Adams upon this subject, and is also interesting as another illustration of the supreme meanness of Yankee sentiment, even in its most exalted type.

"December the 30th, 1803. The Rev. Mr. Coffin, of New England, who is now here, soliciting donations for a college in Green county, in Tennessee, tells me that when he first determined to engage in this enterprise, he wrote a paper, recommendatory of the enterprise, which he meant to get signed by clergymen, and a similar one for persons in a civil character, at the head of which he wished Mr. Adams to put his name, he being then President, and the application going only for his name, and not for a donation. Mr. Adams, after reading the paper and considering, said 'he saw no possibility of continuing the union of the States; that their dissolution must necessarily take place; that he, therefore, saw no propriety in recommending to New England men to promote a literary institution in the South; that it was, in fact, giving strength to those who were to be their enemies, and therefore he would have nothing to do with it."

What was philanthropy in our forefathers has become misanthropy in their descendants, and compassion for the slave has given way to malignity against the master. Consequences are nothing. The one idea pre-eminent above all others is abolition!

It is worthy of notice in this connection that most abolitionists know little or nothing of slavery and slaveholders beyond what they have learned from excited, caressed, and tempted fugitives, or from a superficial, accidental, or prejudiced observation. From distorted facts, gross misrepresentations, and frequently malicious caricatures, they have come to regard Southern slaveholders as the most unprincipled men in the universe, with no incentive but avarice, no feeling but selfishness, and no sentiment but cruelty.

Their information is acquired from discharged seamen, runaway slaves, agents, factious politicians, and scurrilous tourists; and no matter how exaggerated may be the facts, they never fail to find willing believers among this class of people.

In the Church, the missionary spirit with which the men of other times and nobler hearts intended to embrace all, both bond and free, has been crushed out. New methods of Scriptural interpretation have been discovered, under which the Bible brings to light things of which Jesus Christ and his disciples had no conception. Assemblings for divine worship have been converted into occasions for the secret dissemination of incendiary doctrines, and thus a common suspicion has been generated of all Northern agency in the diffusion of religious instruction among the slaves. Of the five broad, beautiful bands of Christianity thrown around the North and the South—Presbyterian, old school and new, Episcopalian, Methodist, and Baptist, to say nothing of the divisions of Bible, tract, and missionary societies—three are already ruptured—and whenever an anniversary brings together the various delegates of these organizations, the sad spectacle is presented of division, wrangling, vituperation, and reproach, that gives to religon and its professors any thing but that meekness of spirit with which it is wont to be invested.

Politically, the course of abolition has been one of constant aggression upon the South.

At the time of the Old Confederation, the amount of territory owned by the Southern States was 647,202 square miles; and the amount owned by the Northern States, 164,081. In 1783, Virginia ceded to the United States, for the *common benefit*, all her immense territory northwest of the river Ohio. In 1787, the Northern States appropriated it to their own exclusive use, by passing the celebrated ordinance of that year, whereby Virginia and all her sister States were excluded from the benefits of the territory. This was the first in the series of aggressions.

Again, in April, 1803, the United States purchased from France, for fifteen millions of dollars, the territory of Louisiana, comprising an area of 1,189,112 square miles, the whole of which was slaveholding territory. In 1821, by the passage of the Missouri Compromise, 964,667 square miles of this was converted into free territory.

Again, by the treaty with Spain, of February, 1819, the United States gained the territory from which the present State of Florida was formed, with an area of 59,268 square miles, and also the Spanish title of Oregon, from which they acquired an area of 341,463 square miles. Of this cession, Florida only has been allowed to the Southern States, while the balance—nearly six-sevenths of the whole —was appropriated by the North.

- Again, by the Mexican cession, was acquired 526,078 square miles, which the North attempted to appropriate under the pretence of the Mexican laws, but which was prevented by the measures or the Compromise of 1850. Of slave territory cut off from Texas, there have been 44,662 square miles.

To sum this up, the total amount of territory acquired under the Constitution has been, by the

Northwest cession	286,681	square miles.
Louisiana cession	1,189,112	" "
Florida and Oregon cession	400,731	" "
Mexican cession	626,078	" "
Total	2,402,602	" "

Of all this territory, the Southern States have been permitted to enjoy only 283,713 square miles, while the Northern States have been allowed 2,083,889 square miles, or between seven and eight times more than has been allowed to the South.

The following are some of the invasions that have been, from time to time, proposed upon the Constitution, in the halls of Congress, by these agitators:

1. That the clause allowing the representation of three-fifths of the slaves shall be obliterated from the Constitution: or, in other words, that the South, already in a vast and increasing minority, shall be still further reduced in the scale of insignificance, and thus, on every attempted usurpation of her rights, be far below the protection of even a Presidential veto.

Next has been demanded the abolition of slavery in the District of Columbia, in the forts, arsenals, navy yards and other public establishments of the United States. What object have the abolitionists had for raising all this clamor about a little patch of soil ten miles square, and a few inconsiderable places, thinly scattered over the land—a mere grain of sand upon the beach—unless it be to establish the precedent of Congressional interference, which would enable them to make a wholesale incursion upon the constitutional rights of the South, and to drain from the vast ocean of alleged national guilt its last drop? Does any one suppose that a mere microscopic concession like this would alone appease a conscience wounded and lacerated by the "sin of slavery?"

Another of these aggressions is that which was proposed under the pretext of regulating commerce between the States—namely, that no slave, for any purpose and under any circumstances whatever, shall be carried by his lawful owner from one slaveholding State to another; or, in other words, that where slavery now is there it shall remain forever, until, by its own increase, the slave population shall outnumber the white race, and thus by a united combination of causes—the fears of the master, the diminution in value of his property, and the exhausted condition of the soil—the final purposes of fanaticism may be accomplished.

Still another in the series of aggressions, was that attempted by the Wilmot Proviso, by which Congress was called upon to prohibit every slaveholder from removing with his slaves into the territory acquired from Mexico—a territory as large as the old thirteen States originally composing the Union. It appears to have been forgotten that whether slavery be admitted upon one foot of territory or not, it cannot affect the question of its sinfulness in the slighest degree, and that if every nook and corner of the national fabric were open to the institution, not a single slave would be added to the present number, or that, if excluded, their number would not be a single one the less.

We might also refer to the armed and bloody opposition to the Fugitive Slave Law, to the passage of Personal Liberty Bills, to political schemes in Congress and out, and to systematic agitation everywhere, with a view to stay the progress of the South, contract her political power, and eventually lead, at her expense, if not of the Union itself, to the utter expurgation of this "tremendous national sin."

In short, the abolitionists have contributed nothing to the welfare of the slave or of the South. While over one hundred and fifty millions have been expended by slaveholders in emancipation, except in those sporadic cases where the amount was capital invested in self-glorification, the abolitionists have not expended one cent.

More than this: They have defeated the very objects at which they have aimed. When Virginia, Maryland, Kentucky, or some other border State has come so near to the passage of gradual emancipation laws that the hopes of the real friends of the movement seemed about to be realized, abolitionism has stepped in, and, with frantic appeals to the passions of the negroes, through incendiary publications, dashed them to the ground, and producing a reaction throughout the entire community that has crushed out every incipient thought of future manumission.

_ Such have been the obvious fruits of abolition. Church, State, and society!—nothing has escaped it. Nowhere pure, nor peaceable, nor gentle, nor easily entreated, nor full of mercy and good fruits; but everywhere forward, scowling, uncompromising and fierce, breaking peace, order and structure, at every step, crushing with its foot what would not bow to its will; defying government, despising the Church, dividing the country, and striking Heaven itself, if it dared to obstruct its progress; purifying, pacifying, promising nothing, but marking its entire pathway by disquiet, schism and ruin.

We come now to the train of historical facts upon which we rely in proof of the foregoing assertions.

From what I have already stated, it may be seen that during the colonial existence of this country, African slavery had been introduced and overspread its whole surface. The Southern Colonies had, from the fertility of the soil and the value of their productions, become the most profitable mart for black labor; but the influx gradually outstripped their productive powers, and began, as elsewhere, to inspire the leading men of this section with serious alarm.* They devised what means they could to check it, but commercial rapacity eluded or overpowered their remonstrances. While

---

* On account of the immense number of slaves imported by the North.

the Southern Colonies were thus suffering, at this early date, both inconvenience and detriment from the blacks who were forced upon them, the Northern or New England Colonies, were driving a brisk and profitable business upon the solitary basis of the African Slave Trade. The principal occupations of these Colonies consisted of Commerce and the Fisheries. The New England ships made the voyage to England with tobacco, rice and other Southern products, and then took in British manufactures for the Gold Coast, [which exchanging for blacks, they returned them to the Southern colonies, and reloaded with tobacco, etc., for the North and Europe, as before, thus completing the round voyage. The fisheries employed a considerable number of persons, and the cured fish found sale chiefly in the Catholic countries of Europe, mostly in exchange for coin,* which was always in demand in England. Large quantities of these fish were sold in the West Indies for sugar and molasses. The latter was distilled into rum, which in the changing character of the Slave Trade on the Coast under the British Governors, rapidly became a favorite article of barter for Blacks, greatly to the dissatisfaction of the English manufacturers of coast-goods. Lord Sheffield in his report to the Parliamentary Committee of 1777, states, that "out of the Slavers which periodically left Boston, thirteen of them were loaded with rum only, and that having exchanged this for $2,888 negroes with the governors of the Gold Coast, they carried them thence to the Southern colonies." The same report mentions that during the three years ending with 1770, New England had sent 270,147 gallons of rum to the Gold Coast. Thus, from what I have stated, the startling fact will be elicited that the Northern and Southern Colonies, long before the breaking out of the Revolutionary War, were engaged in a lively controversy on the subject of slavery; the South resisting

---

* These were almost the only coins that circulated in those Colonies at that time, and consisted of Joes, Half-Joes, Pistoles, etc.

the excessive flow of blacks into their section, and New England persisting in the importation for the profits of the trade. The South was anxious to stop the Slave Trade and manumit their Blacks, but New England, like the mother country, was not disposed to listen to them, and abandon so lucrative a traffic.

Mr. Jefferson, of Virginia, seems to have been one of the most earnest advocates of the Southern sentiment. In 1777, being then a member of the Virginia Legislature, he brought in a bill which became a law, "to prevent the importation of slaves." He also proposed a system of general emancipation, as a preliminary to which he introduced a bill to authorize manumission, and this became a law. In these efforts he had the support and sympathy of the slave-holding States, who were overrun with slaves, that returned no adequate remuneration. At this period their numbers reached some 600,000, a part of whom were employed in raising tobacco and rice. The majority of them, however, were occupied in domestic farm-labor, producing no exportable values. Hence there was no profit in slavery at the South, while at the North it was even a greater burden. Massachusetts found it so unproductive that, in 1780, she abolished it in her own borders, but she did not cease for that reason to force it, by her importations, on the South.

In the Congress of the Confederation, the views of the North and South on the subject of slavery, founded on interests so antagonistic, frequently came into collision. It was at this epoch, too, that Virginia, Georgia and other Southern States ceded to the Federal Government for the common benefit of all the States, their immense Western Territories. All the States were then slave-holding, and the idea that a man could not hold his slaves in any part of the territory of the United States, had never yet been broached. On the contrary, the right to carry them everywhere was undoubted. The policy of Virginia, however, was manumission; and Mr. Jefferson, in 1784, prepared in the Congress of the Confederation a clause preventing slaves being carried into the said territories ceded to the United States, north of the Ohio river. This was a part of the Southern scheme of manumission, which was meant as a check to the trading in Negro slaves, carried on by Massachusetts with unabated activity. This clause did not pass at the time, but in 1787, it was renewed by Nathan Dane, in the Federal Convention. The clause enjoining the restitution of fugitive slaves was then added and it passed unanimously. By a unanimous vote, it became a vital part of the Federal Constitution, and without it, this compact could never have gone into effect. The slave trade carried on by the North became also the theme of much sharp discussion in the Convention. The North was not disposed, of course, to give it up, but with the South it had become an intolerable grievance. They had long and earnestly protested against it when carried on by the mother country, but their minds were now made up to break with the North rather than submit further to this traffic. The North then demanded compensation for the loss of this very thriving trade, and the South readily conceded it by granting them the monopoly of the coasting and carrying trade against all foreign tonnage. In this way it was settled that the Slave Trade should be abolished after 1808.* Without this im-

---

*In corroboration of the above, I append the following extract from the sermon of Rev. Dr. N. Adams, of the Essex Street Church, Boston, delivered on Fast Day, January 4, 1861:

"We at the North are certainly responsible before God for the existence of slavery in our land. The Committee of the Convention which framed the Constitution of the United States, consisted of Messrs. Rutledge, of South Carolina, Randolph, of Virginia, and three from the Free States, viz: "Messrs. Wilson, of Pennsylvania, Gorham, of Massachusetts, and Ellsworth, of Connecticut. They reported, as a section for the Constitution, that no tax or other duty should be laid on the migration or importation of such persons as the several States should think proper to admit; not that such migration or importation should be prohibited. This was referred by the Convention to a committee, a majority of whom being from the Slave States, they reported that the Slave Trave be abolished after 1800, and that a tax be levied on imported slaves. But in the

portant clause, the South would never have consented to enter into a Confederacy with the North. The Federal Constitution, with these essential clauses, having passed into operation, it became, henceforth, a certainty that the Slave Trade would finally expire in the United States at the close of 1808. This left it still a duration of nineteen years, and the North seemed determined to reap the utmost possible advantage from the time-remaining. The Duke de Rochefoucault-Liancourt, in his work on the United States, 1795, states that "twenty vessels from the harbors of the North are engaged in the importation of slaves into Georgia; they ship one negro for every ton burden." Thus we see, that while New England was vigorously engaged in buying and selling negro slaves, Virginia, on the other hand, was steadfastly pursuing her theory of manumission.

In 1793, Congress, on the recommendation of President Washington, passed an act to put in force the clause of the Constitution enjoining the restoration of fugitive slaves. It seems evident they were regarded by the Constitution in the light of property only. It likewise provided for taxing them, and ordained that three-fifths of their number should be a basis of representation. This was, certainly, the view taken by the framers of the Constitution, in their intercourse with foreign nations. John Adams, afterwards President, and Doctor Franklin, signed, in 1783, the Treaty of Peace with Great Britain, which contained provision for payment of "Slaves and other Property" carried away during the war. These Treaties were examined and approved by the Government, composed also of the very men who had taken the leading part in drafting the Constitution. In the Treaty of Peace at Ghent, in 1815, the

---

Convention, the Free States of Massachusetts, New Hampshire, and Connecticut, voted to extend the trade eight years, and it was accordingly done; by means of which it is estimated there are now at least three hundred thousand more slaves in the country than there would otherwise have been."

same clause recurred, and the British Government paid a million and a half of dollars for slaves that had been carried off by the enemy. The accounts of Hon. Richard Rush, when Secretary of the Treasury, contain the various sums paid by the United States Government to the "Owners of Slaves and other Property." Our Government has also made frequent demands for the payment of Slave property since the Peace. Some twenty years since, the American Minister, Mr. Andrew Stevenson, conducted a negotiation with England for the payment of sundry slaves that had been cast ashore from wrecked American vessels, and set free by the authorities of Bermuda. The demand was finally acknowledged, and the sum of £23,500 was paid as an indemnity. In a word, the action of the Federal Government has been uniform and consistent in asserting and protecting the rights of our slave-owners against all foreign Powers. The right to this property has been just as positively recognized in our domestic relations. In all the State Conventions held to discuss the Federal Constitution prior to adopting it, the right of property in slaves was never contested. The law at that time for recovering that property was of a summary nature. The owner might seize his property wherever he found it, and on making an affidavit before a Federal Judge, a warrant was issued for the removal of it. There was no provision for trial by jury, or for writ of *habeas corpus*, which would be indispensable if black slaves were considered as persons.

In 1797, John Adams, who signed the Treaty of Peace, and was the leader of the New England or Federal party, succeeded Washington in the Presidential chair. At this period the Slavery question was frequently agitated by the Democratic party of the South, with a view to its modification. In 1800, January 2, Mr. Waln, of Philadelphia, presented a petition to Congress, from the free blacks of Philadelphia, praying for a revision of the Fugitive Slave Law. On this occasion, Mr. Harrison Gray Otis, a leader of the Federal party, thus expressed himself: "Although he possessed no slaves himself," he said, "yet he saw no reason why others might not; and that their owners and not Congress, were not the fittest persons to regulate that *species of property*." Mr. Brown, of Rhode Island, on the same occasion, declared that the petition was not from negroes, but was the contrivance of a combination of *Jacobins*, (meaning the Democratic party) who had troubled Congress for many years, and he feared would never cease to do so. He therefore moved that the petition be taken away by those who had brought it there. The motion being supported by Messrs. Gallatin, Dana, and other Northern members, the petition was withdrawn. In this debate, the Northern members who represented the slave-trading interests, naturally adhered to the property in blacks, although the new doctrine of the British Abolitionists began to make converts in this country, outside of the body of Quakers, who had always opposed slavery.

It may be as well to remark here, that it does not appear any laws were ever enacted in Great Britain authorizing the trading in, or possession of black slaves as property. Nevertheless, that they were so regarded, is evident from the opinion of the Eleven Crown Judges, given in pursuance of an Order in Council, and in consequence of which the Navigation Act was extended to the Slave Trade, to the exclusion of Aliens. The laws by which England allowed the holding of slaves, extended, of course, to the Colonies; and all those of North America held slaves, without any special enactments for that purpose. The right was inherent, like that to any property; and when the separation of the Colonies from the mother country took place, that legal right, like the Common Law of England, survived the Revolution, and remained in force in all parts of the country.

It is claimed by the anti-slavery party that slavery exists by local law only, and cannot exist out of the State sanctioning it. Whereas, it is maintained by their opponents that it originally existed all over the land, whether as Colonics or States, and that it required a special law to exclude it. This fact is beyond cavil.* It should be also recollected that the Spanish and French Colonies that afterwards became a part of the United States, derived the right to hold slaves from the head of the Church, as well as from the State.

To return to the record of events. During Mr. Jefferson's first term of office, the State of Virginia proposed to the Federal Government that the proceeds of the public lands that had been ceded to it should be appropriated to the manumission and removal of slaves, with the sanction of the respective States. This movement was not successful.

It is necessary to notice two very important events that occurred during the administration of Mr. Jefferson, which wholly changed the destiny of black slavery in the United States. The first was the invention of the cotton-gin, which gave great additional value to this staple, and hence opened a broader field to the employment of the Blacks. The next was the purchase of Louisiana, which added new and valuable territory to the South and its special products. These two events revolutionized completely the value of slave labor in the South, and the Blacks, instead of continuing a burden, as hitherto, became henceforward a source of profit.

On the other hand, the approaching termination of the Slave Trade, which had profitably employed for so many years the commercial interests of New England, rendered that section not only indifferent to the prolongation of slavery, but even out of chagrin from having been forced by the opposition of the South to give it up, they began to

---

*Among other authorities on this question of the day, may be cited that of Chief Justice Parker, of Massachusetts, the leading Abolition State. In 2 Pickering, he says: "We thus, in making the Constitution, entered into an agreement that slaves should be considered as property," etc.

nourish a species of spite against it, and which has since manifested itself with uninterrupted bitterness.

The cessation of the Slave Trade, and the purchase of Louisiana, both of which were so distasteful to the North, were followed, as already stated, by the Embargo Act, in Mr. Jefferson's administration; and all this together, gave nearly a quietus to the commercial interests of New England. The exasperation which followed these measures, that seemed to threaten ruin to this section, led shortly to a desire to break up the Confederacy. In February, 1809, the Governor-General of Canada, Craig, deputed his agent, John Henry, to go to Boston and treat with the leading Federalists there; and by the arrangement then made, Massachusetts was to declare itself independent, and invite a Congress to erect a separate Government. Mr. John Q. Adams, Ex-President, in a letter to Mr. Otis, 1828, states that the plan had been so far matured, that proposals had been made to a certain individual to put himself at the head of the military organization. These schemes went on until they resulted in the Hartford Convention, 1814, where the subject of a Northern Confederacy, in all its bearings, underwent discussion. The sentiment of the North at that time may be seen in the party cry: "The Potomac for a boundary—The Negro States to themselves." This was the favorite phrase of the day all over the Eastern States. The peace with Great Britain soon afterwards occurred, and the stimulus this gave to business of all kinds, together with the conciliatory conduct, as stated of Mr. Calhoun, of South Carolina, diverted New England from her resolute menace to break up the Union.

While this irritation was still lingering in the Northern mind a bill was introduced into Congress, 1818, to authorize the people of Missouri to form a Constitution, preparatory to admission into the Union. This territory was a portion of that same Louisiana whose purchase had been so vehemently resisted by New England. During its ownership by Spain, and afterwards by France, slavery had existed in the whole of this territory, and it remained undisturbed after it its purchase by the United States; nevertheless its admission into the Union as a slave State, was violently opposed by the Eastern States. An ardent political struggle ensued that threatened the safety of the Confederacy, but which was, finally, allayed by admitting Missouri as a slave State, but on condition that no more Slave States should exist north of the 36° 30′ parallel of latitude. This is the well-known Missouri Compromise. It was at this time, also, that the slave trade was declared to be piracy, and punishable with death.

Meanwhile, slavery had become so manifestly unprofitable at the North that most of these States abolished it. New York did so in 1826, and many other States, even Delaware, Maryland and Virginia, were moving in the same direction. New Jersey, Ohio and Delaware passed resolutions desiring Congress to appropriate the proceeds of the public lands to the manumission of slaves, with the consent of the slave States. In 1825, Rufus King, of New York, made the same proposition in Congress, where it had been originally introduced by Virginia. At this period, in the Southern States, the utmost favor was extended to Emancipation. Societies for this purpose were formed to cooperate with the Colonization Society, then in full vigor, and whose object was to free blacks and transport them to Liberia. In March, 1825, Virginia passed an act to furnish the Colonists in Liberia, under the direction of the "Richmond and Manchester (England) Colonization Society," with implements of husbandry, clothing, etc. The emancipation of blacks to be sent to Liberia, were frequent all over the Southern States, and on a liberal scale. Alabama, Louisiana and Missouri passed laws prohibiting slaves to be brought within their borders for sale, and further enacting that those brought in by settlers should not be sold under two years.

The sentiment of Emancipation was making steady progress; but, at the same time, a decided repugnance to free
3

blacks began to manifest itself. Ohio, Illinois, and other Northwestern States, forbade by law free blacks coming into the State, under any pretence; and a white person who brought one in, was required to give bonds in $500. They were not regarded as citizens of the United States, and from their idle habits, were considered as a nuisance everywhere. The Southern States also enacted that free blacks arriving there as seamen, should be under surveillance while in port. In consequence of this general antipathy to free blacks, and in view of the difficulty of deporting them, Mr. Tucker, of Virginia, proposed in Congress, 1825, to set off the territory west of the Rocky Mountains as a Colony for free blacks. This effort failed; but all the leading statesmen of the South, Mr. Mangum, Mr. McDuffie, etc., urged the adoption of some scheme of emancipation.

About this time a new movement was initiated in New England. The doctrine of Abolition was then at the zenith of its popularity in England, where it was already proposed to transplant it to our Southern States, which would then be converted into a great free black cotton-growing country. This utterly impracticable idea was seized upon by various individuals of the New England States, who forthwith began to sow the seeds of agitation. It is impossible to attribute to them any very philanthropic motive; for only twenty years had elapsed since Massachusetts had been forced to give up her slave trading, and it is not at all credible that the tastes thus acquired should, in so short a time have been supplanted by so ardent a love for the negro of the South as to desire his manumission at the risk of breaking the Confederacy. No; it really looked more like a renewed expression of that old grudge which the Eastern States have for so many years nourished against the South.

In 1828, a Mr. Arthur Tappan subscribed, with the aid of friends in Boston, sufficient funds to establish a newspaper in New York, called the "Journal of Commerce," whose object was to promote the borrowed English theory of Abolition. Its editor was a certain David Hale, an auctioneer of Boston, and a teacher in the Presbyterian Sunday-school there. At the same juncture, the Baltimore "Genius of Emancipation" fell into the hands of another Abolition, named W. Lloyd Garrison. This individual was the grandson of what was known as a "Tory" during our Revolutionary War, and who, at the Peace, was compelled to fly the country to Nova Scotia, whence his widowed daughter and her only son returned, some years after, to Boston to seek a livelihood. The young Garrison readily caught up the doctrine of Abolition, as most congenial to his English antecedents and education, and set to work with baleful energy to urge its propagation, fraught with so many dangers to the country of his adoption. On assuming the editorship of the Baltimore paper, he instantly assailed both Colonization and Emancipation as only obstructions to Abolition, and openly avowed that the Union of the States was equally an obstacle to Abolition. By some it was supposed that this treasonable denunciation of the Union was out of deference to the memory of his Tory grandfather, who had done all he could to prevent it.

It may easily be imagined that the startling proclamation of such ultra views as these, led rapidly to a complete revolution of feeling at the South. The excitement against Garrison spread far and wide. The Manumission Society of North Carolina demanded his imprisonment, and the State of Georgia set a price upon his head. The emancipation societies at the South began to suspend their operations and to break up. The Baltimore journal mentioned, it was necessary to suppress. The people of the South generally, becoming more and more alarmed at the aggressive attitude of the Abolitionists, began to ponder over some means of defence.

In the year 1830, the same Garrison founded a new journal in Boston, called "The Liberator," whence he propounded his extreme views in the most extravagant language. In the following year the "New England Anti-

Slavery Society" was formed. This was followed in due course by the "American Anti-Slavery Society," under the leadership of Messrs. Garrison, Tappan and Birney. The Sunday-schools of the Eastern States became active coadjutors in the same cause. These societies adopted precisely the same tactics as their British prototypes. They circulated tracts and books, full of inflammatory appeals. Highly-colored engravings, too, representing the blacks undergoing every kind of torture, were distributed for those who could not read. These were meant more especially to excite the blacks at the South, and were sent through the mails. These proceedings were considered, at the time so dangerous to the peace of the community and to the integrity of the Union, that popular indignation frequently broke out into riot. In New York, in 1832, the dwelling of Arthur Tappan and the church of Dr. Cox were both demolished by a mob. Many influential citizens sanctioned these violent demonstrations of public feeling, and the well-known Editor of the "Courier and Enquirer," Mr. James Watson Webb boasted of his share in this vindication of Southern rights.

The Abolitionists of Boston, meanwhile, continued their operations with all the ardor of their puritanical descent. Garrison was sent to England, to obtain funds by the Anti-slavery societies; and in 1834 he returned home with Mr. George Thompson, a Member of Parliament at that time, and an Abolition lecturer. This led to so violent an outcry, that Thompson, alarmed for his safety, went back to England. A new mode of excitement was then devised by the Abolitionists, who got up a clamor against South Carolina for detaining free Blacks who came into her ports. Massachusetts claimed that free blacks were her citizens, and that as such they had a right to go to South Carolina;

* This gentleman has since changed his ground, and is now a prominent leader of the anti-slavery party.

but as she made no complaint against Ohio, Illinois and other States who also excluded free blacks, it was evident that she sought a quarrel with South Carolina, for the very purpose of spreading the Abolition infection.

A Mr. Hoar was sent by Massachusetts as an agent to Charleston to make a formal complaint of her alleged grievance, and, as was anticipated, Mr. Hoar was summarily dismissed. Upon this the Abolitionists professed great indignation, and the Legislature was appealed to for a measure of retaliation, which was soon got up under the title of a "Personal Liberty Bill," which was designed, under a transparent plea, to obstruct the restoration of fugitive blacks.

Up to this time, Abolition had been discussed merely as a moral question, but the agitation had gained such strength among its unsuspecting converts, that it was thought high time by its designing leaders to carry it into the political arena, where they anticipating making it a stepping-stone to power and emolument.

It will be seen in the sequel that these ingenious schemers were doomed to disappointment, and that the *spolia optima* of the agitation they began were destined to be gathered by the hand of the professional politician, leaving but "a barren sceptre in their gripe."

In 1838, the Abolition party was too weak and too ignorant of political strategy to dare to take the field in person; therefore, they began coquetting with the prominent politicians of the day. Mr. Marcy and Mr. Seward were, at that time, the candidates of the two rival parties for Governor of the State of New York, and perhaps the two most influential men of the North. The occasion was thought opportune by Messrs. Smith and Jay, the New York sponsors for the untoward bantling of Abolition to put these gentlemen to the test. It happened that there existed a statute in New York, called the "Sojournment Law," which allowed a slaveholder to bring his black servants with him, and remain there nine months, without prejudice to his rights;

for it had been decided in the Federal Courts that a slave taken *voluntarily* into a free State could not be recovered. When Mr. Seward was interrogated in relation to this law, he sustained it as "a becoming act of hospitality to Southern visitors." Mr. Marcy made no reply. Mr. Seward, however, changed his views afterwards on this subject, and refused in 1840, while Governor, to restore a fugitive slave on the requisition of Virginia.

The evil results of this sectional issue were foreseen by many States; and among others, Ohio, in 1840, passed resolution in her Legislature, to the effect that "Slavery was an institution recognized by the Constitution," and that the unlawful, unwise and unconstitutional interference of the fanatical abolitionists of the North with the institutions of the South were highly criminal. The violent proceedings of the Northern Abolitionists did not escape the attention of the South, where they created not only alarm, but aroused a deep and natural feeling of indignation. The change of sentiment that had occurred may be seen in an act of the State of Alabama, to the effect that "all free Blacks remaining in the State after August 1, 1840, should be enslaved."

At the very close of 1839, a handful of Abolitionists met in Warsaw, N. Y., and decided formally to transform their doctrine from a moral into a political question; and they set to work at once on a political organization. Determined to eschew any affiliation with the parties of the day, they elected one of their own band, Mr. Birney, as a candidate for the Presidency of the United States. It was now evident to all dispassionate observers, that the motives of the founders of Abolition were not so much the emancipation of the blacks, as their own elevation to place and power. It is clear enough the North regarded them with suspicion at that day, for in the Federal election of 1840 Birney received but 7,000 votes.

The agitation of the Slavery question received a new impulse at this period, from the discussions awakened by the revolt of Texas. This fine country had once formed part of Louisiana, was ceded by France to Spain, and then became a part of Mexico. In 1836, an insurrection, headed by Americans, broke out, and was soon followed by the independence of Texas. Speculations now ran high in the price of her lands, and the project was broached of re-annexing her to the United States. The celebrated Daniel Webster, among others, favored this scheme; but he was afterwards induced to change his views and oppose it. Just as in the case of Louisiana, in 1805, the New England States resisted the Annexation of Texas, during the Presidency of Mr. Tyler, on the same pretext of extending slavery, but on the real ground of jealousy of the South. The leading politicians of the day were sorely embarrassed whether to support Annexation or not; and by opposing it, Mr. Clay lost his election in 1844; and for the same reason, Mr. Van Buren failed to obtain his renomination by the Democratic party. The difficulty was terminated by the admission of Texas, March 3, 1845, but on the agreement that four States should be formed out of the Territory besides the one existing, and that the States so formed south of the line 36° 30′ should be admitted with or without slavery, as their inhabitants should decide, but that slavery should not exist north of that line.*

A temporary lull followed: but the slavery question was soon again evoked to gratify a political grudge. The rejection of Mr. Van Buren as the Democratic candidate in 1844, by Southern influence, in consequence of his opposition to Texas, led him, from motives of irritation, to raise up a new party in New York, on the cry of "Free Soil, or no more Slave States." This act was a violation of the agreement made with the South on the admission of Texas, and was frowned upon by the Democratic party; but the

*The attempt, in 1846, to foist upon the country, to the injury of the South, the infamous "Wilmot Proviso"—a Bill to prevent the right of Southerners to carry their slave property into the Territory acquired from Mexico. The Bill passed the House, but was defeated in the Senate.

issue started by Mr. Van Buren was successful enough to divide the party in the State of New York, and to give the election to the Northern party. This incensed and alarmed the South, who were at last pacified by the Compromise measures of 1850, which, however, were stoutly opposed by Mr. W. H. Seward, who had become already the chosen and wily representative of the anti-slavery sentiments of the North.

I may as well observe here, what I have already stated elsewhere, that the politicians of the North found themselves in the sad predicament of having no political principles to advocate. The settlement of the Tariff question in '46, on the demand of the commercial interests of the North, left them wholly destitute of any policy by which they might hope to ride into power. Under these circumstances, it was natural they should follow with a wistful eye the labors of the Abolitionists, who had certainly succeeded in working up the feelings of the North to a lively pitch of excitement on Southern slavery. They were not, of course, disposed to borrow the extreme views of these zealots, which were wholly incompatible with the existence of the Union; but they thought they might venture to utilize to their advantage the anti-slavery sentiments that had been so skilfully aroused. They set about this very adroitly by raising a cry against extending slave territory, which it was supposed would please the susceptibilities of the North, and not too much exasperate the South. Thus we find that eminent politician, Mr. Seward, already at work in 1850, sowing the seeds of the new anti-slavery party of the North, by opposing the healing policy of Mr. Clay, on the ground of its fostering slavery and increasing its area.

One of the prominent measures of the Compromise of 1850, was the new Fugitive Slave Law, which Daniel Webster declared to be far more favorable to the blacks than that recommended by Washington in 1787. Yet it was seized upon by the cunning of the anti-slavery politicians to keep up the subsiding agitation, and several of the

Legislatures of the Northern States were induced to pass "Personal Liberty Bills," in imitation of the example set by Massachusetts.

I must not omit to remark that the Abolitionists still kept on the even tenor of their way, and were as active as ever in promulgating their impracticable theory by secretly circulating tracts, books and pictures, harping on slavery and all its fancied horrors. They still kept possession of the political field, and still hoped to make a ladder of their hobby by which to ascend to power. In 1852, they dropped Mr. Birney, and selected for their Presidential candidate Mr. Hale, of New Hampshire. He received 157,000 votes, against the 7,000 thrown for Birney, in 1840.

Among other ingenious modes of excitement, a discussion was regularly kept alive at the North as to the citizenship of free blacks. Several States bestowed the suffrage upon them, as a practical proof of their right to rank as citizens. This controversy was rather inflamed than otherwise, by a decision of the Federal Supreme Court, in the Dred Scott case, 1853, which settled that no blacks are citizens of the United States. In 1854, the slavery question re-appeared in Congress, and the action of the North on this occasion was pregnant with serious consequences. Two new territories of the West were pronounced sufficiently occupied to render legislation necessary, and a bill to create a territorial government in Kansas and Nebraska was reported by Mr. Douglas, of Illinois. His bill contained a clause to repeal the famous Missouri line of 36° 30′, running south of the territories in question. This line was the basis of compromise in 1820, and was again a means of adjusting the dispute that arose on the admission of Texas in 1845. The constitutionality of this line was, however, more than doubtful, for the reason that Congress never had any power conferred on it by the Constitution to legislate on slavery; nor was it at all necessary, since individual States could retain or exclude slavery, according to their pleasure. Besides, the line in question was really a nullity, because slavery was so unprofitable to the north of it that it would never be carried there. It was only to the south of this line that the cotton culture made slavery a profit and a necessity. Hence the South made no objection to its repeal, in 1854; but it is difficult to perceive what motive Mr. Douglas could have had in proposing this repeal, unless it was merely to fan the glowing embers of the slavery question.

No sooner was this Missouri line revoked, than a prompt and significant movement was made in the New England States. Emigrant Aid Societies were formed, as already mentioned; and settlers for Kansas, one of the territories just organized, were lustily summoned as recruits in the new crusade against slavery, and funds in the way of bounty were liberally distributed. This unusual means to stimulate emigration was designed to secure Kansas as a free State, by obtaining a majority for the Northern people. Such an attempt made with demonstrations of vehement hostility to the South, was sure to provoke anger and resistance. This, of course, was calculated upon by the anti-slavery propaganda, and they were not disappointed. The slave State of Missouri, directly adjoining Kansas, was not disposed to be forestalled, and, as it were, forced out of their legal share to territory in such close proximity; so they did their best to encourage emigration too, but the slaveholders were naturally chary to carry their blacks with them, as they were sure to be tempted away. As a matter of course, it was impossible for the people of the two opposite sections, in their intemperate state of mind, to live long in peace together. Collisions occurred, and occasional loss of life ensued. The Abolitionists were eagerly waiting for some such news as this, for it was rightly anticipated that a conflict, sooner or later, was inevitable.

When the looked-for intelligence at last arrived, a wild and furious shriek for "bleeding Kansas" vibrated in a thousand echoes through all the valleys of New England. The organs of the Abolitionists teemed with the most discordant appeals to the passions of the people, and nothing but imprecations of the most startling description were launched against the "Border Ruffians," as the settlers from Missouri were forthwith christened. Public meetings were called in the Eastern States, and the pulpit soon became a rostrum for clerical agitators. Subscriptions were rapidly set on foot to buy arms and ammunition for the sacred defenders of anti-slavery in Kansas, whose brows were encircled with the halo of martyrdom. Speculators in "Sharpe's rifles" joined in the well-sustained chorus of the Abolitionists, and a considerable profit was the result. At a public meeting in New Haven, a well-known Abolitionist, Rev. H. Ward Beecher, of Brooklyn, and brother of the authoress of "Uncle Tom's Cabin," aided by his presence and language to swell the clamor fast rising in the North. He desired his name to be subscribed for "twenty-five Sharpe's rifles," and announced he would collect the money to pay for them, in his church, the following Sabbath, which was done.

Such ingenious modes as these, and so skilfully handled, could not fail to excite the sympathies and stir the passions of any community. Ever since 1828, the Abolition party had been laboriously engaged in sapping the mind of the North on the subject of black slavery; nor must it be forgotten that they appealed to something more than its philanthrophy, when they raised the cry of "No more slave territory," which simply meant that all that vast extent of country stretching from the Mississippi to the Rocky Mountains, should be given up to Northern emigration. It was natural, certainly, that so palatable a doctrine should be acceptable at the North: but just as natural that it should be unwelcome at the South, whose equal claims were so unceremoniously ignored.

The harvest so industriously tilled by the Abolitionists, was now ripe; and the leaders of the old Whig, or Northern party, experienced, astute, and with an organization extending over the entire North, stepped forward, and brushing from their path the noisy fanatics who had sown the seed, they gathered for their own garners the luxuriant crop of anti-slavery sentiment now sprouting all over the North. They met in convention in Philadelphia, June, 1856, and unfurling the flag of the "Republican Party," made, for the first time, a sectional issue the basis of party action. They selected for their Presidential candidate Mr. John C. Fremont, known in the country as an officer of the army, but without any political antecedents. It was thought judicious not to nominate a politician too closely identified with the anti-slavery movement, lest the possible consequences might alarm the "sober second thought" of the North. Thus accoutred, the Republican party went to the polls, November, 1856, and brought off a vote of 1,334,553. They were defeated by the Democratic party, which was now the only link between North and South; but the Republican leaders felt quite sanguine that, with the tactics their experience would suggest, they would carry off the Presidential prize in 1860. It was thus that the moral question as to the sin of slavery, borrowed from England by our Abolitionists, and kept alive by their address till the North was thoroughly infected by it, was at last, converted into a political question and made party issue.

The Republican politicians felt a dread, lest the Northern masses, who had conscientiously imbibed the anti-slavery poison, might force them reluctantly to carry their unconstitutional theories into legislation. It is certain they had their misgivings, but there was no alternative. Without a principle or a measure to brandish against their political opponents, there was nothing but to abandon the hope of office, or to do battle with the dangerous arm they had taken from the hands of the Abolitionists. Ambition outweighed patriotism; and during the four years just elapsed, the country has been distracted with the din of the anti-slavery propaganda. Orators, writers, lecturers, and preachers, have all joined in the *melee*, and their united efforts were directed to the apotheosis of the negro, and the excommunication of the slaveholder. Every church, public hall, and hustings through the North, has rung with anathemas against the vilified South ; and it is not strange, therefore, that people accustomed to this unbroken strain of vituperation, should begin to believe, at last, that slavery was quite as hideous as it was painted.

In October, 1859, an event occurred which amazed the whole country. We allude to the invasion of the State of Virginia, by John Brown and his retinue of men. This man Brown had figured in "bleeding Kansas" as a daring ring-leader of the anti-slavery bands that had contended for the mastery there. When these bloody contests subsided, he was reduced to inaction ; and he chafed at the loss of the stern excitement congenial to his fierce nature. Whether it was fanaticism or ambition that inspired him, no one can say ; but he conceived the horrible project of setting on foot a servile insurrection. Followed by a handful of desperate men, he suddenly entered the State of Virginia, seized the arsenal of the Federal Government, to obtain the arms he needed, and raised the cry of "Freedom to Slaves." To his astonishment, no doubt, the affrighted blacks ran to their masters for protection, and some were shot in seeking to escape. This nefarious attempt was quelled by the arrest of Brown and his confederates, and their subsequent trial and execution.

One thing was proved by the utter failure of this daring outrage, for it showed that the blacks were contented with their homes, and desired not the emancipation of the sword. Another thing, if not quite so clear, at least looked ominous. This madman, Brown, had been known as an efficient instrument in the hands of the anti-slavery party of New England ; and it was, therefore a matter of conjecture at the South how far he was incited to this fearful attempt against their very existence. Had they not some reason to think the act met the approval of the Abolitionists of the North, when 300 bells tolled for the fate of Brown, and when the organs of the party honored his memory, while affecting to disapprove his conduct?

This event sunk deep into the mind and heart of the Southern States. They were led to believe, for the first time, that the ultra wing of the Republican party contemplated the confiscation of their property and the destruction of their lives.

Another incident occurred in the summer of 1860, which deepened their conviction that the Northern States had entered into a dark conspiracy to desolate their land with fire and sword. It was discovered that a book, called the "Impending Crisis," was being secretly circulated all over the North as a "campaign document." The purport of this volume was to show, by assertion, as well as by figures, that the free labor of the North was more profitable than the black labor of the South. The tone of the book was violent in the extreme. We will add a few extracts, which will enable the reader to form a correct opinion of the character and object of the work:

"Slavery is a great moral, social, civil, and political evil, to be got rid of at the earliest practical period."—(page 168.)

"Three-quarters of a century hence, if the South retains slavery; which God forbid! she will be to the North what Poland is to Russia, Cuba to Spain, and Ireland to England."—(p. 163.)

"On our banner is inscribed—No co-operation with Slaveholders in Politics; no Fellowship with them in Religion; no Affiliation with them in Society. No Recognition of Pro-slavery men except as Ruffians, Outlaws, and Criminals."—(p. 156.)

"We believe it is, as it ought to be, the desire, the determination, and the destiny of the Republican party to give the death-blow to slavery."—(p. 234.)

"In any event, come what will, transpire what may, the institution of slavery must be abolished."—(p. 180.)

"We are determined to abolish slavery at all hazards—in defiance of all the opposition, of whatever nature, it is possible for the Slavocrats to bring against us. Of this they may take due notice, and govern themselves accordingly."—(p. 149.)

"It is our honest conviction that all the Pro-slavery Slaveholders deserve to be at once reduced to a parallel with the basest criminals that lie fettered within the cells of our public prisons."—(p. 158.)

"Shall we pat the bloodhounds of slavery? Shall we fee the curs of slavery? Shall we pay the whelps of slavery? No, never."—(p. 329.)

"Our purpose is as firmly fixed as the eternal pillars of heaven; we have determined to abolish slavery, and, so help us God! abolish it we will."—(p. 187.)

The volume containing the above quotations, not by any means the most bitter, was endorsed by 68 members of Congress of the Republican party, whose names were given for publication. The South, under manifestations like these, felt they had a right to infer that, if a party making such declarations of hostility were elected to power by the North, they must either consent to the early abolition of black slavery, or retain it by seceding from the Union.

When the British Government emancipated the blacks in her colonies. she acted with the strictest commercial equity; but the book in question repudiates any compensation to the "curs and whelps of slavery." One more extract:

"The black god of slavery, which the South has worshipped for 237 years."—(p. 163.)

Now, the writer is ignorant that the South protested for years, first, against the mother country, and, next, against New England, importing slaves within her borders. However, the object of the book was to inflame the mind of the North against the South, and therefore falsehood was just as good as truth.

In April, 1860, the delegates of the Democratic party met in Convention at Charleston, South Carolina, to make their nomination for the Presidency. The Northern wing of the party proposed Senator Douglas as the most eligible candidate at the North, from his doctrine of "Popular Sovereignty."* The Southern wing objected, as they considered said doctrine only a concession to the Anti-slavery dogma. Mr. Douglas did not withdraw his name, and a

---

* Mr. Douglas proposed giving the people of a Territory the right to retain or exclude slavery, instead of reserving the decision till the Territory was admitted as a State, the practice hitherto.

rupture of the party ensued. The Northern delegates nominated Mr. Douglas, in Baltimore, June 18; and on the same occasion, the Southern delegates nominated Vice-President Breckinridge.

This schism doubled the chances of the Republican party, which met in convention to select their candidate at Chicago, Illinois, May, 1860. It was generally supposed that Mr. W. H. Seward, the acknowledged leader of the Anti-slavery party at the North, an able and wily statesman, would be its chosen champion in the electoral lists about to open; but, to the surprise of all, an almost unknown politician of the West, Mr. Abraham Lincoln, was selected as its standard-bearer.

On the 6th of November, 1860, the long agitation on the slavery question, that began in 1803, ended with the election to the Presidency of Abraham Lincoln, the representative of the Republican party, but which contained within its bowels, like the Trojan horse of old, the armed men of the Abolition party. Shortly after this event, Gov. Andrew, of Massachusetts, declared at a public meeting, that "the election of Mr. Lincoln was only the first step towards forcible emancipation."

RESUME.

The whole territory of the States, North and South, was originally slaveholding—English, Spanish, and French. Not from any local law, but from the laws of the mother country.

Slaves were regarded only as property in all the thirteen States that formed the Union; since it would have been a manifest absurdity for the slaveholders who made the Declaration of Independence, to declare "all men were born free and equal," had they not considered their slaves as property.

In forming the Union, the thirteen slave States conferred upon the Federal Government the power to tax slave property: to protect it from foreigners, as well on the national territories as at sea, and also from domestic escape; and conferred no other power, either to prohibit or to extend it.

The North clung to the profits of the Slave Trade as long as possible, and attacked the slave system when they were deprived of those profits.

The territory that was once all slave, has become free;— 1st, by the Ordinance of 1787, prohibiting slaves north of the Ohio; 2d, by eight Northern States abolishing slavery in their borders; 3d, by the Missouri Compromise of 1820, prohibiting slaves north of 36° 30'; 4th, the act admitting Texas re-enacting that line. Thus the North has driven slaves out of half the Territories of the United States, showing a constant and large aggression upon the South.

The duty of the Government is undoubtedly to protect the property upon the Territories. until people there settled form their own laws.

The agitation of the slave question grew originally out of the chagrin of New England, at being deprived of the slave trade and its profits. It was prolonged by the mutual irritation that the opposition of Massachusetts to the purchase of Louisiana occasioned.

Emancipation made steady progress in all the States. until Abolition forced the slaveholders upon the defensive.

Abolition made little progress, until unscrupulous partisans coquetted with it for party issues.

The question of the power of the Government to exclude slavery from the Territories, has been blended with the moral question as to the " sin of slavery."

The cry of "Free Soil" was raised in 1848, by Mr. Van Buren, to avenge his non-nomination by the South, at Baltimore.

The compromise measures of 1850, were carried by the influence of Henry Clay.

Violation of these compromises, by the "Personal Liberty Bills" of the Northern States, soon followed.

Repeal of the Missouri Compromise, in 1854.

4

Attempt, by the Abolition party, to make Kansas a Free State by force, which was resisted by the South.

Rise of Republican party, under the lead of Mr. W. H. Seward, and its defeat in 1856.

Violent agitation of the slavery question at the North, followed by the invasion of Virginia by John Brown, in 1859, and the circulation of the Helper Book, in 1860.

The theory of a "Higher Law" at the North, to justify resistance to the Constitution and laws of Congress, has begotten the Higher Law of self-preservation at the South, to justify resistance to a dominant party, which embraces the "sin of slavery" among its tenets.

The Southern States have been for nearly sixty years the object of political persecution by the North, which they have borne with patience and returned with kindness. In 1820, the North entered into a compromise, which has been broken. In 1850 they made new agreements, which have since been violated. In 1860 a legal majority elected a President on the "Platform" that "slavery must be restricted to its present limits." Outraged in our rights, and threatened in our interests, what course is left the South? To fold their arms and await more injury and endure more obloquy? Would this check the aggressions of the North till both North and South were swallowed up in the vortex of ruin? It is clear that the South has no alternative. Far better they should have abandoned the Confederacy than remain only to engage in bitter feuds that compromise the dignity of the country, and sow the seeds of undying hatred.

In 1789, according to our view, the South entered into a civil compact with the North, on certain conditions and guarantees. These have been broken, and the South returns, in her opinion, to her original "sovereignty.* Even

* This principle of sovereignty was repeatedly asserted by New England during the last war, and on January 4, 1815, a report of a committee was made in the Hartford Convention, in favor of immediate secession

were it otherwise—were it true that the South owed allegiance to the Federal Government—still, she asserts our own Declaration of Independence in 1776, and the present practice of Europe justify all people in repudiating a government which assails their rights and sacrifices their best interests. If the Northern States do not acknowledge these truths, then are they false to their origin, and seek to substitute for a government of opinion the tyranny of force. The South will adhere to its rights of secession at all hazards, and at every sacrifice.

A few general considerations, and we conclude our narrative. After-tracing the course of events recorded in the foregoing pages, the questions naturally arise—What has been the result? What have the Abolitionists gained? The answers may be briefly summed up as follows:

1. They have put an end to the emancipation which originated among the real philanthropists of the South. In their wild and fanatical attempts they have counteracted the very object at which they have aimed. In the language of another, "The worst foes of the black race are those who have intermeddled in their behalf. By nature, the most affectionate and loyal of races beneath the sun, they are also the most helpless; and no calamity can befal them greater than the loss of that protection they enjoy under

from the Union, on the plea that the Constitution had been violated the Embargo Act, and the ordering of the militia into the service of the United States. The report defended the right of secession as follows:

"That Acts of Congress, in violation of the Constitution, are absolutely void, is an undeniable position. . . . . But in cases of deliberate, dangerous, and palpable infractions of the Constitution, affecting the sovereignty of a State and liberties of the people, it is not only the right, but the duty, of such State to interpose its authority for their protection, in the manner best calculated to secure that end. When emergencies occur, which are either beyond the reach of the judicial tribunals, or too pressing to admit of the delay incident to their forms, States which have no common umpire, must be their own judges and execute their own decisions. The States should so use their power as effectually to protect their own sovereignty and the rights and liberties of their citizens."

this patriarchal system. Indeed. the experiment has been tried of precipitating them upon a freedom which they know not how to enjoy; and the dismal results are before the world in statistics that may well excite astonishment."*

In striking confirmation of the above, we extract from the mortuary records of the last year the following cases of Negro slaves who lived to over a hundred years:

1850 February 2. Female slave, Virginia 105
1860 " 15. Milly Lamar, Georgia................. 135
1860—March 25. Sam, Georgia........................140
1860 April 17. Glasgow, Kentucky............. 112

" With the fairest portions of the earth in their posses-sion, and with the advantage of a long discipline as the cultivators of the soil, their constitutional indolence has converted the most beautiful islands of the sea into howling wastes. It is not too much to say, that if the South should at this moment, surrender every slave, the wisdom of the entire world, united in solemn council, could not solve the question of their disposal. Freedom would be their doom. Every Southern master knows this truth and feels its power."

2. Touch the negro, and you touch cotton—the main-spring that keeps the machinery of the world in motion. In teaching slaves to entertain wild and dangerous notions of liberty, the Abolitionists have thus jeopardized the com-merce of the country and the manufacturing interests of the civilized world. They have likewise destroyed confi-dence. In short, all the kind relations that have ever existed between the North and the South have been interrupted,

---

* "Compared with European laborers, the black lives like a prince. He has his cabin generally neat and clean, and always weather-proof. He has likewise his own garden-patch, over which he is lord paramount. He is well fed, well lodged, well clothed, and never overworked. His holidays are numerous, and enjoyed with infinite gusto. Sleek, happy, and con-tented, the black lives to a great age. The slaveholder finds it to his interest to treat his negroes liberally, and takes every means to make them healthy and contented."

and a barrier erected, which, socially, commercially, and politically, has separated the heretofore united interests of the two sections.

3. They have held out a Canadian Utopia, where they have taught the slaves in their ignorance to believe they could enjoy a life of ease and luxury, and having cut them off from a race of kind masters, and separated them from comfortable homes, left the deluded beings, incapable of self-support, upon an uncongenial soil, to live in a state of bestiality and misery, and die cursing the Abolitionists as the authors of their wretchedness.

4. They have led a portion of the people of the North, as well as of the South, to examine the question in all its aspects, and to plant themselves upon the broad principle that that form of government which recognizes the institution of slavery in the United States, is the best, the condition of the two races, white and black being considered, for the development, progress, and happiness of each. In other words, to regard servitude as a blessing to the negro, and, under proper and philanthropic restrictions, necessary to their preservation and the prosperity of the country.

5. Step by step they have built up a party upon an issue which has led to a dissolution of the Union. They have scattered the seeds of Abolitionism until a majority of the voters of the Free States have become animated by a fixed purpose to prevent the further growth of the slave power.

The power of the North has been consolidated, and, for the first time in the history of the country, it is wielded as a sectional weapon against the interests of the South. The Government is now in the hands of men elected by Northern votes, who regard slavery as a curse and a crime, and they will have the means necessary to accomplish their purpose.

The utterances that have heretofore come from the rostrum, or from irresponsible associations of individuals, now come from the throne. "Clad with the sanctities of office, with the anointing oil poured upon the monarch's head, the decree has gone forth that the institution of Northern slavery shall be constrained within assigned limits. Though Nature and Providence should send forth its branches like the banyan tree, to take root in congenial soil, here is a power superior to both, that says it shall wither and die within its own charmed circle."

Abraham Lincoln, President of the United States, says:

"I believe this Government cannot endure permanently, half slave and half free. I do not expect the Union to be dissolved; I do not expect the house to fall, but I do expect that it will cease to be divided. It will become all one thing, or all the other. Either the opponents of slavery will arrest the further spread of it, and place it where the public mind shall rest in the belief that it is in the course of ultimate extinction, or its advocates will push it forward until it shall become alike lawful in all the States, old as well as new, North as well as South."

"I have always hated slavery as much as any Abolitionist. I have always been an old line Whig. I have always hated it, and I always believe a course of ultimate extinction. If I were in Congress, and a question come up on a question whether slavery should be prohibited in a new territory, in spite of the Dred Scott decision, I would vote that it shall."

"Abolitionism and fanaticism is a blood-hound that never bolts its track when it has once lapped blood. The elevation of their candidate is far from being the consummation of their aims. It is only the beginning of that consummation: and if all history be not a lie, there will be coercion enough till the end of the beginning is reached, and the dreadful banquet of slaughter and ruin shall glut the appetite."

And now the end has come. The divided house, which Lincoln boastfully said would not fall, has fallen. The ruins of the Union are at the feet as well of those who loved and cherished it as of those who labored for its destruction. The Constitution is at length a nullity.

THE CONFEDERATE STATES OF AMERICA.

The secession from the old Union, or the dissolution of the United States, which has resulted in the formation of a new Republic called "The Confederate States of America," commenced by the withdrawal of the sovereign State of South Carolina from the Union. The Ordinance of Secession was passed on the 20th December, 1860. The secession movement thus inaugurated, was taken up and followed by other States. Mississippi passed Ordinance of Separation on January 9th, 1861; Florida, January 11th, 1861; Alabama, January 11th, 1861; Georgia, January 19th, 1861; Louisiana, January 25th, 1861, declaring their sovereign independence and separate existence from the Union.

A Convention of Delegates from the six seceding States was called, and assembled in Congress at Montgomery, Ala., to organize a Provisional Government. The assembly met on the 4th day of February, 1861. A Provisional Constitution for the States was adopted on the 8th day of February. On the 9th day of February Congress proceeded to the election of a President and Vice-President. Jefferson Davis, of Mississippi, as President, and Alex. H. Stephens, of Georgia, as Vice-President, were unanimously elected for the term of one year. On the 18th day of February, President Davis was inaugurated. On February 1st, 1861, the State of Texas passed an Ordinance of Secession, which was followed by the following States: Virginia, April 17th, 1861; Tennessee, May 6th, 1861; Arkansas, May 6th, 1861; North Carolina, May 20th, 1861; Missouri, October 28th, 1861; Kentucky, November 20th, 1861.

The Permanent Constitution was adopted, and approved by the President on the 11th March, 1862.

An election for President and Vice President was held on the 6th day of November, 1861, for the first regular term of six years under the permanent Constitution.

The Provisional Government ended on the 18th day of February, 1862.

The permanent Government was organised on the 22nd of February, 1862, by the inauguration of Jefferson Davis, as President, and Alex. H. Stephens, as Vice President for the first regular term of six years.

CHRONICLE OF EVENTS

AND

DIARY OF THE PRESENT REVOLUTION.

1860.

*November 6. Abraham Lincoln and Hannibal Hamlin, the Republican candidates for President and Vice-President were elected by a sectional vote of the United States.

November 13. Georgia Legislature appropriated one million dollars to arm the State.

November 19. A detachment of State troops ordered to guard the arsenal at Charleston, S C.

December 14. Cass, Secretary of State, resigned, because President Buchanan refused to reinforce Fort Sumter.

December 17. The Convention of the people of South Carolina, called together by the Legislature of the State, meets in Columbia, S. C., to decide on measures relative to the aspect of affairs, arising from the election of a President and Vice President who were known enemies of the South. The Convention adjourned to meet in Charleston.

December 20. The South Carolina Convention, on the second day of its session in Charleston, with but few dissenting votes, passed an ordi-

---

*The election for President and Vice-President was held in the States, and resulted as follows:

Total number of votes in Southern States	1.310,907
Total number of votes in Northern States	3,429,075
Whole number of votes in the Union	4,739,982
Vote for Lincoln	1,865,840

Vote against Lincoln:—

Douglas received	1,288,043	
Breckinridge	836,801	
Bell	742,747	
		2,867,591

Majority in the Union against Lincoln	1,872,301

nance of secession, declaring the State free and independent from the Federal Union.

December 26. Sudden evacuation of Fort Moultrie by Major Anderson, United States ——— . He spikes the guns, burns the gun-carriages and retreats to Fort Sumter, which he occupies.

December 27. Capture of Fort Moultrie and Castle Pinckney by the South Carolina troops. Captain Coste surrenders the revenue-cutter Aiken.

December 30. Gov. Floyd, Secretary of War, resigned because President Buchanan sustained Anderson's occupation of Fort Sumter, after pledges that the previous status should be preserved.

December 30. The U S Arsenal in Charleston, S C, taken possession of by Carolina troops, the Federal troops evacuating it by agreement. The arsenal contained a large number of arms and military stores, etc.

1861.

January 3. The South Carolina Commissioners left for Washington. Fort Pulaski, Savannah, taken and garrisoned by State troops, in anticipation of its occupation by Federal troops. Mount Vernon Arsenal, Alabama, occupied in like manner. Revenue cutter Dolphin taken possession of, but returned by Gov Brown, of Georgia. Florida Convention met.

January 4. Fort Morgan, in Mobile Bay, taken by the Alabama troops.

January 8. President Buchanan sent in special message to Congress, on the condition of the country. Jacob Thompson, Secretary of the Interior, resigned because the Star of the West had been sent to Fort Sumter, and without the promised notification to himself. Forts Johnson and Caswell, at Wilmington, N. C., taken possession of and garrisoned by Smithfield Guard.

January 9. The steamship Star of the West fired into and driven off by the South Carolina batteries on Morris' Island. Failure of the attempt to reinforce Fort Sumter.

January 9. Mississippi Convention passed the ordinance of Secession. Steamer Marion seized at Charleston by State authorities.

January 10. Forts Jackson, St. Phillippe and Pike, near New Orleans, captured by the Louisiana troops.

January 11. The Florida Convention, by a vote of 62 to 7, passed the ordinance of secession.

January 14. The military expedition from New Orleans, under command of Lieut. Col. Walton, having formed a junction at Baton Rouge with volunteer companies from Gross Tete and the parishes of East and West Baton Rouge, took unopposed possession of the Federal Arsenal in Baton Rouge, Major Haskin, the Federal commandant, surrendering it to

Gov. Moore, and being permitted to remove his command, with their arms and equipments.

The Alabama Convention by a vote of 61 to 39, passed the ordinance of secession.

January 12. Capture of the Pensacola Navy Yard, and Fort Barrancas. Major Chase shortly afterwards takes command, and the siege of Fort Pickens commences.

January 13. The Federal troops, under command of Major Haskin, which had been in garrison at the arsenal, Baton Rouge, left that city on board the steamer Magenta, for St. Louis.

January 15. The Mississippi ordinance of secession was signed by every member of the convention, except two who were absent, thus making it the unanimous act of the convention.

Lieut Slemmer, who commanded the Federal troops in Fort Pickens, Pensacola harbor, refused to surrender. The fort was manned by about one hundred men.

January 17. A Washington dispatch announced that the Cabinet would not recognize the South Carolina Commissioners in their official capacity, and refused to hold intercourse with them.

January 18. A party of volunteers took possession of Fort McRae, Pensacola harbor, and found in it several valuable guns, but none mounted.

January 19. The Georgia Convention, by a vote of 208 to 89, passed the ordinance of secession. There was great rejoicing throughout the State as the news spread.

January 23. The Washington Artillery, of New Orleans, was organized as a battalion, under command of Major Walton.

January 24. The Federal arsenal near Augusta, Ga., containing a large quantity of arms, and garrisoned by a company of Federal troops, surrendered to Gov. Brown, of Georgia, who had about 700 State troops with him to support, and, if necessary, enforce his demand.

January 26. The Louisiana Convention, by a vote of 113 to 17, passed the ordinance of secession, adopted a resolution in relation to a free navigation of the Mississippi river, and then adjourned to meet in New Orleans on the 29th. Previous to adjournment the ordinance was signed by all the delegates but ten.

February 1. Under orders of the Louisiana Convention, the Custom House, Mint and Sub-Treasury, N. O., were taken possession of by the State, and the old officers were reinstated and empowered to continue in the discharge of their duties. The Collector of the Port, the Naval Officer, the Surveyor and the Sub-Treasurer, had previously resigned the appointment they held from the Federal Government.

February 1. The Texas Convention by a vote of 166 to 7, passed the ordinance of secession.

February 4. Surrender of the revenue-cutter Cass to the Alabama authorities. Members from the seceding States assembled in Congress to form a Provisional Government. The 4th of February will be a somewhat memorable day in the history of the country. On that day the Confederate Congress met at Montgomery; the Peace Convention assembled at Washington—several of the Northern States refusing to be represented; and the Virginia election was held for members to a State Convention.

February 8. The Provisional Constitution of the Confederate States adopted. The States of South Carolina, Georgia, Florida, Alabama, Mississippi and Louisiana represented. Little Rock Arsenal, with 900 stand of arms, and a large quantity of ammunition, surrendered to the Arkansas troops.

February 9. Jefferson Davis, of Mississippi, and Alexander H. Stephens, of Georgia, were elected President and Vice-President of the Provisional Government.

February 13. In the Federal Congress the electoral votes were counted, and Lincoln and Hamlin were decided duly elected President and Vice-President. The ceremony was brief and very dull. The Lincolnites had pretended to fear a violent outbreak, and Gen. Scott had made disposition of the imposing military force of his command in reference to the reported intended attack on the Capitol, but unnecessarily, as there was not the slightest demonstration of hostility.

February 18. General Twiggs transfers the public property in Texas to the State authorities. Col Waite, U S A, surrenders San Antonio to Col Ben McCulloch and his Texas Rangers.

Inauguration of President Davis at Montgomery, Ala.

February 22. Lincoln raises a flag of thirty-four stars in Independence Square, Philadelphia, and "puts his foot down firmly" for "universal freedom and equality."

February 23. Lincoln passed through Baltimore incognito, on his way in a hurry to Washington, early in the morning. He had suddenly and mysteriously left Harrisburg in the night, by a special train, and was disguised by wearing "a Scotch plaid cap and a very long military cloak." On arriving in Washington he was met by several of his partisans, and taken to Willard's Hotel. Soon afterwards, accompanied by Seward, he paid his respects to President Buchanan. The cause of this strange night journey of Lincoln has never been clearly explained. His partisans tried to make it appear that there was a plot to take his life, but they failed to bring forward any evidence of it. His exit from the Federal capitol, it is very probable, will be as undignified as his entrance into it.

March 1. P. G. T. Beauregard appointed Major-General in Confederate Army.

March 2. The Revenue-cutter Dodge seized by the authorities of Texas.

March 4. General Beauregard assumes command of the troops beseiging Fort Sumter.

March 4. Inauguration of President Lincoln took place in Washington, It differed from all former inaugurations of the Chief Magistrate in this, that a large body of military under some pretext, was concentrated in Washington, prepared and under orders for active service, and that it was the inauguration of a President whose authority was totally repudiated by seven of the once United States, and was fast waning in several others.

The surrender of Fort Brown to the Texas authorities was agreed to by Captain Hill, commander of the Federal garrison, on the demand of the Texas Commissioners, who were supported by a strong force of volunteers under command of Col. Ford.

March 7. The Confederate Congress confirmed the nomination of Col. Braxton Bragg, of Louisiana, as Brigadier-General of the Provisional army; also of Col. Hardee, of Ga., as Colonel of the 1st regiment of Confederate States infantry.

March 11. The Permanent Constitution of the Confederate States adopted by Congress at Montgomery.

March 13. The Constitution of the Confederate States ratified by Alabama, by a vote of 87 to 5.

March 16. Georgia ratifies the Constitution of the Confederate States by a vote of 87 to 5.

March 21. Louisiana ratifies the Constitution of the Confederate States, by a vote of 101 to 7.

March 23. Texas ratifies the Constitution of the Confederate States by a vote of 68 to 2.

March 30. Mississippi ratifies the Constitution of the Confederate States by a vote of 78 to 7.

April 3. South Carolina ratifies the Constitution of the Confederate States, by a vote of 149 to 29.

Gen. Beauregard, the Confederate commander at Charleston sent a dispatch by telegraph to the Confederate Secretary of War, at Montgomery, stating that an authorised messenger from Lincoln had just informed Governor Pickens and himself that provisions would be sent into Fort Sumter, peaceably, if possible, but by force, if necessary.

The steamship Baltic left New York for Fort Sumter (so reported) heavily loaded with arms, munitions of war, stores, provisions, gunny bags, &c.

April 12–13. Battle of Fort Sumter. Brilliant victory gained by Gen. Beauregard and the South Carolina troops. After thirty-four hours' bombardment the fort surrenders to the Confederate States. No lives lost.

Fort Pickens was reinforced by the Federals, and a meditated assault on it was, consequently, abandoned.

April 14. Evacuation of Fort Sumter by Major Anderson and his command. Abraham Lincoln, President of the United States, issues a proclamation calling for 75,000 volunteers to put down the "Southern rebellion."

April 15. Colonel Reeves, U. S. A., surrenders Fort Bliss, near El Paso to Colonel J. W. McGriffin, the Texas Commissioner.

April 15. Seizure of the North Carolina forts and the Fayetteville arsenal by the State troops.

President Davis issued his proclamation calling for 32,000 troops.

April 17. Capture of the steamship Star of the West by Colonel Van Dorn, C. S. A.

April 17. The Virginia Convention passed the ordinance of secession, subject to ratification by the vote of the people on the 23d day of May. The Convention also ratified the constitution of the Provisional Government of the Confederate States.

April 18. The garrison in Harper's Ferry Armory, under command of Lieut. Jones, hearing of the approach of a body of Virginia troops, attempted the destruction of the Armory, and evacuated the place, which was immediately occupied by the Virginia troops.

April 19. The Baltimore massacre. The citizens of Baltimore attack with missiles the Northern mercenaries passing through their city en route for the South. The Massachusetts regiment fires on the people, and many are killed. Two mercenaries are also shot. Great excitement follows, and the Maryland people proceed to burn the railroad bridges and tear up the track.

Considerable excitement was created throughout the Confederate States by a report that Gen. Scott had resigned his commission in the Federal army.

Lincoln issued his proclamation that he had set on foot a blockade of the ports of the seceded States; also, that any Confederate privateer molesting a vessel of the United States would be held amenable to the laws for the punishment of piracy.

A New York letter thus sketches the state of things in that city: No open friend of secession is safe here now. The press is gagged. Free speech, except only in behalf of the Union, is not allowed, and a sympathizer with the South hardly dare call his soul his own. And this a free country! Even the 'Napoleon of the press,' the great Herald, which has defended the cause of the South unflinchingly, has cowered before a mob and changed from your friend to your enemy. Other journals have, in like manner, been threatened with pillage, or blown sky high with gunpowder, unless they came out boldly and unequivocally for the Union; one printing establishment has been entirely sacked, and the mob reigns supreme."

April 20. Capture of the Federal army at Indianola, Texas, by Colonel Van Dorn, C. S. A. The Federal officers released on parole.

April 20. Attempted destruction of Norfolk Navy-yard by the Federal authorities. The works set on fire and several ships scuttled and sunk. The Federal troops retreat to Fortress Monroe. The Navy-yard subsequently occupied by the Virginians.

April 21. The steamboat Decatur, bound to New Orleans, and loaded with provisions and Western produce, was boarded at Cincinnati by a mob, and detained by the "Committee of Safety."

April 22. Florida ratifies the Constitution of the Confederate States unanimously.

April 23. Federal troops were stationed at Cairo, Illinois, ostensibly to prevent steamboats and other craft, bound South with provisions, &c., passing down the river.

Fort Smith, Arkansas, captured by the Arkansas troops under Colonel Solon Borland.

April 26. The Washington States and Union—a thorough Southern paper—suspended publication, apprehending violence from the Lincolnites.

May 1. The new tariff of the Confederate States went into operation.

May 6. Tennessee seceded from the Union. Arkansas seceded from the Union. War declared by President Davis against the United States. The Confederate States issue letters of marque to privateers.

May 9. The blockade of Virginia commenced.

A body of Federal troops under command of Brevet Col. Reeve (315 men of the 8th infantry) surrendered as prisoners of War to Col. Van Dorn's command, near the San Lucia Springs, 22 miles west of San Antonio. This was the last body of Federal troops in Texas.

May 10. A body of 5,000 Federal volunteers, under Captain Lyon, U. S. A., surround the encampment of 800 Missouri State troops, near St. Louis, and oblige them to surrender. The St. Louis Massacre. The German volunteers, under Colonel Francis P. Blair, Jr., wantonly fire upon the people in the streets of St. Louis, killing and wounding a large number.

May 11. The St. Louis massacre; repetition of the terrible scenes of May 10. The defenceless people again shot down. Thirty-three citizens butchered in cold blood. The blockade of Charleston harbor commenced by the United States steamer Niagara.

May 14. Gen. B. F. Butler, with a body of Federal troops, having occupied Baltimore, issued a proclamation to the people of that city, setting forth the objects of such occupation.

May 15. Sterling Price was appointed Major-General of the Missouri State forces.

May 19, 20, 21. Attack on the Virginia batteries at Sewell's Point near Norfolk, by the United States steamer Monticello, aided, by the steamer Minnesota. The assailants driven off with loss. No one hurt on the Virginia side.

Federal officials entered the principal telegraph offices in Lincolndom, and seized the records to obtain evidence against Northern sympathizers with the South. The besotted Lincolnite papers lauded the tyrannous act.

May 22. At Pensacola, and in the vicinity, there were some 12,000 Confederate troops, from Louisiana, Mississippi, Alabama, Georgia and Florida, under command of Gen. Bragg,

Wheeling, Va., was occupied by Federal troops.

May 23. Gen. Joseph E. Johnson takes command of the Confederate forces at Harper's Ferry, Va.

May 24. Alexandria, Virginia, occupied by 5000 Federal troops, the Virginians having retreated. Killing of Colonel Ellsworth by the heroic Jackson.

May 25. Hampton, Va., near Fortress Monroe, taken by the Federal troops. Newport News occupied.

May 26. New Orleans and Mobile blockaded.

May 29. President Davis arrives in Richmond.

May 30. Grafton, Western Virginia, was occupied by Federal troops, the Confederates retiring.

May 31. General Harney removed from the Federal command in Missouri, because of his not using proper efforts to subdue the Missourians, and was succeeded by General Lyon.

May 31. Fight at Fairfax Court House—the first encounter of the campaign after the fall of Sumter. Federal cavalry, commanded by Lieutenant Tomkins, attacked the Virginia troops and were repulsed, with heavy loss, by Warrenton Rifles, commanded by Captain Marr. Captain Marr was killed in the beginning of the action. Ex-Governor Smith and Colonel Ewell successively led the Virginia troops after Marr's fall.

June 1, 2, 3. Engagement at Aquia Creek, between the Virginia batteries and the United States steamers Wabash, Anacosta and Thomas Freeborn. The enemy withdrew, greatly damaged.

June 3. Battle of Phillippa, in Western Virginia. Col. Kelly, commanding a body of Federal troops and Virginia tories, attacks an inferior force of Southerners at Phillippa, under Colonel Porterfield, and routes them. Colonel Kelly severely wounded, and several on both sides, reported killed.

Senator Douglas died in Chicago.

June 5. Fight at Pig's Point Battery, between the Confederate troops and the United States steamer Harriet Lane, resulting in the discomfiture of the enemy. The Harriet Lane badly hulled.

June 8. The people of Tennessee ratify the Constitution of the Confederate States, by a vote for separation of 108,511 to 47,238.

June 10. Battle of Great Bethel, near Yorktown, Va. This splendid victory was gained by eleven hundred North Carolinians and Virginians, commanded by Colonel J. Bankhead Magruder, over four thousand five hundred troops, under Brigadier General Pierce. The Federal troops attacked the Southern entrenchments, and after a fight of four hours were driven back and pursued to Hampton. Southern loss, one man killed and seven wounded. Federal loss is believed to be several hundred. They confess to thirty killed and one hundred wounded.

June 13. Governor Jackson, of Missouri issues a proclamation, calling the people of that State to arms. He commences to concentrate troops at Jefferson City, burning the bridges on the route to St. Louis and the East.

June 16. Gen J E Johnston, with nearly all his forces, withdrew from Harper's Ferry, having previously blown up the stupendous railroad bridge over the Potomac, and fired the eight large buildings in the armory yard. He moved towards Winchester, and the army bivouacked in the vicinity of Charleston.

Mr. Tucker, editor of the Missouri State Journal, was arrested in St. Louis on the charge of treason.

Federal troops occupied Jefferson City, Mo., without resistance. Gov. Jackson and his party had left two days previously for Booneville.

June 16. Fight near Leesburg. Va. Federals driven off by Colonel Hunton.

June 17. Another murderous outrage by Federal troops (German Home Guards) occurred in St. Louis. The gun of one of the soldiers accidentally exploded as they were on the march, when opposite the Recorder's court-room, and they immediately, without any provocation, fired indiscriminately among the people, seven of whom were killed and a large number wounded. One of the men killed was in the court-room at the time, and the Recorder had a narrow escape.

June 17. Battle at Kansas City between 1300 Missourians, under Col. Kelley, and 1300 Federals. The latter defeated. Federal loss 100 killed and wounded. Confederate loss 49 killed and wounded.

June 17. General Butler demanded 15,000 additional troops at Fortress Monroe. The Southerners burn seventy locomotives on the Baltimore and Ohio Railroad. An order from Governor Magoffin, that no Tennessee troops shall occupy any portion of Kentucky. The thermometer at Alexandria 105 degrees in the shade. Wise moving opposite McClellan's advance. Sawyer's cannon mounted at Rip Raps.

5

June 18. Skirmish at Vienna, Va., between Colonel Gregg's South Carolina Regiment and the 5th Ohio Regiment. The enemy routed with the loss of several killed. General Robert Schenck, the Federal leader, unfortunately not among the number. This was represented as a trivial affair, but was important in the chain of events, and indicative of after results.

June 20. Gen. Lyon lands a large force, and attacks the State militia near Booneville, Mo. The militia retreated successfully. Federal loss 100 killed and wounded. Confederate loss, 7 killed and 30 wounded.

June 19. Serious fight at New Creek, near Romney, Va. Col Vaughan, with a body of Virginians and Tennesseans, routes a body of Federals, killing a number. No Confederates killed.

Scott boasts of the evacuation of Harper's Ferry as in perfect accordance with his plans, and that no Southern movements can in the slightest degree affect his programme. Aquia Creek defences increased.

The State of Virginia ratified ordinance of secession by vote of 73 to 3. State seal ordered.

June 21. The Western Virginia Lincolnite Convention elected Frank Pierpont, Governor; also a Lieutenant Governor, and a full Governor's Council. The bogus Governor was inaugurated at Wheeling.

Southerners erecting masked batteries opposite Rip Raps. Rosseau has authority to raise two Kentucky regiments, with blank commissions in his hands. Surveyor Cotton orders that permits shall be obtained for freights over the Louisville and Nashville Railroad. A battle between McDowell's division and Beauregard at Vienna, anticipated—the main blow, with 45,000 men, to be struck from Washington, intending to effect a surprise.

June 23. Mississippi Sound blockaded by Federal war-vessels. Coasting schooners fired on by the fleet: no damage done.

June 24. Serious bank riot in Milwaukie, Wis. Military ordered out, and fire on the people, killing nearly 100.

Fight in Lancaster county, Va. A force of Federal marauders land on the shore of the James river and commit depredations. They are driven off and several killed by a company of Virginians.

June 26. Brilliant affair near Romney. Captains Richard and Turner Ashby, of the Fauquier company, with a handful of followers, cut to pieces fifty or sixty of the enemy, the Ashbys fighting half a dozen Hessians each, at the same moment. Captain Dick Ashby mortally wounded.

June 27. Engagement at Mathias Point, between the Confederate troops and the United States steamer Freeborn. Captain Ward, of the Freeborn, killed. Marshal Kane, of Baltimore, arrested by order of the Lincoln Government, and incarcerated in Fort McHenry.

June 28. Skirmish near Alexandria. Sergeant Hanes, of Richmond, killed.

Skirmish near Cumberland, Va., in which the Federals took to inglorious retreat.

June 29. The jury, with regard to the late bloody tragedy in St. Louis, brought in a verdict that the shooting of citizens by the Federal troops was done without provocation.

St. Nicholas steamer captured on passage from Baltimore to Washington, by Col. Thomas, (Zarvona) and together with three prizes subsequently taken, carried into the Rappahannock.

July 1. General Patterson crosses the Potomac with the Federal army near Williamsport.

Seizure of the Baltimore Police Commissioners by order of General Banks. They are confined in Fort McHenry, and afterwards removed to Fort Lafayette, (New York.)

July 2-3. Blockade of Galveston, Texas, commenced.

July 3. Battle of Haynesville on the Potomac, between Gen. Patterson's army and the Southern advance under Col. Jackson. After a sharp fight the Confederates retired. Federal loss 90 killed and wounded and 87 captured. Confederate loss, 5 killed and 7 wounded.

The Lincoln Cabinet decides to make a grand advance and a triumphant entry of the Federal army into Richmond, Va. Fremont commissioned as Major-General in the Federal army.

July 5. Battle of Carthage, Mo., between the State troops, under command of Governor Jackson, and the Federals, under Gen. Siegel. The battle was a bloody one. Siegel's forces were nearly surrounded and cut to pieces. The Federal loss, 500 killed and wounded; Southern loss, 270 killed and wounded. Federal forces, under General Patterson, take possession of Martinsburg, Va. Patterson advances and attacks the Confederate forces, under command of General Johnston. The Federals are defeated with great slaughter, and forced back to Martinsburg. A heavy skirmish occurred near Newport News, between a body of Federals and a Louisiana battalion, under command of Lieutenant-Colonel Drew. Col. Drew was killed in leading the attack. The Federals were forced to retreat, after suffering a loss of 50 killed and wounded.

July 5. A body of Confederates, under command of Gen. McCulloch, captured 80 Federal troops, with a quantity of arms, ammunition and provisions, at Neosho, Mo.

Lincoln, in his message to the Federal Congress, recommended measures to make the contest with the Confederate States "short and decisive." He denied States' rights and assumed every attribute of sovereignty for the Federal Government.

July 7. The Privateer Sumter runs the blockade from the Mississippi river. She is chased by the Federal blockading steamer but succeeds in making good her escape.

Engagement at Acquia Creek between the Confederate batteries and an United States steamer.

July 8. General Johnston's army near Martinsburg was reinforced, and he prepares to move his forces to effect a junction with General Beauregard, near Manassas. General Lyon marched towards Boonville, Mo.; he compels the people to take the oath of allegiance to the Federal Government as he advances.

July 9. Engagement near N. Orleans. An United States war steamer is fired off by the batteries on Ship Island.

July 10. Brush at Hatteras Inlet, N. C., between the Confederates and an United States steamer.

McClellan marching on Beverly, Va.; constant skirmishing occurring between the Federals and Southerners.

July 11. The St. Louis State Journal, for its able advocacy of Southern rights, and its stinging denunciation of Lincoln, his advisers and his policy, was suppressed by order of Gen. Lyon.

July 12. Rich Mountain fight, between a regiment of Virginians, under command of Colonel Pegram, and a large body of Federals. After a hard fought battle, Colonel Pegram was forced to retreat before a greatly superior number. Virginians lost 100 killed and wounded; Federal loss, 70 killed and wounded. Laurel Hill evacuated by Gen. Garnett and the Confederate forces. A peace petition, gotten up by the citizens of New York City, is seized by the City Marshall. McClellan pursues General Garnett, and attacks the rear of his retreating forces.

July 13. Battle of St. George, in Western Virginia. The Confederates routed and five hundred captured by Gen. McClellan. Gen. Garnett killed.

July 17. Battle of Scary Creek, Kanawha Valley, between a body of Federals, 2800 strong, and a body of Virginians, 700, under General Wise. The Virginians achieved a signal victory over the Federals, and took many prisoners.

July 18. The Federal Grand Army, under the command of General McDowell, advances in three divisions towards Manassas. Battle of Bull Run, Va. A great and decisive victory was achieved by Gen. Beauregard, over the Federal forces. Federal loss, 450 killed and wounded; Confederate loss, 55 killed and 100 wounded.

July 20. Provisional Congress, 3d session, of the Confederate States met in Richmond, Va.

The main body of the army of the Shenandoah, under command of Gen J E Johnson, arrived at Manassas. Gen Johnson arrived about noon.

July 21. A naval engagement took place on Oregon Inlet, N. C., between the Confederate steamboat Beaufort and a Federal steamship, name unknown. The latter having received three shots in her hull, hauled off.

July 21. Great battle of Manassas Plains, Va. The Confederate army, under Gens. Johnston and Beauregard, achieved a glorious and triumphant victory over the United States army.

The Federal army, commanded by Gen. McDowell, according to best informed Lincolnite journals, was 55,000 strong, and had 119 pieces of cannon. The Confederate army, under command of Gens J E Johnston and Beauregard, was about 28,000 strong, and had 50 pieces of cannon. The battle commenced soon after sunrise, and raged until nearly 4 o'clock in the afternoon, when the Federals, defeated at all points and panic stricken, fled from the field in the utmost disorder, in all available directions, closely pursued by the victorious Confederates. The vaunted "On to Richmond" movement was changed into a general and inglorious rout. "The admirable character of our troops," Gen. Johnston says, in his official report, "is incontestably proved by the result of this battle; especially when it is remembered that little more than 6000 men of the army of the Shenandoah, with 16 guns, and less than 2000 of that of the Potomac, with 6 guns, for full five hours successfully resisted 35,000 U. S. troops, with a powerful artillery and a superior force of regular cavalry." "The brunt of this hard-fought engagement fell upon the troops who held their ground so long with such heroic resolution." "The victory," says Gen. Beauregard, "was dearly won by the death of many officers and men of inestimable value, belonging to all grades of our society." Among the Confederates killed were Gens. Bee and Bartow. The Confederate loss, according to Gen. Beauregard's report was—killed 369; wounded 1483; making an aggregate of 1852. The Federal loss cannot be accurately stated. Their official reports only afford data for an approximate estimate. Gen. Beauregard says, in his report: "We are warranted in placing the entire loss of the Federals at over 4500 in killed, wounded and prisoners. To this may be legitimately added, as a consequence of the battle, the thousands of fugitives from the field who have never rejoined their regiments, and who are as much lost to the enemy's service as if slain or disabled by wounds." In addition, the Confederates captured on the field and in the pursuit, 28 pieces of cannon, about muskets, nearly 500,000 cartridges, a garrison flag, 10 colors, 64 artillery horses, with their harness, 26 wagons, much camp equipage, and a great quantity of clothing, blankets, knapsacks, subsistence stores, &c. President Davis arrived on the field of battle in time to witness the final charge of the Confederates, and the recoil and complete rout of the grand Federal army, which, in the morning had marched on the field in full confidence of victory.

July 21. Capture of four prizes off Cedar Keyes, Florida, by the Confederate steamer Madison. Lieut Selden, U S A, and nineteen sailors, taken prisoner.

July 22. J W Tompkins shot dead in the streets of Louisville, Ky., by a Federal officer, while hurrahing for Jeff Davis.

July 25. Battle of Mesilla, Arizona Territory. The Confederate forces, under Lieutenant Colonel Baylor, attacked a large body of the Federals at Fort Fillmore. After a desperate fight, the Federals were severely defeated, and compelled to evacuate the Fort. Federal loss, 32 killed and 500 taken prisoners.

Federal army retreats to Alexandria and Washington City. Gen. McClellan takes command of the remnant of the Grand Army at Washington.

July 28. Surrender of 750 Federal troops to Col Baylor, C S A, at Fort Stanton, Arizona.

July 30. Retreat of Gen Wise, in Western Va. He reaches Gauley Bridge, near Lewisburg, in safety.

Gen Pillow occupies New Madrid, Mo. The Confederate army concentrating in Southern Missouri.

August 2. Gen Magruder commences his march down the York Peninsula.

August 3. Skirmish near Cassville, Mo. A body of 75 Southrons, after a sharp contest, defeated and routed a detachment of 123 Federals. The Federal war steamer Dart made an attempt to bombard the city of Galveston, Texas. The attack was unsuccessful; the steamer was compelled to retire. The Federal forces, under command of Major Lynde, desert all the Federal Forts in Arizona, after destroying property and provisions. The Forts taken possession of by Lieutenant-Colonel Baylor, of the Confederate army.

August 7. The village of Hampton, Va., was burnt by order of Gen Magruder, to prevent its occupation by the Federals as winter quarters.

An express arrived at Mesilla, Arizona, announcing the firing and hasty abandonment of Fort Stanton by the Federal troops, and the immediate occupation of the Fort by a party of Arizonians who put out the fire, and preserved the property and stores, estimated to be of the value of $50,000, including a battery of flying artillery, a huge amount of ammunition, and full supplies for six months.

August 8. The Southerners erecting batteries on the Potomac river at Acquia Creek.

August 10. Battle at Oak Hill, near Springfield, Mo. The Federal forces 10,000 strong, under Gens Lyon and Seigel attacked the Confederates, 12,000 men, under command of Gen Ben McCullough, after a desperate fight the Federals were severely defeated and put to rout. Gen Lyon was killed. The battle was fought under great disadvantage to the Confederates, only two-thirds of them being armed, principally with shot guns and muskets. Federal loss 800 killed, and 1,000 wounded and 300 taken prisoners. Confederate loss, 265 killed, 800 wounded, and 30 missing.

August 10. Fight at Edina, Mo., between a body of Southerners and the Home Guards. The latter were completely routed. Loss, 50 killed and wounded, on each side. The newspaper office of the Democratic Standard, at Concord, N. H., demolished by a mob, for reflecting on the cowardice of the returning three months' volunteers.

August 12. Skirmish at Leesburg, Va. A large force of Federals crossed the Potomac on a marauding expedition. The Southerners attacked the expedition, and compelled the Federals to make a cowardly retreat.

August 13. The Federal government despairs of finding able Generals and officers at home, to engage in its unholy war against the South ; makes overtures to all the broken down Generals and officers of European nations to come and assist them.

August 13. About 16 miles back of New Madrid, 60 Missourians routed 200 Federals, killing and capturing many.

August 15. Skirmish at Matthias Point. A boat load of Federals from the U S steamer Resolute landed and were fired upon by the Confederate troops. Five were killed, when they retreated.

Three newspapers in St. Louis—the Morning Herald, Evening Missourian, and War Bulletin—were suppressed by order of Gen Fremont, for advocating Southern rights, and denouncing Lincoln's policy.

The houses of many Southern rights men in St. Louis were searched by Fremont's myrmidons.

Many persons were arrested by order of Gen Fremont, in St. Louis, for treason. The Federal Marshall had warrants for the arrest of a large number of others, who sympathized with the Southern cause.

August 16. The Grand Jury of the Federal district of New York presented the following newspapers, for expressing sympathy with the Southern cause: Journal of Commerce, New York News, Day Book, Freeman's Journal, and Brooklyn Eagle.

August 17. Lincoln's proclamation forbidding trade and travel with the seceding States.

August 18. The Confederate Privateer Jeff Davis went ashore on St. Augustine bar and was lost.

August 20. Fight at Hawk's Nest, Western Virginia, between Wise's Legion and the 11th Ohio Regiment. The enemy fled, after losing 50 in killed and wounded. Gen Wise's loss, one man killed.

August 20. Gen Jeff Thompson occupies Commerce, Mo., and erects batteries on the river. Steamers City of Alton and Hannibal City fired on and sunk by the Confederate batteries; 400 Federals taken prisoners. Riot in Philadelphia. The newspaper office of the Pennsylvania Sentinel destroyed by the mob, for advocating a peace policy; Jefferson printing office destroyed by the mob. A S Kimbal, editor of the Essex County Democrat, is tarred and feathered for opposing the war policy of the North. The Louisville Courier suppressed by Federal authority, for advocating the rights and cause of the South.

August 21. Fight at Charleston, Mo. Confederates defeated, with a small loss.

August 25. Commencement of the Reign of Terror throughout the Northern States. Men and women arrested and imprisoned for sympathizing with the Southern cause. Newspapers friendly to the South suppressed by order of the Federal Government. Citizens compelled to take the oath of allegiance to the Federal Government.

Mason's Hill, near Alexandria, occupied by the Confederate troops.

August 26. General advance movement of Beauregard's army upon the Federal lines on the Potomac.

August 26. Battle of Cross Lanes, Western Va. The Confederate forces, under Gen Floyd, attacked and surrounded a large body of Federals. The Federals were repulsed and defeated after a severe fight; losses not known.

The despotic Government of the North pursues its tyrannical course. They arrest and imprison innocent women, who sympathise with the Southern cause. Mrs. Greenhow, widow of a former Librarian of the United States Congress, is imprisoned on some suspicion against the Government. Mrs. Gwin's trunks and private property are searched by the Federal detectives. A lady from the South is arrested in Philadelphia, for some imaginary suspicion. The United States Government has given orders to arrest several ladies who are suspicioned of expressing sympathy with the secessionists.

August 27. Fight at Bailey's Cross Roads, near Alexandria. The Confederates rout a body of the enemy and take Munson's Hill. Five Federal captured and one killed.

August 28-29. Battle of Fort Hatteras. The Confederate entrenchments on Hatteras Island attacked by the Federal fleet under Commodore Stringham and Gen Picayune Butler. After a bombardment of 24 hours the commander of the Confederates, Commodore Barron, surrendered. The enemy captured 691 prisoners, and carried them all to New York. The Island occupied by the Federal troops.

August 31. Gen Fremont, commander of the Federal forces in St. Louis, issues his infamous proclamation, ordering all persons found in arms

against the Federal Government, to be shot, and also declaring the slaves
of persons sympathizing with the Southern cause, to be manumitted.

September 2. Skirmish at Big Creek, on the Kanawha. The enemy
driven back.

September 5. Governor Magoffin proclaims the neutrality of Kentucky.

September 6. Engagement at Hickman, Ky., between two Federal gun
boats and one Confederate steamer. After firing several ineffectual shots
the Federals were forced to retire.

Advance of the Federals in Kentucky. Paducah captured.

September 7. Fight at Fort Scott, Mo.; the Confederate force under
Gen Price, and the Federals under Lane and Montgomery. A severe
battle was fought, which resulted in a fine victory for the Southerners.
Losses not known.

September 7. The occupation of Columbus, Ky., by the Confederate
forces, under Gens Polk and Pillow.

September 10. The Confederate forces take possession of Munson's
Hill, Va. Skirmishes constantly occurring in the neighborhood of Arling-
ton Heights, between Federals and Southerners.

Battle of the Gauley, at Carnifax Ferry, Western Va. Gen Rosencranz
attacked Gen Floyd's position with 15,000 men. After several ineffectual
attempts to carry it, he fell back baffled and disheartened. At least 150
of the enemy were killed and 250 wounded in these vain efforts. Floyd
had but five men wounded, as his force was well protected. At night,
fearing that Rosencranz might cross above and attack him in the rear,
Floyd retreated.

September 11. Battle of Lewinsville on the Potomac. Several regiments of Federal troops under Col Isaac J Stevens, of the New York
79th, marched from Chain Bridge on a reconnoisance. They were attacked by the Confederates under Col J E B Stuart, and after a sharp
fight, fled in Bull Run fashion. Federal loss, 5 killed and 9 wounded,
Confederate loss none.

September 11. Battle of Toney's Creek, on the Kanawha. Wise's
cavalry, under Col Clarkson, defeat the enemy, whose loss is 50 killed
and wounded. Clarkson took 50 prisoners and lost not a man.

The Legislature of Kentucky orders the Confederate forces to leave
the State. Several heavy skirmishes occurred near Munson's Hill, Va.
A detachment of the New Orleans Artillery attacked a large body of
Federals; a sharp engagement took place, which compelled the Federals
to beat a hasty retreat.

September 12. The Dubuque, Iowa, Herald suppressed for being friendly to the cause of the South.

September 13. Col John A Washington, of Va., killed in a skirmish in

September 17. The Southern Rights members of the Maryland Legislature were seized, while in session at Frederick City, by order of Lincoln, the Legislature thereby broken up, and the prisoners conveyed to Fort Lafayette.

September 17. Battle of Blue Mills, Mo. A party of Unionists and Jayhawkers were defeated and routed by the Missourians. Federal loss 300 killed and wounded. Confederate loss 5 killed and 20 wounded.

September 18. Bowling Green, Ky., occupied by the Southern forces, under Gen Buckner.

September 19. Battle of Barboursville in Kentucky, between 800 Confederates under Gen Zollicoffer, and 1800 Federals. The enemy routed, as usual, with a loss of 50 killed and 2 prisoners.

September 19-20. Battle and siege of Lexington, Mo. The Confederate forces, under Gen Price, attacked the city of Lexington, which was in possession of the Federals, under Col Mulligan. The siege lasted three days, when the Federals were forced to surrender. Federal loss, 39 killed, 120 wounded, and 3500 taken prisoners; Confederate loss, 25 killed. 72 wounded.

September 21. Attack on Osceola, Mo. A large party of Federal Jayhawkers from the Kansas borders attacked a small party of Southerners. The Southerners made a brave defence, but were finally overpowered and compelled to surrender. The town was then pillaged and burned by the enemy; 40 Federals were killed and wounded during the fight.

September 23. Skirmish near Fort Craig, Arizona. A severe conflict took place between a detachment of Southerners and a body of United States regulars. The latter were badly defeated. Loss not known.

September 23-24-25. Heavy skirmishing on Sewell Mountain, Western Va., between Rosencranz and Wise. Two Confederates killed.

September 25. Fight at Chapmansville, Va. A party of Confederate militia were defeated and put to rout. Confederate loss 7 killed and wounded. Federal loss 40 killed and wounded.

Battle of Alamosa, Arizona Territory. A splendid and decisive victory won by the Confederates. Federal loss, 30 killed, 17 captured. Confederates lost only 2 killed.

September 29. Col J W Spaulding, of Wise's Legion, killed while on a scouting expedition in Western Va.

September 30. Hopkinsville, in Kentucky, taken by Gen Buckner, C S A.

October 1. Capture of the Federal steamer Fanny, in Albemarle Sound, by the Confederate steamers Curlew and Raleigh. Forty-five Federals taken prisoners, and $100,000 worth of stores captured.

October 2. President Davis visits the Confederate army at Manassas. Grand review of the troops.

The Confederate forces, under Gen Zollicoffer, take possession of Manchester, Ky.

October 3. Battle near Greenbrier River, in Western Va., between 1500 Confederates, under Gen Henry R Jackson, and 3000 Federals, under Gen Reynolds. After six hours battle, the enemy withdrew, leaving Jackson still master of the ground. Jackson's loss 50 in killed, wounded and missing. Enemy's loss at least 250.

October 4. The Potomac River effectually blockaded by the Confederates.

October 5. Retreat of Rosencranz from Sewell Mountain. He fled with his whole army to the other side of the Gauley, 20 miles distant.

October 6. The Chickamacomico Races, on Roanoke Island, N C. An entire Indiana regiment chased 20 miles by Col Wright's 3d Ga. regiment. Thirty-two Federal prisoners and valuable munitions of war captured. Col Wright's loss, one man, who ran after the enemy until he fell exhausted. The Northern papers claimed a magnificent Federal victory.

October 8. Expedition to Chickamacomico Creek, coast of N Carolina. Three Confederate steamers, under command of Commodore Lynch, made a successful attack on the Federal defences, and captured one Federal steamer, and took a large quantity of arms and ammunition. Fight on Santa Rosa Island, Gulf of Mexico. A small body of the Confederates, under command of Gen Anderson, planned and executed a successful attack on a large encampment of Federal "roughs," under the notorious "Billy Wilson." The Federals were completely routed and cut to pieces.

October 12. Expedition to the Passes of the Mississippi river. The celebrated iron-clad vessel, "Manassas," accompanied by three small steamboats, under the command of Commodore Hollins, accomplished a splendid victory, by attacking the Federal blockading fleet at the head of the Passes. The "Manassas" ran into one large steamer, the "Preble," and sunk her; also, badly disabled another large steamer, the "Richmond," and drove the remainder of the fleet out of the river.

October 15. After occupying Mason's and Munson's Hill, for seven weeks, in vain expectation of getting a fight from McClellan, the Confederate army fell back upon Centreville.

October 16. Fight at Bolivar, near Harper's Ferry. Col Ashby, with a small body of Virginia militia, succeeded in repelling an attack of the Federals, in large force.

October 17. Gen Thompson attacks and captures a large guard of Federals at Big River Bridge, Mo.

October 21. Three companies of an Indiana regiment mobbed and destroyed the offices of the Daily Journal and Democrat newspapers, in Terre Haute, Indiana. The mob also threatened to destroy the residences of several private citizens, who favored the Southern cause.

October 21. Fight at Rock Castle Ford, Ky. The Confederate forces, under Gen Zollicoffer, attacked the Federals and drove them from their entrenchments. Confederate loss, 11 killed and 70 wounded. Federal loss, 24 killed and 47 wounded.

Fight at Fredericktown, Mo. Jeff Thompson attacks a large force of Federals; after a brisk contest, the Confederates fell back.

October 21. Brilliant victory at Leesburg. The enemy with twelve regiments (7000 men,) under Gen E D Baker, crossed the Potomac and attacked the Confederate army, near Leesburg, consisting of three regiments, (1500 men,) under Gen Nathan G Evans, of South Carolina. The Federals were terribly defeated, losing 500 in killed, 800 in wounded, and 726 in prisoners, also 4 pieces of artillery and 1600 stand of arms. Gen Baker was killed, and on our side Col Burt was mortally wounded. Confederate loss 35 killed, 118 wounded and 2 prisoners. Many of the enemy were lost in the river.

October 22. Fight in Carrol county, Mo. A large body of Federals made an attack on a small force of Confederates. The Federals were severely repulsed.

October 24. Fight at Romney, Western Va. The Federal forces, under Gen Kelly, made an attack on the Confederate defences at Romney. The Federals were forced to retire several times, and finally returned with a superior force. The Confederate forces, under Col McDonald, were compelled to withdraw from their defences. Losses unknown.

October 25. Gen Fremont, having advanced from St Louis, occupies Springfield, Mo.

October 28. The State Legislature of Missouri, which met at Neosho on the 28d inst., passed an ordinance of secession this day, declaring the State of Missouri free and independent from the Union.

October 29. The great Federal armada sails for the Southern coast. Fight on the Centreville road, near Leesburg. A Mississippi regiment, under Col Barksdale, encountered a large body of Federals. After a spirited fight, the Federals were badly repulsed.

October 31. Gen Scott, of the Federal army resigns, and is succeeded by Gen McClellan.

November 2-3. Skirmish near Springfield, Mo. A Federal force of mounted men attacked a body of Confederate cavalry. After a sharp encounter, the Federals were completely routed, with a severe loss.

Great storm on the Atlantic coast. Several of the Lincoln armada lost.

November 5. Gen Fremont removed from his command in Missouri and succeeded by Gen Hunter.

November 7. Battle of Belmont, Mo.; one of the hardest fought battles of the present war. The Federal forces, under Gens McClernand and Bowlin, attacked the Confederates, under Gens Pillow and Polk.

After a desperate contest, the Federals were defeated, with heavy losses. Confederate loss, 105 killed, 419 wounded and 117 missing. Federal loss 473 killed, 627 wounded and 227 captured.

November 7. Urbanna, on the Rappahannock, shelled by the Federals. The small body of Confederates made a brave and gallant defence, and were forced to evacuate their Forts and positions before an overwhelming force.

November 7. Naval attack and capture of Port Royal, S C. The great Federal fleet under Gen Dupont attacked and captures Forts Walker and and Beauregard, S C.

November 8. Battle at Piketon, Ky. The Federals under Gen Bull Nelson, in superior force, attacked the Confederates, under Col Williams, who fought the enemy for two days, repulsing them in every attack Confederate loss during the two days fight was 11 killed, 20 wounded and 7 missing. Federal loss, 220 killed.

Mason and Slidell, Confederate States Ministers, arrested on the high seas, by Lieutenant Wilkes, of the Federal navy.

November 8–9. Several bridges on the Tennessee and Virginia Railroad burned by the East Tennessee tories.

November 9. Fight at Guyandotte, Va. Resulted in a complete victory for the Southerners. The Federal forces were surrounded and cut to pieces. Several skirmishes occurred at Bristol, Tenn., between the Union men and the Southerners. The Union men were completely routed, and great numbers captured.

. November 13. The Great Northern Expedition ("The Wildcat Brigade,") to Cumberland Gap, meets with a signal failure. The expedition, after accomplishing nearly one-half of their journey, took fright, when they commenced a retreat which ended in a disgraceful stampede.

November 14. Fight at McCoy's Mill, Western Va., between the Federal forces, under Gen Benham, and a detached force of Gen Floyd's Brigade. The Federals had every advantage, in numbers, artillery, and position. The Confederates had no artillery. After a gallant fight the Confederates were compelled to fall back. The most serious loss to the Confederates was in the death of Col Croghan.

November 15. The Lincoln followers and Union men burned and destroyed several large railroad bridges in East Tennessee.

November 16. Capture of 30 Federals near Upton Hill, (Potomac,) by Major Martin, of the Natchez Cavalry. Several Federals killed.

November 18. Skirmish at Fairfax Court House. A heavy skirmish took place at Fairfax Court House, between a large force of Yankees and a detachment of Virginians. The Yankees were driven from the field, after losing 10 men killed and eight wounded. Fight at Jacksonboro', Tennessee river. Two Federal gun boats attacked the Confederate battery. After a brisk engagement, the boats withdrew: quite a number of the enemy were killed, and one boat disabled. A force of Federals 8000 strong, invades and takes possession of Accomac county, Eastern Va. The Confederate forces, being small, and nearly without arms and ammunition, were compelled to give way to an overwhelming force.

November 20. Kentucky secedes from the Union, and prepares to seek admission into the Confederate States. Provisional Constitution formed; G W Johnson elected Governor.

November 22. Fight at Pensacola, Fla. The Federals in command at Fort Pickens opened their batteries on two small Confederate steamers in the bay. Gen Bragg, of the Confederate forces, promptly replied by opening his batteries. A general engagement commenced. Incessant firing was kept up by both parties for nearly two days, when the Federal batteries suddenly ceased firing. Little or no damage was sustained by the Confederate Forts or batteries. The Federals must have suffered very seriously, as they have not since been able to renew their unfinished attack. The Confederate loss was 16 killed and wounded.

November 24. Occupation of Tybee Island by the Federals.

November 26. Missouri admitted into the Confederacy.

Cavalry fight near Vienna, Virginia, between the enemy and Col Ransom's North Carolina Cavalry. Many of the enemy killed and 26 captured. One Federal regiment ran, the officers leading. Ransom's loss, none.

November 30. Crisis at hand. Reasons now exist which go to show that the last remnants of the old Federal Union are preparing their final and most desperate efforts, to crush out of existence our young giant Confederacy. The Federal grand army, under McClellan, is preparing for its second onward march toward Manassas. The long talked of expedition down the Mississippi river is nearly ready to start. Two new naval expeditions are about starting for the Southern coast. Another attack is looked for at Columbus, Ky. A heavy force is expected to attack Bowling Green, Ky.

December 2. Secretary Cameron's report has been issued. He boasts of the immense army that the North now has in the field (over 600,000 men;) he proposes to employ all the negroes captured from their owners, and says that the negroes should never be returned to their rebel masters. The Federal invaders on the Carolina coast commit all kinds of depredations—stealing everything within their reach. The Carolina planters destroy their mansions and burn their cotton, to prevent them from falling into the hands of the enemy.

Skirmish at Anahdale, Potomac. Col C W Fields, 6th Regiment Virginia Cavalry, kills four and captures fifteen of the enemy. Fields' loss two.

December 2. Skirmish near Cumberland river, Ky. Gen Zollicoffer had a brisk encounter with a body of Federals, who retreated badly whipped.

December 13. Battle of Alleghany Mountains, Va. The Federals, under Gen Reynolds, were most signally defeated after a hard fight by the Confederates, under Col Edward Johnson. Confederate loss, 20 killed, 96 wounded and 28 missing. Federal loss, 95 killed 178 wounded and 7 missing.

December 14. Great conflagration in Charleston.

December 17. Gen T J Jackson destroys dam No. 5 on the Chesapeake and Ohio canal, thus cutting off canal communication between Washington and the West.

December 17. Battle of Woodsonville, in Ky. A large body of the enemy attack Gen Hindman, who had 1100 infantry and 40 pieces of artillery, but were defeated with a loss of 75 killed and wounded. The Confederates lost the gallant Col Terry, of Texas.

December 18. News received from Europe report that all the leading European powers highly censure the United States Government for unjustly arresting Mason and Slidell. The English Government demands their immediate surrender, and that they be delivered on board a British vessel.

December 18–19–20. The newspaper office of the St Croix Herald, at Calais, Me., was destroyed by the people, for opposing the war policy of the North. Gen Pope surprises and captures 960 Southerners, under Col Magoffin, in Missouri.

The Federal blockading fleet at Charleston sink 15 hulks, loaded with stone, in the harbor.

Gen Price and forces retreat from Springfield, Mo., to the Arkansas State line, and is pursued by the advancing Federals. Several sharp skirmishes occurs during the retreat, in which the Federals were kept at bay, and Price, with the main body of his army, made a safe retreat. Confederate loss, 5 killed, 18 wounded and 200 captured during the retreat. Federal loss, 15 killed and 60 wounded.

December 20. Battle of Dranesville—a fight between heavy foraging parties, the Confederates under Gen Stuart, the enemy under Gen McCall. Gen Stuart, though vastly outnumbered, kept up the fight until his wagon train was saved, and then retreated. Soon after which, the enemy fell back also, yielding the position. Confederate loss, 21 killed, 149 wounded and 8 missing. Federal loss, 65 killed, 110 wounded.

December 21. Alfred Ely, M. C., New York, exchanged for C J Faulkner, of Va.

December 26. Battle of Chustenahlah on the Arkansas river, Indian Territory. The Confederates, under command of Gen McIntosh, attacked a large body of hostile Indians, under the notorious Indian Chief, Opothleyhold. The Indians were completely routed, and over 200 killed. The Confederate loss, 75 killed and wounded.

December 27. The Confederate Ministers, Mason and Slidell, are released by the U. S. Government, and delivered on board an English vessel.

December 28. Exploit in Hampton Roads of the Confederate steamer Seabird, under Capt Lynch, who attacks the Federal steamer Express, takes schooner Sherwood in tow, and after a fierce fight, in which the Federal batteries at the Rip Raps take a part, succeeds in driving off the Express and capturing the schooner, taking her into Norfolk in triumph.

Fight at Sacramento, near Green river, in Kentucky, between a detachment of Col Forrest's cavalry and the enemy, who were routed after a fight of half an hour. Confederate loss, 2 killed 1 wounded. Federal loss, 10 killed, 20 wounded, 18 prisoners.

1862.

January 1. Engagement at Fort Pickens. The Federals, in command at Fort Pickens, opened fire on a Confederate vessel in the bay. Col. Anderson, being in command of the Confederates, promptly opened his batteries on Fort Pickens. The firing lasted nearly half a day. No casualties reported by the Confederates.

Battle near Port Royal river South Carolina. The Federals advanced up Port Royal river and gave battle to the Confederates, after a brisk fight the Federals driven back defeated. Federal loss 17 killed 9 wounded. Confederate loss 8 killed 15 wounded.

January 4. Judge Hemphill, of Texas, died in Richmond, Va.

January 5. Skirmish at Hanging Rock, near Romney, Va. Confederate loss, 5 killed and 7 captured.

January 6. French man-of-war approached Ship Island under a neutral flag for the purpose of business with the French Consul at New Orleans, and was fired into by the Federal vessel. An apology soon made.

January 8. Skirmish on Silver Creek, Mo. Confederates defeated.

January 9. Col. Lubbock, of the Texas Rangers, died. Burnside expedition left Annapolis.

January 10. Battle of Middle Creek, near Prestonburg, Ky.— The Confederate forces under Gen. Humphrey Marshall was attacked by the Federals. The Federals severely defeated. Gen. Marshall in his official report says:

"My loss in the action of the 10th inst., is accurately stated at 10 killed and 14 wounded. The loss of the enemy was severe, estimated by the officers of my command, who had an opportunity to see them dead, at over 200 killed and more than that wounded. The enemy had some 4,500 or 5,000 men on the field, and at least 500 cavalry (for that number was counted.) I had some 1,600 men fit for duty and present on the field. He engaged probably 2,500 or 3,000 of his men ; I about 900 or 1,000 of mine."....Senators Johnson and Polk, of Mo., expelled from U. S. Senate, charged with treason to the Government.

January 12-13. Burnside expedition left Old Point, and caught in a succession of damaging storms before reaching Hatteras.

January 14. Secretary Cameron, of the Lincoln Cabinet, resigns, and is succeeded by Stanton, of Pa., as Secretary of War.

January 15. The Federal gun boats made an attack on Fort Henry, Tennessee river, and retired without doing any damage to the Fort.

January 16. Battle near Ironton, Mo. Confederate troops under Jeff. Thompson, drove the enemy towards Pilot Knob.

January 17. Ex-President Tyler, died in Richmond, Va.

January 19. Battle at Fishing Creek, or Mill Springs, Ky. The Confederate forces, under command of Gen. Crittenden and Zollicoffer, advances from their entrenchments and attack the Federals under Gens. Thomas and Schoepf. The Confederates were repulsed and Gen. Zollicoffer killed. His death is thus described;

Soon after the fight began, not far from the entrenchments of the enemy on Sunday morning, Gen. Zollicoffer mistook a regiment of Kentuckians for one of his own command. He rode up very near the Colonel. The first intimation he had of his position was received when it was too late. "There's old Zollicoffer," cried out several of the regiment in front of him. "Kill him!" and in an instant their pieces were leveled at his person. At that moment Henry M. Fogg, aid to Gen. Zollicoffer, drew his revolver and fired, killing the person who first recognized Gen. Z. With the most perfect coolness, Gen. Z. approached to the head of the enemy, and drawing his sabre cut the head of the Lincoln Colonel from his shoulders. As soon as done, twenty bullets pierced the body of our gallant leader, and Gen. Zollicoffer fell from his horse a mangled corps.

The Confederate force engaged was only 4,700 while the Federals numbered 14,000. Confederate loss was 114 killed, 102 wounded and 15 taken prisoners. Federal loss, 92 killed, 194 wounded.

January 22. A brisk skirmish took place near Boston, Ky. The Federals were badly whipped and lost 8 killed and 5 wounded. Confederate loss, 3 wounded.

January 27. Reported fight at James Island, Fla. Sixty Federals reported killed, 35 captured. Confederate loss, 13 killed and wounded.

January 29. Reported skirmish near Occoquan, Va. Nine Texans killed and 1 wounded.....Naval engagement near Fort Pulaski, Ga. No lives lost.

January 30. The state of affairs in the North is thus described:

The most candid of the Northern people confessed their disappointment, especially with reference to two topics—the integrity of the slave population and the tremendous amount of resistance the South has offered to the resources and best exertions of the North. Expressions opposing the prosecution of the war were every day becoming more open and more careless of restraint. It was commonly said that the Democratic party would soon be in power again in the North, and that its programme would be to upset the whole present system of Yankee government and deal terrible vengeance upon those responsible for the

6

consequences of the war. We are told that public expressions were more than once heard that "Cameron and Welles should be hung," and that the work of retribution should go on until "every man who had loaned money to the government had been treated to a halter." Regrets, at once pitiful and ridiculous, were lavished on the destruction of "the Union."

The resignation of Cameron, Lincoln's Secretary of War, was treated with congratulations by the less ultra people of the North; and it was said that Welles' resignation would soon follow. The "emancipationists" were excessively annoyed, and were showing the most infamous exasperation of feeling. The pages of Harper's Weekly were adorned with scurrilous cuts and illustrations given of an exasperated policy of conquest, in pictures of Southern ladies "of the first families" delving at wash tubs under Massachusetts task masters.

There was a general feeling of despair at the financial aspects of the war. It was stated, on authority, that no more specie would be paid out of the Federal Treasury except for interests on the old public debt. The financial programme at Washington was understood to be an additional issue of demand notes to the amount of a hundred and fifty to two hundred millions of dollars, and a war tax to the amount of a hundred and fifty millions; although it was estimated in well-informed quarters that the increased expenses of the war would run up to $1,000,-000,000 a year. All private loans had ceased, and the full coming of crisis was awaited in a sort of dreary despair. The newspapers were endeavoring to animate confidence, but the influence of the press in the North—owing to its long course of deception in the war—had positively expired.

February 1. Skirmish at Bloomery, Western Va. A large party of Federals surprised and captured 45 Confederates The Federals lost 15 killed and wounded. The Federals elated with their success, committed great outrages on the inhabitants of the neighborhood.

February 4-5-6. Attack and capture of Fort Henry, Tennessee river. The Fort was attacked by Federal gun boats, and a force of 10,000 men under Gen. Grant. Gen. Tilghman made a brave defence, but was forced to surrender before an overwhelming force; two gun boats were badly damaged. Confederate loss was 10 killed, 13 wounded, and Gen. Tilghman with 57 men were taken prisoners. Gen. Heiman with 3,000 men succeeded in making a safe retreat to Fort Donelson. Federal loss 45 killed, (32 scalded to death on one gun boat) and 60 wounded.... Santa Fe, New Mexico, evacuated by the Federals who retreated to Fort Union..... Sixty Federal war vessels appeared at Roanoke Island, North Carolina.

February 7-8. The Federal gun boats ascend the Tennessee river to Florence, Ala., creating great excitement among the people living along the river. Several Confederate Steamboats were burned and destroyed to prevent their falling into the hands of the enemy. The Federals seized on a quantity of Confederate stores at Florence; after committing many depredations, the Federals returned with their boats to Paducah.

...., Battle of Roanoke Island, North Carolina. The Federals landed 10,000 men, and attacks the Confederate batteries and captured the Island. Capt. O. J. Wise was killed and 2,437 Confederates taken prisoners. Our entire loss is but 23 killed, and some 58 wounded, while that confessed to by the foe, and reported to us by one of the party, who accompanied Capt. Wise's body home, was 35 commissioned officers, including two colonels, and 175 privates killed, and between 300 and 400 wounded. This fact attests more strongly than language could do, the heroism of the defense. Let the battle of Roanoke Island be classed no longer among the disasters of the war ; rather let us cherish the memory of the deeds that there ennobled our arms, and shed fresh lustre upon the brilliant historic fame of the Southern volunteers. The enemy admit 300 killed and wounded,.while our estimate of their loss is from 400 to 600.

February 7. Rev. R. J Stewart, of St. Paul's Church, Alexandria, Va., was arrested by Federal soldiers while holding services in his church, charged with being a secessionist, and for omitting to mention the name of the President of the United States in his prayer. He refused to leave the church and was dragged by force from the pulpit.

February 10. Newspaper office of the "Local News" was destroyed by Federal soldiers in Alexandria, Va. Large numbers of the citizens of Alexandria are arrested on charge of conspiracy against the Federal government.....Battle at Cobb's Point, near Elizabeth City, North Carolina. The Federals from Roanoke Island attack the Confederate steamers at batteries. Commodore Lynch made a brave defence, but was forced to retreat. The Federals captured 7 Confederate steamers and some army stores, guns, &c. Confederate loss 6 killed, 3 wounded. Federal loss 11 killed, 4 wounded.

February 11. Elizabeth City, North Carolina, partly burned by its inhabitants to prevent its falling into the enemy's hands.

February 12. Edenton and Hartford, North Carolina, occupied by the Federals.

February 12. Battle of the trenches.	Battle of Fort Donelson.
February 13. Battle with gun boats.	Cumberland river, Tennes-
February 15. Battle at Dover.	see.

The fighting at Fort Donelson was the most bloody and desperate ever witnessed on the American continent, excepting, perhaps, the earlier conquest of Mexico by the Spaniards. The fighting commenced on Wednesday, 12th, the enemy was driven back with heavy loss ; the battle of the 13th was fought mainly with the Federal gun boats. Seven boats attacked the Fort. The gun boats were entirely defeated by the heavy guns at the Fort. Some of the balls passed through a thickness of 25 inches of the iron and wood casing of the boats ; 42 Federals were killed and wounded on the boats. The main fight was on Saturday, when our forces marched out of our entrenchments and attacked the enemy, killing not less than 1000, capturing 7 pieces of artillery, 250 prisoners and a large lot of small arms, blankets and knapsacks. The enemy had, with a large force, surrounded us, pre paratory to cutting off our communication with Clarksville and Nashville. This was the cause of our going out and attacking them on Saturday. The result of the fight on Saturday made us feel triumphant. About sun down on Saturday we sent off the sick, wounded and prisoners in the two small boats we had at Donelson. Early in the night, our scouts brought up the information that fourteen steamboats were landing fresh troops one mile and a half below us. Three hours after our cavalry informed us that the enemy, in large force, had again surrounded us, occupying the position from which we had driven them in the morning.

The complete state of exhaustion of our army, and its manifest inability to make or sustain another attack, determined the surrender. The snow was six inches deep, the weather severely cold, and our men had been working and fighting for several days and nights, with no means of rest except when they found in the trenchments. They had been hurriedly carried there, without their tents or camp equippage.

Gens. Pillow and Floyd gave up their command to General Buckner, and ignominously left the Fort. The noble General Buckner refused to desert his men and was captured prisoner. As an evidence of the desperate character of the contest, the following paragraph is copied from a Federal account of the battle.

" The heaviest loss to any one of the Federal regiments at Fort Donelson, was the 11th Illinois, which went into the fight with 590 men and officers, and came out with 170. Two companies of this regiment, company K, Capt. Carter, of LaSalle, went into action with 62 men, and came out with nine! Company H, Capt. Contes, of Peru, went in with 51 men and came out with 10. This will give an idea of the hard fighting and terrible loss sustained."

The Federal loss is estimated at 1,200 killed, 2,000 wounded and 270 captured prisoners. Confederate loss 231 killed, 1,007 wounded, and 5,079 taken prisoners.

The whole amount of the Confederate force on first day of battle was nearly 13,829 men. The Federal force on the last day amounted to nearly 55,000 men.

February 14. Skirmish near New Concord, Ky. Five Federals killed, several wounded.

February 15. Bowling Green, Ky., evacuated by Gen. Johnson and Confederate forces.

February 16. Tennessee Rolling Mills burned by the Federals..... Skirmish near Moorfield, Va. Col. Ashby made a successful attack on a large force of Federals, killing many and driving them from their position.

February 17. Skirmish near Galveston, Texas. A large force of Federals, in attempting to make a landing near Galveston Bay, were surprised by the Confederates and driven back ; several Federals wounded.

Gen. Johnson notifies Gov. Harris that he cannot hold the city of Nashville against the Federals. Gov. Harris causes the State Archives to be removed to Memphis. The Governor and members of the Legislature leave Nashville for Memphis.

February 17-18-19. Great panic in Nashville, Tenn., caused by the fall of Fort Donelson and the threatened occupation of the city by the Federals. Great amount of army stores and provisions ($500,000 worth) destroyed, to prevent its falling into the enemy's hands. All the bridges and fortifications destroyed. Great numbers of people leave the city.

February 20. Winton, N. C., captured by the Federals. Confederate loss, 7 killed and 5 wounded.

February 22. Jefferson Davis inaugurated President of the Confederate States for the first regular term of six years.

February 24. Mayor Cheatham formally surrenders the city of Nashville to the Federals.

February 25. Skirmish near Occuquan, Va. Several Yankees reported killed.

February 26. The Federal forces, 40,000 strong, under Gen Buell, occupy Nashville, Tenn.

February 22. Gen. Johnson falls back to Stephenson and Decator, on the line of the Memphis and Charleston Railroad.

March 1-2-3. Skirmish on the Tennessee River, near Savannah, between a party of Louisianians and Federal gun boats. The Federals defeated, 22 killed, 45 wounded. Confederate loss, 7 killed, 14 wounded.

Invasion of the Virginia Valley. Martinsburg and Charleston occupied by the Federals, under Gen. Banks.

Skirmishing near New Madrid, Mo., between the advancing Federals and Jeff. Thompson's forces; 20 Federals reported killed and 10 captured.

Columbus, Ky., evacuated by the Confederate forces. All the Confederate property removed to New Madrid and Island No. 10.

City of Pensacola and the Confederate Forts partly evacuated by the Confederates.

Gen. Bragg leaves Mobile for Memphis, Tenn. Fort Pickens partly evacuated by the Federals.

Brunswick, Geo., and Fernandina captured by the Federals. Commodore Dupont takes possession of all Confederate property. No resistance offered by the Confederates.

Columbus, Ky., occupied by the Federals, under General Cullum.

Martial law declared in Richmond, Va. John M. Botts and several prominent Union men arrested in Richmond for aiding the enemy.

March 5. Martial law declared in Memphis, Tenn.

General Beauregard takes command of the army of the Mississippi. Headquarters at Jackson, Tenn.

March 5-6. Skirmish near New Creek, Western Virginia. Col. Ashby made a successful attack on a large force of Federals routing them and capturing 40 prisoners. Confederate loss, 3 killed.

March 21. Battle of Valverde, Arizona Territory. The battle was fiercely contested, and undoubtedly the severest of the present war—as desperate as any on record for the amount of men engaged. The Confederate forces were mostly native Texans, who fought with all their well known courage and bravery, capturing the enemies batteries of 7 guns, at the point of the bayonet and knife, winning a glorious victory over the Federals. Maj. Lockridge, of the Confederates, was killed while leading a charge. Confederate loss, 86 killed and 156 wounded. Federal loss, 230 killed, 200 wounded and 500 captured prisoners. The Confederate force amounted to only 2,300 ; the Federals were 6,000 strong.

Running the blockade. Over 120 vessels have run the blockade from Southern ports since March, 1861, to the present time. During the past year 7 vessels have been captured by the Federals in attempting to run the blockade. It is estimated that 70 vessels have entered Southern ports during the same time.

The great debt and cost of the war to the Northern government:

"By a late statement of the chairman of the committee of Ways and Means in the Federal House of Representatives, it was shown that there will be required, in order to pay the outstanding debts of the treasury, for which there are no funds on hand, and to carry on the war until the next session of Congress, upwards of seven hundred millions of dollars. The aggregate debt, on the 1st day of December next, will be, by the same statement, $925,000,000. But Congress must also provide for the remainder of that current fiscal year, which will terminate on the 30th of June, 1862. Including these sums, the official Federal estimate is, that the public debt will amount on the 1st of July, 1863—only sixteen months hence—to $1,350,000,000.

This estimate does not take into account the effects of a depreciated currency upon the cost to Government of its loans in bonds and treasury notes. Many additional millions must therefore be added to the aggregate to represent correctly the debt which will have to be redeemed, at some time, unless bankruptcy and repudiation come in first, with only a reasonable allowance for that excess of expenditure over estimates, which is universal at Washington ; the Federal debt will, by the middle of next year, reach fully up to fifteen hundred millions of dollars."

March 7. McClellan commences moving his troops from Washington to the Peninsula, Va.

March 6–7–8. Battle of Elkhorn, or Pea Ridge, Ark. A great and desperate battle was fought between the Federals, under Generals Curtis and Seigel, with a force of 20,000 men, and the Confederates, under Generals Price, McCulloch and VanDorn, with 14,000 men. After three days hard fighting the Confederates withdrew on account of the death of McCulloch. Confederate loss, 169 killed, 431 wounded and 200 taken prisoners. Federal loss, 390 killed, 900 wounded and 500 captured prisoners. [From Gen. VanDorn's official report.] Generals McCulloch and McIntosh, of the Confederates were killed. Gen. Seigel of the Federals, badly wounded. Thirty Federals were killed by the Confederate Indians in the battle.

March 7. Leesburg evacuated by the Confederates ; large amounts of Confederate and private property destroyed to prevent its falling into the enemy's hand.

March 8-9. Naval battle in Hampton Roads, near Norfolk, Va. The new Confederate steamer Virginia, (late Merrimac) otherwise known as the "Norfolk Turtle," "Colossus of the Roads," attacks five of the largest Federal blockading ships. The Virginia was assisted in the attack by the Confederate gun boats, "Patrick Henry," "Jamestown," "York-town" and "Teaser." The Virginia won a most glorious victory, having destroyed the following war vessels : Congress, burnt. 430 men, 50 guns ; Cumberland. sunk, 360 men, 22 guns ; Minnessota, riddled, 550 men. 40 guns; St. Lawrence, peppered, 480 men, 50 guns ; gun boats two or three disabled, 120 men, 6 guns ; Forts silenced, 200 men. 20 guns ; Ericsson, 150 men, 3 guns. Total—men, 2890—guns, 230. The Virginia also engaged the Federal iron clad vessel "Monitor." The encounter was a drawn battle, both vessels retiring at the same time. The Monitor was considerably damaged. The Virginia suffered only a trifling loss on the breaking of her iron prow. Federal loss estimated at 700 killed, wounded and drowned. Confederate loss, 9 killed, 18 wounded.

The self abnegating heroism of Capt. Buchanan, commander of the Virginia in the recent memorable conflict, will be generally appreciated when it is known that his younger and favorite brother was the purser of the frigate Congress, at which the fire of the Virginia was most pertinaciously directed, and is supposed to have perished on board of her.

March 1. Skirmishing near Charleston, Va., the federals routed and several killed, and 17 taken prisoners.

March 7 -8-9. The Confederate forces evacuates Centreville. Manassas and Occuquan, and falls back to a new line of defence on the Rappahannock River, Va. In retiring from Manassas, everything that could give aid and comfort to the enemy was destroyed ; guns, ammunition and stores were brought off in good order ; and the railroad tracks both that leading to Manassas Gap and that to Orange, torn up. The continuation of the former to Mount Jackson, in the direction of Stanton, will also be torn up as fast as General Jackson, of the Army of the Shenandoah, retires to the mountains. The New York Post says the retreat from Manassas was the most masterly effort in ancient or modern warfare. That it changes the character of the war, and protracts the contest for a long time.

March 8. Traffic in gold and silver. Gold and silver was sold by speculators as high as 80 per cent. premium in New Orleans, and in Memphis, Tennessee, gold was reported to have been sold at 140 per cent. premium. Dealing in gold and silver was suppressed by authority in New Orleans.

March 8-9. Capturing and harrassing the enemy near Nashville, Tenn. The gallant "partizan leader," Captain Morgan, is making him self famous in exploits ; he is giving the enemy great trouble. During a late skirmish, there were sixty Federals captured, also a large amount of property belonging to the enemy.

March 9. Skirmish near Nashville, Tenn. Captain Scott made an attack on the Federals, completely routing them; killing thirty and capturing a large amount of guns, ammunition, &c. Confederate loss, 3 killed 5 wounded.

March 11. The Federal army occupies Manassas, Va. On Tuesday evening, being about to be attacked by 18,000 of the enemy, General Jackson, with his small force of only 5000 fell back from Winchester, and stayed that night about four miles from that town. On Wednesday morning 1000 of the enemy took possession of Winchester. On the afternoon of Wednesday, Gen. Shields' column advanced toward Newtown, but were met and driven into Winchester by Col. Ashby's command. Before evacuating Winchester, General Jackson succeeded in removing all his stores, baggage, etc., so that not a dollar's worth of public property fell into the hands of the enemy. Skirmish near Cumberland Gap, Tenn. The Federals were severely repulsed and forty taken prisoners. Confederate loss, 2 killed and 1 wounded.

March 12. The dark days of the Confederacy. The peaceably defensive policy of the Confederate Government, during the past six months, has nerved the Federal Government to redoubled exertions in the scheme of conquering the South. The consequence to the Confederacy has been the loss of several important battles, reverses and loss of positions, not a few of which has been owing to bad Generalship on the part of Confederate commanders. The timid and discontented portion of the Southern people see in such reverses the doom of the South. But all true Southerners feel confident that the worst has come, and are certain of glorious success in the future. A new spirit of energy has been infused into the government, and the army, all true patriots, are resolved to conquer or die for the cause of freedom and their rights....Jacksonville, Florida, occupied by the Federals, who erect batteries. The people destroyed part of the city before surrendering to the Federals.... Skirmish near Paris, Tenn. The Confederates withdrew their pickets.

March 12–13. Skirmishing at Eastport, Tenn. The Confederate batteries attacked by the Federal gunboats; no damage done....Attack on New Madrid, Mo. The Federals advanced and attacked the Confederate at New Madrid, a brisk fight took place, during which the Federals were repulsed and driven back; during the following night the Confederates suddenly evacuated the place, as it was expected that the Federals were returning with large reinforcements to renew the attack. The Confederates left behind a large number of cannon, guns and army stores. Confederate loss during the fight 16 killed, 9 wounded. Federal loss 25 killed, 47 wounded.

March 13. Hon. W. L. Yancey, Confederate minister, arrives in New Orleans from Europe, he makes a speech to the citizens of New Orleans, during which he said that "He came back convinced that we had no friends in Europe, that we must fight the battle alone, and rely only on our own firm hearts."....The Federals landed a force of 2,500 men, and attacks and capture the Confederate batteries at Newbern, N. C. The Confederates, who numbered only 700, fought bravely before surrendering. After capturing the batteries the Federals advanced to the city of Newbern and shelled the place, before the women and children could escape. Confederate loss, 45 killed, 55 wounded and 202 taken prisoners. Federal loss estimated at 650 killed and wounded.... General Lee assigned the command of the Confederate army under the consent of President Davis....Andy Johnson, the traitor, arrives in Nashville, Tennessee, and assumes the office of Governor under Federal authority. Johnson was accompanied by his fellow traitors Etheridge and Maynard.

March 14. Gen Fremont appointed to a new command in the West —"The Mountain Department."....A party of Confederate cavalry was surprised by the enemy near Cumberland Gap, Tennessee. Five Confederates killed and wounded.

March 15. Bombardment of New Madrid and Island No. 10 commences....The Federal Senate has passed the bill for the "occupation and cultivation" of such cotton lands as the Federal armies may acquire in the South....They are going to take the cotton lands, and work negroes thereon for the benefit of the government. It is, to be sure, an absurd project and will be, whenever attempted, a miserable and costly failure. It is a Yankee scheme, to become slaveholders in fact, while giving the slaves a nominal freedom; to work them by agents, underlings and drivers, without one motive to produce that kindly humanity, which is the glory of the system in Southern hands. It is a grand national sham, which has in it all the elements of cruelty to the negro, and the certainty of breaking up speedily under circumstances of wretchedness to the poor slave, and losses to the speculating government ....Cavalry fight near Warrenton, Va. Gen. Stewart engaged a large force of Federal cavalry and succeeded in completely routing them, killing forty and captured one hundred with their horses, &c. Confederate loss was six killed and one hundred and eighty wounded.... General McClellan, commander of the Federal army, takes the field in person, commanding the "army of the Potomac" he delivers a long speech to his soldiers.

March 17. Attack and bombardment at Island 10, Mississippi river, continued by the Federals. The Island is vigorously defended.

March 18. Skirmish near Point Pleasant, Mo. The Federals erecting batteries below Island 10. The Confederate gunboats advances and shells the batteries, a brisk firing took place when the Federals retired from their batteries. Three of the Confederate steamers were slightly damaged. A gun bursted on board one of the boats while being fired. No lives lost.

March 19. Financial condition of the Confederate States. We learn that the official report of the Secretary of the Treasury shows that our financial system has proved adequate to supplying all the wants of the Government, notwithstanding the unexpected and very large increase of expenditures resulting from the great augmentation in the necessary means of defence. The report exhibits the gratifying fact that we have no floating debt; that the credit of the Government is unimpaired, and that the total expenditure of the Government for the year has been, in round numbers, one hundred and seventy millions of dollars—less than one third of the sum wasted by the enemy in his vain effort to conquer us—less than the value of a single article of export—the cotton crop of the year.

March 22. Fighting at Cumberland Gap, Tennessee. The Federals were repulsed with considerable loss. Confederate loss 2 killed, 5 wounded....Andy Johnson, the Yankee military Governor of Tennessee, makes a speech at Nashville in which he adroitly seeks to throw all the blame for the present condition of affairs upon the South.... In his opinion, Lincoln is our friend, and has no idea of interfering with our institutions.

March 22. A federal gunboat with a large force on board attempted to land and occupy a fortification on Mosquito Inlet, Florida. The Federals were fired on by a party of Confederates and forced to retreat. Federal loss 9 killed, 15 wounded and 2 captured.

March 23. Battle at Bolton's Mill, or Kernstown, Va., Gen. (Stone-Wall) Jackson with 6000 men engaged the Federals under Gen Shields, numbering 18,000 strong, after a severe contest the Federals were repulsed and fell back. General Jackson also fell back for reinforcements. Federal loss 175 killed, 460 wounded. Confederate loss 93 killed, 163 wounded and 230 captured....Guerrilla fighting near Jefferson City, Mo. Federal cavalry attacked Guerrilla parties dispersing them, 78 were captured prisoners, 3 killed, the Federals lost during the attack 400 killed and wounded.

March 25. The Federal bombardment at Island No. 10 has been continued for nine days, without doing any material damage to the fortifications. Two Federal gunboats were sunk and three badly disabled during the attack. It is estimated that the enemy fired 2500 shot and shell at the batteries on island 10 and vicinity during the first four days of the bombardment, and wasted 60,000 pounds of powder, with iron in proportion, killing one and wounding two of our men. The shells which they throw at us, weigh from 190 to 200 pounds. It is estimated that one thousand Federals were killed and wounded during the bombardment....Bay St. Louis A lively naval battle occurred in this vicinity to-day between the Confederate gunboats Oregon and Pamlico and the famous Federal gunboat New London. The fight lasted three hours, and resulted in the defeat of the New London....Peppering the Yankees, St. Mary's river, Georgia. A Federal gunboat with a large force on board went in pursuit of a Confederate steamer. The Federals unexpectedly encountered a body of Confederates who opened fire on them, killing forty and wounding sixteen Yankees. The Confederates retired without loss.

March 27. Battle of Glorietta, New Mexico. The Federals completely routed, with a loss of 700 killed and captured. Confederate loss, 68 killed and wounded.

March 29. Another attack on the Yankees at Edisto, North Carolina. General Evans, with one thousand men, proceeded to attack the

enemy, which was supposed to be 2500, but found them to be 5000 to 6000. The Confederates drove in the enemy's pickets, killing one, mortally wounded and capturing twenty. We retired in good order....
Fight in Polk county, Mo. An engagement took place between the Confederate forces and State troops; large number of Federals killed and wounded. Confederate loss reported to be 15 killed and wounded ....THE PECULIARITIES OF THE DAY.— In the whirl of passing events we scarcely notice the strange things that are daily happening and existing around us. How astonishing it will appear, in a few years, that a time existed when planters raised corn and potatoes, fattened hogs and cultivated garden vegetables, while cotton was by universal consent neglected, and this at a time when cotton was worth in Liverpool 28 cents a pound, yet selling on the plantation at 5 cents....Our newspapers have felt the martial influence as strongly as other things. They never had so much variety as now, since Faust first pulled the press; they are of all sizes and colors, and sometimes contain four pages, and sometimes two. They are short enough for a pocket handkerchief one day, and big enough for a table cloth another. They assume as many hues as Niagara in the sunshine, and are by turns blue, yellow, green, red, purple, grey and common brown packing paper....How odd it will be to remember that certain merchandize was forbidden to be brought into the city, and certain kinds of produce to be taken out; and that in many places in the markets and stores, dealers could sell only at prices dictated to them by a provost marshal....Politics are dead. A political enemy is a curiosity only read of in books. We have no whigs, no democrats, no know nothings, no nothing. Our amusements have revolutionized. The winter has passed by without a company having been engaged at the theatre, or a single circus having spread tent. Our people have done their own playing and their own singing, and the ladies have spent the mornings in sewing coarse shirts or pantaloons for the soldier to wear, and sung in public at night to gain money for the soldiers' equipments....The President's message to Congress, asking the repeal of all existing military laws and making conscript laws instead, recommends a law subjecting every man between 18 and 35 years to militia service....Skirmish near Rappahanock River, Va. Colonel Wheat engaged the enemy, driving them back, killing 3, and capturing 29 Yankees.

March 30. Federal raid at Union city, Tenn. A large force of Federals surprised a small squad of Confederates at Union city, after a sharp engagement the Federals retreated; Confederate loss 2 killed, 7 wounded and thirty taken prisoners. The enemy captured a large number of horses and army stores; 2 Federals killed.

March 31. Three companies of Georgians attacked the Yankees on Wilmington Island, killing one and wounding several; Georgians lost one killed....Skirmish near Jacksonville, Fla. A detachment of Col. Dilworth's Guard attacked the Federals, killing 4 and capturing 3 of the enemy; Confederate loss 2 killed and wounded.

April 1. A party of Federals secretly landed at Island 10, and spiked several guns of the Confederate battery, and successfully escaped from the Island.

April 4. Several Federal gunboats and transports passed Island 10 during a heavy storm and under cover of the night.... Naval engagement near Bay St. Louis, Miss. The Confederate gunboats engaged the Federal boats. The Federals withdrew, one of their boats being badly damaged; Confederate loss 1 wounded.

April 5. Two thousand Federals landed at Pass Christian, Mississippi, and attacked the Confederate camps. The Confederates being in small force, were compelled to retire, no one hurt. The Federals after committing many depredations on private property, returned to their boats.

April 5–6 Skirmishing near Yorktown, Va. The Federals are reported to be landing in large force in the neighborhood. A heavy battle will take place at an early day.

April 6. Skirmish in East Tennessee. Colonel Vaughn has penetrated Scott county, Tennessee, to Huntsville, whipped the enemy and routed him, and brought off meat, shoes, cattle and horses. He killed about forty of the enemy, and took seventeen prisoners, losing only five men. He also destroyed all the commissary stores he could not bring away.

April 6–7. Battle of Shiloh, Tenn. The Confederates, under Gens. Beauregard and Johnson, advanced from their encampment and attacked the enemy. The battle commenced early on Sunday morning. The fighting was the most terrible of any during the war, both sides contending with great desperation. Towards evening the Federals commenced falling back and retreated to their gunboats on the Tennessee river, being severely defeated, leaving behind nearly all their batteries (18) which were taken by the Confederates. General Prentiss, with 3000 men, were taken prisoners. An immense number of guns, army stores, &c., were captured by the Confederates. The lamented General Albert S. Johnson was killed early in the evening. During the night of Sunday, the Federals were largely reinforced by General Buell with 25,000 troops, and on Monday morning the battle was renewed with vigor, and continued throughout the day. The Federals were again repulsed and defeated, retiring to their gunboats. The Confederates moved back to their positions after accomplishing a most brilliant success ....The Confederate forces in the two days' fight numbered 38,000 men. The Federal force on the first day's fight was over 58,000, on the second day the Federals were reinforced to 70,000 men. The Confederate loss was 1,728 killed, 8,012 wounded, and 959 missing; Federal loss, 2,500 killed and 9,800 wounded and 3,700 taken prisoners. The Federals suffered severely in the loss of officers, nearly all being killed, wounded and captured. Generals Sherman, Tom Crittenden, Major Wallace and Lew Wallace were killed. Gens Grant, Smith and Buell were wounded.

April 7. The loss of Island 10, Mississippi river. After being bravely defended from a constant bombardment of twenty days, the Federal gunboats, with a large force, succeeded in passing below the Island and attacked the rear batteries, and compelled the Confederates to leave their

guns and surrender the Island. The Confederates, before surrendering, destroyed nearly all the property on the Island, spiking their guns.
The steamboats, floating batteries and wharf boats were scuttled and
sunk. About one thousand of the Confederates escaped from the Island,
after suffering severe hardships. Gen. Mackall and two thousand men
were taken prisoners on the Island. Many of the Confederates were
drowned in making their escape through the overflowed swamps near
the Island....Picket skirmish at Shepardstown, North Carolina. The
Confederates killed two Yankees and captured nine... Reported insurrection in Southern Illinois. A general disposition on the part of the
people to resist the payment of the war tax, followed by a protest of some
twenty members of the Legislature, against the doctrines of Lincoln's
message, is said to be the origin of the difficulty. The recusant members were arrested by the abolition authorities. Trouble followed, which
a single regiment found it impossible to quell, when several others were
sent out and the peace party was crushed at the point of the bayonet.

April 8. When our army commenced retiring from Shiloh on Monday
evening, General Breckinridge's brigade, with the cavalry, was ordered
to bring up the rear, and prevent the enemy from cutting off any of our
trains. The cavalry mentioned were attacked by a Federal force of two
regiments of infantry and one of cavalry, the latter being in the advance.
At the first fire the cavalry of the enemy turned and fled, actually breaking the ranks of their own infantry in endeavoring to escape the missiles
of the Confederates. The result of this dashing affair was—Federal
loss, killed and wounded, two hundred and fifty, and forty-eight prisoners; Confederates, ten killed and wounded.

April 11. Battle of Fort Pulaski, Georgia. The fort was attacked
by a large force of Federals. After a most gallant defence the Confederates surrendered. Three balls had entered the magazine, and a clear
breach had been made in it. The balls were conical, steel pointed, and
propelled with such force as to pass entirely through the wall at nearly
every fire No lives were lost during the bombardment, and only four
were wounded....The Federals take possession of Huntsville, Alabama,
and Decatur, on the Memphis and Charleston Railroad; the enemy seized
several railroad cars at Decatur.

April 13. Engagement at Fort Jackson and Fort Philippe, La.
(The first firing since the forts were built.) Several Federal gunboats
commenced bombarding Fort Jackson at "long range." The Fort
promptly replied by opening their batteries.

April 12–13. Heavy skirmishing continues daily on the Peninsula,
Va. The Federals repulsed in every attack. In the fight on the 12th
the Confederates lost 5 killed and 13 wounded; the Federal loss was
much heavier....The seige of Fort Macon, North Carolina, commences. The Federals land a large force near the fort. Col. White
who commanded the Confederates, sent out a detachment and gave
them battle, repulsing the Federals after a hot conte't. Confederate
loss, 15 killed and several wounded.

April 16. Skirmish near White Marsh Island, Georgia. The Federals repulsed with a loss of 20 killed and wounded. Confederate loss, 5 killed and 4 wounded.... Battle of Lee's Farm, Va. The Federals made a spirited attack on the Confederate lines. After a hard contested battle the Federals were severely defeated. Confederate loss, 30 killed and 55 wounded. Federal loss, 385 killed and wounded. The Confederates were commanded by Gen. Magruder.... Skirmishing near Fredericksburg, Va. The Confederates were attacked and driven into the city with severe loss. The Federals under Gen. McDowell advances and compels the Confederates to evacuate the city; large amounts of public and private property was destroyed during the hasty evacuation.

April 18. Bombardment of Forts Jackson and St. Phillippe, below New Orleans, continued.

April 19. Battle of South Mills, or "Sawyers Lane," Va. The Federals were defeated. Confederate loss, 18 killed and 50 wounded. Federal loss, 200 killed and wounded.... Fight near Elizabeth City, North Carolina. The Confederates were defeated with a loss of 6 killed and 31 wounded.... The Confederate Senate passed a bill providing for the organization of partizan bands.... Skirmishing continues on the Peninsula, Va. The Confederates generally repelling all attacks of the enemy; in the battle to-day, the Confederate loss was 18 killed and 50 wounded; the Federal loss was very heavy.

April 20. The seige of Fort Jackson, La., continues day and night. Such a tremendous bombardment has never been known in modern war. It is estimated that the enemy have fired 370,000 pounds of powder, and 1000 tons of iron. No damage has yet been done to the fort. Two gunboats have been sunk and one disabled.

April 23. Guerrilla fighting in Logan county, Va. A large party of Federals were routed, with a loss of 50 killed and wounded.

April 24. Great gunboat battle above Fort Jackson. On the morning of 24th inst., the Federal fleet succeeded in passing the forts. The fleet was immediately attacked by the Confederate gunboats, when a most desperate battle took place. The Confederate boats were all disabled and sunk. The Federal fleet advanced up the river to New Orleans. The Confederate fleet consisted of 10 gunboats, including the great ram Louisiana and "Manassas." The Federal fleet consisted of 8 mortar boats and 14 war steamers, including 4 iron clads. The Federals lost 3 war vessels; one of the largest vessels, the Pensacola, with a crew of 400 persons, was sunk with all on board. Confederate loss, on board of the boats, 38 killed and 125 wounded. Federal loss estimated at 1000 killed, wounded and missing. The garrison, under Gen. Duncan, still held possession of the forts.

April 25. The Federal fleet attacks the Chalmette Batteries, below New Orleans; after a fight of two hours, the batteries were silenced.... On the night of the 25th inst., the Confederate garrison at Fort Jackson mutinously revolted, spiking their guns, which compelled the brave Gen. Duncan to surrender the forts to the Federals. The bombardment of the fort lasted seven days, unintermittingly. Sixteen lives were lost inside the fort, and 26 wounded. No injury was done to the guns; the fort could have been held; had the garrison continued faithful....Fort Macon, North Carolina, surrenders conditionally after a well contested defence. Confederate loss inside the fort, was seven killed and 18 wounded.

April 25-27. Skirmishing in Tennessee and North Alabama between Colonel Scott's cavalry and the Federals under General Mitchell. Colonel Scott captures a large amount of stores and takes several prisoners.

April 26. Great excitement in New Orleans. The advance fleet of Federal gunboats arrives in front of New Orleans, a party of Federals landed and demanded the surrender of the city; immense quantities of sugar and molasses was destroyed to prevent its falling into the Federal hands; General Lovell retreats with his troops up the Jackson railroad.

April 27-28. Battle of Cassville, Mo. Confederates defeated with a loss of 30 killed and wounded, and 62 taken prisoners.

April 28. Skirmish at Pittsburg Landing, Tenn.; Federal loss 27 killed, wounded and prisoners.

April 28-29. Heavy skirmishing at Cumberland Gap, Tenn.; Federals repulsed with a loss of 100 killed, and 284 wounded; Confederate loss 27 killed and 61 wounded.

April 29. Fight at Bridgeport, Tenn.; Confederates defeated.

April 30. and May 1. Forts Macomb and Pike, on Lake Pontchatrain, La., was destroyed and abandoned by the Confederates; four Confederate gunboats were destroyed in a very hasty manner.

May 1. The city of New Orleans formally occupied by the Yankee General Butler ...General Morgan captures a large amount of Federal stores at Pulaski, Tenn.

May 5 Skirmish near Lebanon, Tenn.; the Confederates were severely defeated, and lost 20 killed and 35 wounded and 45 captured prisoners....Battle of Williamsburg, Va.; a signal victory was gained by the Confederates, under General Johnson, over the Federals, under General McClellan: Confederate loss, 520 killed and 1100 wounded; Federal loss, 1000 killed and 2700 wounded.

May 7. Battle of Barhamsville. or West Point, Va; the Yankees were badly defeated.

May 8. Battle at McDowel's, or Sitlington's Mill, Va.; Gen. Stonewall Jackson achieved a great victory over the Federals, who were commanded by General Milroy, Confederate loss, 350 killed and wounded; Federal loss, 175 killed and 255 wounded.

May 9. The Confederate forces evacuates Pensacola navy yard destroying vast amounts of property....Battle of Farmington, (near Corinth,) Tenn; the Federals, under General Pope, were badly defeated and put to route, with a loss of 35 killed and 100 wounded: Confederate loss, 15 killed and 109 wounded.

May 10. Skirmish near Elkhorn River, North Carolina; Confederate loss, 5 killed, 7 wounded; Federal loss, 7 killed and 45 wounded.

May 11. Colonel Morgan captures a train of cars on the Louisville railroad, near Cave City.

May 10–11. Fighting at Parisburg, or Gibbs Courthouse, Va. The Federals were defeated and driven from the town, with a loss of 20 killed and wounded, and 100 captured; large quantities of Federal stores were taken; Confederate loss, 1 killed and 14 wounded.

May 11. Skirmish near Pollocksville, North Carolina; the Federals defeated with a loss of 10 killed; Confederate loss, 3 wounded and 4 captured.

May 12. The advance fleet of Federal gunboats arrives at Natchez, Miss., and demands the surrender of the city.

May 13. Skirmishing near Purdy, Tenn.; several killed on both sides.

May 15. The fleet of Federal gunboats attacks the half finished batteries at Drewry's Bluff, Va; the Federals were repulsed with a loss of 13 killed and 11 wounded; Confederate loss, 7 killed and 8 wounded.

May 17. Battle of Princeton, Va.; the Confederates, under General Heth, defeated the Yankees; Confederate loss, 5 killed and 17 wounded; Federal loss, 150 killed and wounded.

May 18. Skirmish near City Point, Va.; Federals repulsed, with a loss of 8 killed and 9 captured.

May 18–19–20. Skirmishing near Corinth, Miss.; several severe fights occurred without important results; the Federals generally worsted: in the action of the 20th instant 25 Confederates were killed and 65 wounded.

May 18. The advance division of Farragut's Federal fleet arrives below Vicksburg, Miss.; the surrender of the city was demanded.

May 19. Skirmish near Warrenton, Va.; result was 4 Yankees killed; 2 Confederates killed....Skirmish below Vicksburg, Miss.; 4 Yankees killed and wounded.

May 18–19. Battle near Searcy, Arkansas; Federals defeated; Confederate loss 5 killed and 11 wounded; Federal loss 45 killed and wounded.

May 21. Bombardment of Fort Pillow, Tenn., resumed....The Federals commenced bombarding the batteries at Cole's Island, near Savannah.

May 20. A party of Federals in approaching St. Marks, Fla., were surprised by the Confederates; 17 Yankees were killed.

May 23–24. Battle at Front Royal, Va.; the Federals were defeated and driven from the town; 1470 were taken prisoners; large quantities of Federal stores were captured.

May 23–24. Battle of Lewisburg, Western Va.; the Confederates were defeated after a hard fight; Confederate loss, 230 killed and wounded; Federal loss was much heavier.

May 24. The Federal army, under Gen. Banks, in retreat from Front Royal, is pursued by the Confederates, who captures several prisoners, and takes large quantities of stores, &c., near Middleton, Va. ....Skirmish on the New Kent Road, Tenn.: the Yankees repulsed; Confederate loss 2 killed and 5 wounded.

May 23–24. Skirmishing at Garnett's Farm, near Richmond, Va. A severe engagement took place, in which the Confederates were defeated, with a loss of 100 killed and wounded; Federal loss, 122 killed and wounded.

May 25. Battle at Winchester, Va. General Stonewall Jackson defeats the Federal army; and takes 800 prisoners, and captures vast quantities of Federal stores; Confederate loss, 124 killed and wounded; Federal loss, 50 killed and 259 wounded.

May 26. Skirmish near Grand Gulf, Miss.; Federals repulsed..... The first bombarding at Vicksburg, Miss., takes place.

May 26–27. Skirmish at Hanover Courthouse, Va. A desperate engagement took place, in which the Federals were defeated with a loss of 63 killed and 279 wounded; Confederate loss 90 killed and 232 wounded.

May 28. A Confederate scouting party was surprised near Oakfield, Fla., and one man killed.

May 28–29. Corinth, Miss., evacuated by the Confederates, under General Beauregard; skirmishing occurred during the retreat; General Price engaged the Yankees and repulsed them.

May 31. General Stonewall Jackson falls back from Winchester, Va.

May 31, and June 1. Battle of Seven Pines, or Fair Oaks, Va. The Federal army, under General McClellan, was defeated by the Confederates under Gens. Hill, Longstreet, and Huger; Federal loss, 2070 killed, and 4900 wounded, and 550 prisoners; Confederate loss, 1035 killed, and 2700 wounded.

June 1. Fight near Strausburg, Va. Gen. Jackson defeats the Federals under Fremont.

June 2–5. Skirmishing near Washington, N. C. The Federals defeated, with a loss of 9 killed and 17 wounded; Confederate loss, 3 killed and 4 wounded; Colonel Singletary was killed.

June 3. Skirmish on James Island, near Savannah; the Federals repulsed, 20 captured prisoners; Confederate loss, two killed and eight wounded.

June 4. Fort Pillow evacuated by the Confederate forces. ... Fight near Sweeden's Cave, Tenn. A party of Confederates were surrounded by a large force of Federals; the Confederates cut their way out with a loss of 15 killed.

June 5. Skirmishing on the Chickahominy, Va. Four Confederates wounded.... Skirmish near Harrisburg, Virginia. The Federals repulsed; Confederate loss 40 killed and 100 wounded; General Turner Ashby killed.

June 6. Naval battle in front of Memphis, Tenn. The Yankee fleet under Com. Davis, attacks our gunboats; after three hours hard fighting we were defeated; our loss 80 killed and wounded, and 75 taken prisoners, and four gunboats sunk.... The city of Memphis formally surrendered and was occupied by the Yankees.

June 7. W. B. Mumford was publicly hung in the city of New Orleans by the order of Gen. Butler, for tearing down the United States flag from the mint.

7

June 7-8. Fighting on James Island, near Savannah; the Yankees were again repulsed; our loss 55 killed and wounded.

June 8-9. Battle of Port Republic, Va. Gen. Jackson defeats the Yankees under Gen. Shields and Fremont; our loss 550 killed and wounded; Yankee loss 1000 killed and wounded, and 700 taken prisoners.

June 10. Skirmish near York River Railroad, Va. Yankees defeated with a loss of 45 killed; our loss 4 killed.

June 11. Battle of Cross Keys, Va. Gen. Ewell defeats the Federals under Fremont. Federal loss 1,000 killed and wounded; Confederate loss 124 killed and wounded.

June 11-15 Gen. Stuart makes a successful raid among the Yankees near Hanover Court House, and destroys a large amount of Federal property and captures 175 prisoners. The brave Capt. Latane was killed in the action.

June 14. Battle of Languelle, on White River, Ark. Federals defeated.

June 16. Battle of Secessionville S. C A complete victory was gained over the Federals. Confederate loss 40 killed and 100 wounded. 26 missing; Federal loss 300 killed and wounded.

June 18. Skirmish near Richmond, Va. Federals repulsed; Confederate loss 9 wounded.

June 25. Battle on the Williamsburg Road, Va. The First Louisiana Regiment engaged Sickles' Brigade. After a sharp fight the Yankees were driven back. Confederate loss 200 killed and wounded.

Battles of the Chickahominy, before Richmond, Va. June 26, battle of Mechanicsville; 27, battle of Gainesville; 29, battle of Frazer's Farm; 30, battle of Willis' Church; July 1, battle of Malvern Hill. The great Federal army under Gen. McClellan was defeated and utterly routed after seven days hard fighting. Confederate loss 1,850 killed and 6,920 wounded; Federal loss 1,985 killed. 8,800 wounded and 6,000 taken prisoners.

June 28. Great bombardment at Vicksburg, Miss. Seven of the Federal gunboats advanced in front of the city, passing the batteries, when a most terrific bombardment took place. No injury was sustained by the forts.

July 1. A Confederate battery opened fire on the enemy near Coggins Point, James River. After a sharp contest the Federals retreated. Confederate loss 2 killed and 6 wounded.

July 3. Gen. McClellan evacuates his position before Richmond, Va., and retires to the James River.

July 4. The army of the Potomac was originally 230,000 strong. Prior to the 5th of April, according to the testimony of the Assistant Secretary of War, McClellan had 120,000 men at Yorktown. From the time he landed at Yorktown to the beginning of the great battles, he lost, it seems, in various ways, 78,000, and between the landing and close of the seven days' fighting, 98,000 out of 158,000 had been killed, had died in the swamps, or had by sickness been rendered unfit for service. In less than a year, he lost nearly 100,000 out of 230,000 men, without accomplishing anything.

July 8. Skirmish at Culpeper Cross Roads, Va. The Federals defeated.

July 13. Col. Forrest attacks and captures the Yankee garrison at Murfreesboro, Tenn. Federal loss 60 killed and 140 wounded and 1,900 taken prisoners.

July 15. Skirmish at Fayetteville, Ark. Confederates defeated. ....The great ram Arkansas engages the Federal fleet near Vicksburg Miss., and successfully run the gauntlet between 30 gun and mortar boats, without sustaining any injury. Nearly all of the Federal fleet was damaged, and one 'sunk by the guns of the Arkansas. Federal loss on board the boats was 63 killed and 84 wounded; Confederate loss on board the Arkansas 9 killed and 4 wounded. The Arkansas came down and moored under the batteries at Vicksburg; about seven o'clock in the evening five of the Federal gunboats came down and attempted to cut the Arkansas from the shore; the effort was unsuccessful, and the fleet was driven off.

July 21. Skirmish near Carmel Church, Va. The Federals claimed a victory.

July 22. The Confederate and Federal Governments make an agreement for a general exchange of prisoners.....Lincoln publishes an order authorizing the confiscating of Confederate property for the use of Federal soldiers.....The Federal fleet makes another attack on the ram Arkansas, in front of Vicksburg. The fleet was repulsed..... The Confederates attack the Yankees at Florence, Ala., and destroy a large amount of stores.

July 23. Gen. Bragg leaves Tupelo, Miss., for Kentucky.

July 24. The combined Federal fleet retires and abandons the seige of Vicksburg, without accomplishing anything, after a seige of six weeks. No injury was sustained by any of the batteries at Vicksburg. The number of shells thrown into the city and at the batteries will amount to 25,000. The casualties in the city was one woman and one negro man killed, and among the soldiers on guard and at the batteries there was 22 killed and wounded. The lower bombarding fleet, under command of Coms. Farragut and Porter, consisted of 18 gun and mortar boats, 5 sloops of war and 70 transports; the upper fleet consisted of 11 gunboats and rams, and 13 transports, under command of Com. Davis. It is estimated that 500 Federals died from sickness during the seige of Vicksburg.

July 25. Col Armstrong attacks the Yankees at Courtland, Ala., and captures 133 prisoners.....Col. Kelly attacks and routs a large party of Federals at Jonesboro, Tenn. Federal loss 9 killed and 5 wounded; 3 Confederates wounded.

July 26. Guerilla fighting in Missouri. The Confederate guerillas have been successful in several attacks on the Federals in Missouri.

July 29. Fight at Mt. Sterling, Ky. The Confederates were repulsed with a loss of 13 killed and 20 wounded; Federal loss 3 killed and 7 wounded.

July 31. Gen. **Morgan**'s official report of his successful raids through Kentucky and Tennessee, amounts to the capturing of 20 towns, and taking of 1,200 prisoners, and destroying Federal property to the amount of $600,000. The Confederate loss in all the engagements was 23 killed and 47 wounded..... Engagement on the James River near Richmond, Va. The Federal fleet repulsed. Confederate loss 3 killed and 4 wounded.

July 27. Skirmishing near Bolivar, Tenn. The Confederates repulsed with a loss of 15 killed and wounded.

July 27-30. Skirmishing near Stevenson, Ala. The Yankees defeated in two severe fights. Loss of both sides, 17 killed and 40 wounded.

July 28. Battle of Moore's Mill, Mo. (near Fulton.) The Confederates were routed with a loss of 22 killed and 60 wounded.

July 28. Skirmishing near Humboldt, Tenn.

June —. The Confederates attacked and captured the Federal garrison at Summerville, Va. Federal loss, 6 killed and 23 wounded. Confederate loss, 5 wounded.

Aug. 1 Bombardment on James River, near Westover. Four Federals killed and 8 wounded.

Aug. 2. Fight near Madison, Ark. Gen. Parsons surprised a Federal camp and put the Yankees to flight.

Aug. 2. Cavalry skirmish at Orange Court House, Va. Confederates defeated, 2 killed and 10 wounded.

Aug. 3. Skirmish at Cox's Mill Creek, Va. Confederate loss 2 killed and 5 wounded.

Aug. 3. Fight near Memphis, Tenn. The Confederates under Jeff. Thompson defeated with a loss of three killed and five wounded.

August 4. Skirmish near Hanover Court House, Va. Gen. Stuart captures 80 Yankees. Federal stores destroyed.

August 5-6. Fighting near Malvern Hill, Va. The Federals after a hard battle defeated the Confederates with a loss of five killed and nine wounded. The Federals afterwards evacuated the place. Federal loss 30 killed and wounded.

August 5. Battle of Tazewell, near Cumberland Gap. Tenn. Federals repulsed with a loss of 94 killed and wounded. Confederate loss 21 killed and 35 wounded.

August 5. Battle of Baton Rouge, La. The Confederates under Gen. Breckinridge, gained a signal victory. Federal loss 630 killed and wounded. Confederate loss 42 killed and 173 wounded.

August 5-8. Guerilla fighting near Stockton, Mo. The Federals claimed a victory. Confederate loss 90 killed and wounded. Federal loss 85 killed and wounded.

August 6. Fight at Pack's Ferry, Western Virginia. Gen. Loring repulsed a large force of Federals.

August 6. The great ram and gunboat "Arkansas" destroyed and abandoned by her officers. The machinery of the boat became disabled, which compelled the crew to destroy the boat to prevent her falling into Federal hands.

August 6th. The notorious Federal General McCook was killed by Partisan Rangers in Tennessee.

August 7. Skirmish near Decatur, Ala. Capt. Roddy defeats a force of Federals, killing several and capturing 123 prisoners. Confederate loss 2 killed and 7 wounded.

August 8th. Fight near Culpepper court-house, Va. The Federals were badly routed, 5 killed and 19 wounded, and 21 taken prisoners.

August 8. Lincoln issues a proclamation calling for 600,000 more men to put down the rebellion.

August 8–9. Battle of South West Mountain, or Cedar Run, Va. The Confederates, under General Jackson, defeated the combined divisions of the Federal army under Banks, McDowell and Seigel. Confederate loss 220 killed and 670 wounded. Gen. Winder killed. Federal loss 300 killed and 900 wounded, and 400 taken prisoners.

August 11. Battle of Independence, Mo. The Confederate Partisans under Col. Hughes and Quantrell, defeated the Federals, killing 29.

August 11. Skirmish at Friar's Point, Miss. The Yankees defeated and put to route, several taken prisoners.

August 15–16. Battle at Lone Jack, Mo. Col. Tracy, the Partisan leader, gained a great victory over the Federals, putting them to route with a loss of 300 killed and wounded. Confederate loss, 73 killed and wounded. Previous to this battle, Colonel Tracy had defeated the enemy in Greenfield, Osceola and Harmonsville, Mo, causing great havoc among the Yankees, capturing large amounts of Federal stores, and took 300 prisoners, and killing over 100 of the enemy.

August 16. A party of Confederates were defeated near Mammoth Cave, Ky.

August 16–17. Skirmish at Bayou Sara, La. The Federals destroyed part of the town—several persons killed.

August 17. Skirmish at Loudon, Ky. The "Kirby Smith Brigade" of cavalry, under Col. Scott, routed the Federals and drove them from the place, capturing 111 men ; Confederate loss two killed.

August 18. Barboursville, Ky., taken by the Confederates ; 45 Yankees taken prisoners.

August 19. Gen Lee crossed the Rapidan in pursuit of the retreating Federal army under Gen Pope.

August 20. Fight near Union Mills, Buchanan county, Mo ; Federals defeated, with a loss of 5 killed and 4 wounded.

August 20. Fort Donelson, Tenn, taken by the Confederates, 1100 Federals taken prisoners.

August 20–21. Fighting near Gallatin, Tenn. The Confederates under Gen Morgan defeats and routes the Yankees under Gen Johnson. Federal loss 200 killed and wounded, and 500 taken prisoners : Confederate loss 27 killed and 39 wounded.

August 22 Battle of Big Hill, near Richmond, Ky. Colonel Scott defeats the Federals, putting them to route with a loss of 23 killed and 65 wounded.

August 22. Skirmish at Warrenton, Va. Federals defeated with great loss.

Aug. 22. Gen Stuart surprises the Yankees at Catlett Station, Va, routing the enemy and capturing a large amount of Federal stores, and took 350 prisoners ; Confederate loss 2 killed and 5 wounded.

August 26. Skirmishing at Kienzi, Miss. A Confederate party made a dash into the Federal camps, capturing 17 prisoners.

August 27 The Federals evacuate Huntsville, Ala.

August 25. Fighting near Danville, Ky. Our forces defeated and 40 taken prisoner .

August 26 Our forces capture the Yankee camps and stores at Manassas Junction.

August 27. Fighting near Bridgeport, Tenn. Gen Armstrong defeated the Federals after a sharp fight. Federal loss 70 killed and wounded and 213 taken prisoners.

August 29–30. Skirmish near Bolivar, Tenn. Federals routed with a loss of 90 killed and wounded, and 70 taken prisoners. Confederates 85 killed and wounded.

August 28. Fight at Thoroughfare Gap, Va. The Federals severely defeated, and driven from their strong entrenchments.

August 29–30. Battle of Mt. Zion, or Richmond, Ky. Gen. Kirby Smith achieved a signal victory over the Federals in two hard-fought battles. Federal loss 178 killed and 450 wounded, and 4300 taken prisoners. Confederate loss 125 killed and 800 wounded.

August 29–30. Second battle on Manassas Plains, Va. Gen. Lee won a glorious victory over the Federal army, under Gen. Pope. Confederate loss 1800 killed and 4,000 wounded. Federal loss 8,000 killed and wounded, and 7,000 taken prisoners.

August 30. Fighting near Richmond, Ky. The "Kirby Smith Brigade," under Col Scott, defeats and routes a large force of Abolitionists, killing 50 and capturing 3,000. Southern loss 5 killed, 20 wounded.

August 31. Fight at Stevenson, Tenn. The Federals were defeated and compelled to evacuate their strong fortifications.

August 30–Sept. 2d. Col. Jenkins defeated the Federals in several fights in the Kanawha Valley, capturing several prisoners, Federal stores, &c.

September 1st. Battle near Centreville, Va. Federals again defeated by Gen. Jackson Confederate loss, 45 killed and 135 wounded. The Federal General Kearney killed.

September 1. Skirmish near Germantown, Va. Federals routed.

September 2. Bombardment of Natchez, Miss. A party of Federals landed at Natchez, and were driven back to their gunboats. The boats then shelled the city for several hours. Two persons were killed in the city.

September 3d. Col. Scott takes possession at Frankfort, Ky., and captures several Yankees.

September 7–10. Guerilla fighting near Salt River, Ky. Federals routed.

September 9. The Confederate Army under Generals Lee and Jackson enters Maryland.

September 9–10. Col. Jenkins defeats the Federals at Buchanan and Ravenswood, Western, Va., capturing large amounts of Federal stores.

September 9th. The Yankee garrison at Williamsburg, Va., was surprised and captured by the Confederates. Federal loss 15 killed and 70 taken prisoners. Confederate loss 17 killed and wounded.

September 9. Washington, North Carolina taken by the Confederates ; the Federals re-captured the place after a hard fight.

September 10. Skirmishing near Helena, Arkansas. Federals defeated.

September 11. Great excitement was created in the country by the report of the capture of Cincinnati.

September 11. Engagement on the St. Johns River, Florida. Federal gunboats repulsed. Our loss two killed and five wounded,

September 13–14. Battle of Cotton Hill, Western Va. Gen. Loring defeats the Federals, capturing all their fortifications, stores, &c. Federal loss 400 killed and wounded. Our loss 25 killed and wounded.

Sept. 15. Fighting at Charleston, Western, Va. Gen. Loring again defeats the Yankees, driving them from the town.

Sept. 14. Battle of Fort Craig, opposite Mumfordsville, Ky., Gen. Chalmers attacked the Federals, after a day's hard fighting, our forces were compelled to fall back with severe loss. General Chalmers is much to be censured for his unnecessary attack and sacrifice of lives. Our loss 65 killed and 275 wounded. Federal loss 18 killed and 30 wounded.

September 13–14. Skirmishing near Opelousas, La. Several fights occurred between Confederate partisans and marauding parties of Yankees. 150 Yankees were captured in one skirmish. The Confederates lost 15 men killed and 13 wounded, and fifty captured in different conflicts.

September 13, 14, 15. Seige and capture of Harper's Ferry, Va. Gen Stonewall Jackson captures the Yankee garrison after three days' hard fighting. 11,583 Yankees were taken prisoners. Our loss 31 killed and 40 wounded. Yankee loss 200 killed and wounded. An immense amount of Federal stores, guns, &c. were taken.

Sept 14. Battle of Boonsboro Gap or South Mountain, Maryland. The Confederates under D. H. Hill fought a most desperate battle, repulsing the Federals and holding possession of the Pass against the enemy who outnumbered them five to one. Federal loss 4,500 killed and wounded. Confederate loss 600 killed and 1,800 wounded.

Sept. 14. Confederate Debt. Up to the first of August, 1862, our debt was $328,748,830.70; and for outstanding requisitions, $18,524,-128.15. Receipts at the Treasury, grand total, $302,555,196.60. Funds to be raised by January 1, 1863, $209,550,487.06, most of which is to be raised by Treasury Notes.

Sept. 13, 14. General Armstrong surprises the Federals at Iuka, Miss., and routes the garrison. Gen. Price enters the town on the 15th, and captures a large amount of Federal stores, &c. Confederate loss 5 killed and wounded. Federal loss 10 killed, 21 wounded.

Sept. 13. Fight at Newtonia, Mo. Federals defeated with a loss of 150 killed and wounded, and 100 taken prisoners.

Sept. 15. Fight at Ponchatoula, La. Federals routed after a brisk engagement. Yankee loss 5 killed and 6 wounded. Confederate loss 2 killed.

Sept. ,. The Federal garrison at Mumfordsville surrendered to Gen. Buckner. 4,800 Yankees taken prisoners.

Sept. 17. The Federals evacuates Cumberland Gap, Tenn.

September 17. Battle of Sharpsburg or Antietam, Maryland. A signal victory was won by the Confederates under Gen. Lee. The Federals under command of Gen. McClellan numbered 90,000 men. The Confederate force amounted to 56,000 men. The Confederates held possession of the battle-field for 24 hours after the fight, and made a successful retreat. Confederate loss 1,900 killed and 6,915 wounded and 800 taken prisoners. Federal loss, 2,010 killed and 9,416 wounded and 1,044 taken prisoners.

September 18. Fight near Jacksonville, Fla. Federal gunboats repulsed.

September 19. Gen. Lee retreats across the Potomac from Maryland.

September 19-20. Battle of Iuka, Miss. Gen. Price defeated the Federals in the first day's fight, driving them from their fortifications. The second day's battle resulted in the complete rout of the Confederates, with a loss of 265 killed and 687 wounded. Federal loss, 188 killed and 582 wounded.

September 20 Battle of Sheppardstown Ford, Maryland. Gen. A. P. Hill achieved a fine victory over the Federals, repulsing and driving them back across the Potomac with great loss. Confederate loss, 250 killed and wounded. Federal loss, 2,500 killed and wounded.

Sept 21. Mumfordsville, Ky., evacuated by the Confederates,

September 22. Lincoln issues a proclamation declaring all negroes in the Rebel States free after the 1st of January, 1863.

September 26. Gen. Beauregard takes command of the army at Charleston S. C.

September 27. Sabine city taken by the Federals.

September 29. Fight near New Haven, Ky. Confederates defeated Col. Crawford and 290 Confederates taken prisoners.

October 1. Skirmishing near Middleton, Ky. Federal loss, 11 killed and 19 wounded. Confederate loss, 7 killed and 13 wounded....Skirmish at Fern Creek, Ky. Federals repulsed with a loss of 7 killed and wounded....A report was presented to the Confederate Senate, showing the whole number of sick and wounded soldiers admitted into the Hospitals in and around Richmond, since their organization to the present time, was 99,505, of whom 9,774 have been furloughed, and 7,603 have died.

October 3. Fight near Franklin, N. C. Federals defeated, with a loss of 20 killed and 18 wounded and 40 prisoners.

October 3-4-5. Battle at Corinth, Miss. Confederates won signal victories on the first and second day's fighting; on the third day they lost the battle and were compelled to retreat. Confederate loss, 1200 killed and 2,300 wounded, and 2000 taken prisoners. Federal loss, 450 killed and 1.820 wounded and 320 taken prisoners.·

October 3. Skirmish at Olive Hill, Ky. General Morgan.defeats the Home Guards.

· October 5. The Confederates make an attack. on a fleet of Federal steamboats near Donaldsonville, La, killing several Yankees on board of the steamers.

October 6 Skirmish near Big Burch Mountain, Western Va., several Yankees taken prisoners.

October 7. A party of Confederates under Gen Anderson were surprised and captured at Lavernge, Tenn.

October 8. Battle of Perryville or Chaplin Hill, Ky. A decided victory was gained by the Confederates under Gens. Polk and Hardee, over the Federals. Federal loss 4,000 killed and wounded and 2,000 taken prisoners. Confederate loss 2,700 killed and wounded.

October 9. The city of Galveston, Texas, occupied by the Federals ...Skirmish at Middleburg, Va. Federals defeated.....Cavalry skirmish near Chaplin Hill, Ky. The Confederates under Col. Scott defeated, with a loss of 9 killed and 5 wounded. Federal loss 5 killed and 11 wounded....Fight near Frankfort, Ky. Confederates suffered a defeat by the Federals under Dumont. Confederate loss, 4 killed and 75 taken prisoners. Federal loss 5 killed.

October 10–11. Gen. J. E. B. Stuart, with a force of 2,000 men, makes a successful reconnoisance through Pennsylvania, destroying large amounts of Federal property and causing a great panic among the Yankees. During this expedition Gen. Stuart made one of the most extraordinary marches on record, marching 90 miles in 24 hours.... Fight at Augusta, Ky. A party of Confederates after surrendering were fired upon by the Yankees. Lt. Col Prentice was killed. The Yankees were afterwards attacked in force and a large number killed.

October 17. Fight in Harlan co., Ky. The Confederates attacked and defeated a large.party of Union men, killing 4, and 20 taken prisoners....Guerilla fighting near Island 10, Tenn. Confederates defeated with a loss of 5 killed and 11 wounded. Federal loss, 3 killed and 7 wounded.

October 18. Skirmish near Thoroughfare Gap. Va. Confederates repulsed....Murder of Confederates. Ten Confederate prisoners were shot dead by the order of the Federal General, McNeil, at Palmyra, Mo., on account of a raid which the Confederates had made into the town.

October 18–20. Gen. Bragg's army reaches Knoxville, Tenn., on retreat from Ky.

October 18. Skirmish at Lexington, Ky. Morgan's cavalry makes another successful dash into the city, routing the Federals, killing 8 and capturing 150.

October 20. Fighting at Pittman's Ferry, Ark. A party of Confederate Partisans were attacked and defeated by a large force of the Federal army.

October 21. Skirmishing near Nashville, Tenn. Federals defeated and driven into the city.

October 22. Fight at Pocotaligo and Coosahatchie, S. C. Federals repulsed and driven back. Our loss 22 killed and 50 wounded. Federal loss 100 killed and 287 wounded....Battle at Maysville, Ark. Our forces defeated, with a loss of 32 killed and wounded. Federal loss 7 killed and 19 wounded.

October 23. Skirmish near Waverly, Tenn. Our forces defeated.

October 27. Battle of Albemarle, Bayou Lafourche, La. A desperate fight occurred in which our forces were defeated by a vastly superior force of Federals. Our loss 17 killed, 15 wounded, and 208 taken prisoners. Col. McPheeters of our forces was killed after surrendering to the Yankees....A Confederate camp in Clarkson, Mo., was surprised and routed; 4 killed and 40 taken prisoners....Skirmish at Snicker's Gap, Va. Federals repulsed and several killed.

October 28. Fight near Fayetteville, Mo. Our forces defeated, with a loss of 5 killed. Federal loss 3 killed and 4 wounded.....A company of Confederates were surprised and routed with a heavy loss, at Gonzella, Fla.

October 30. Fight at Bollinger's Mills, Ark. Our forces defeated, several taken prisoners.

October 31. Skirmish near Catlett's Station, Va. Federals routed.

October 31. Bombardment at Lavaca, Texas. The Abolitionists kept up the bombardment of the town for two days, when they were forced to retire.

November 4. Battle at Williamston. Our forces defeated by a superior force of the Yankees. Our loss, 4 killed and 32 wounded. Federal loss, 7 killed and 28 wounded.

November 5. Skirmishing near Warrenton, Va. Our forces driven from the place, but returned again reinforced, and defeated the Federals, compelling them to retreat. Federal loss, 1 killed and 6 wounded. Our loss none.....Gen. McClellan, of the Yankee army removed by the Government. Gen. Burnside appointed in his place.

November 7. Fight at Haymarket, Va. Major Andrews attacked a large body of Federals, routing them and capturing 30 prisoners, besides taking a large amount of Federal stores.

November 7. Fight near Vera Cruz, Mo. The Abolitionists defeated, and their garrison captured, with 300 prisoners.

November 7. Skirmish near Donaldsville, La. Abolitions repulsed and put to flight.

November 8. A party of Confederate cavalry was surprised and captured near Cold Water, Miss. 18 Confederates wounded.

November 9. The Federals made a raid into Fredericksburg, and were driven from the town, with a loss of 5 killed and wounded. Confederate loss, 1 killed and 3 wounded....A large force of Federals attempted to land at St. Mary's Ga., and were repulsed by the Confederates. The Federals afterwards shelled the town.

November 11. Fight at Castleman's Ferry, Va. Gen. A. P. Hill repulsed a large force of Federals who attempted to cross the river at that point.

November 12. Skirmish near Nashville, Tenn. Gen. Forrest defeated the Abolitionists near Nashville, killing 15 and wounding 37....Fight at Madisonville, Ky. Col. Johnson's cavalry made a dash into the town and scattered the Federals, killing 23 and wounding 100.

November 13–15. Fighting near Lebanon, Tenn. Gen. Morgan routed the Abolitionists and captured 180 prisoners.

November 16–17. Skirmishing at Fredericksburg, Va. Abolitionists repulsed and 25 captured. Confederate loss, 2 killed, 7 wounded.

November 17. The famous Gen. Morgan of the Confederate army came near being captured, near Tyree Spring, Tenn. He succeeded in making his escape by a ruse.

Nov. 17–18. Skirmishing at Franklin, Va. The Abolitionists defeated and driven back in several brisk engagements, and 17 captured.

November 19. Bombardment of Fort McAllister, Genesis Point, Ga. A heavy bombardment by the Federals was kept up for several hours, when the Yankees retired.

November 27–28. Skirmishing near Mill Creek and Lavergne, Tenn. A severe fight took place near Lavergne, in which the Abolitionists were completely routed, with a loss of 170 killed and wounded. Confederate loss 20 killed, 85 wounded.

November 20th. The following will show some of the means and appliances by which the Abolitionists are trying to subjugate the South and restore the Union :

The World editorially says it is not alone the purpose of the Administration to subdue the Southern armies, but to impoverish the people by a wholesale confiscation of their property.

Our enemies prohibit the introduction of medicines into the South. Since the Federal occupation of Memphis and New Orleans, druggists in those cities have been subjected to the confiscation of their property and to imprisonment as felons, for the sale of medicines that passed within our lines.

On the march from Corinth, Federal troops set fire to fields and fences, which communicated to the houses, etc. Great destruction of property ensued. The route of the army can be tracked by the cinders, blackened stumps and remains of dwellings, barns and fences, fired maliciously. The line of march was lighted by conflagrations. Houses were entered and pillaged by lawless stragglers, and indignities heaped on families without regard to age or sex.

Rosencranz intends to hang all guerillas, and defies the threatened rebel retaliation. As he proceeds South, the alternative will be offered, he says, of allegiance to the Union, or forced within the rebel lines. He will apply the same law to women and children. His idea is to throw an immense population on the South in order to consume what it considers our limited supplies, and thus starve us into subjugation.

A List of Killed, Wounded and Missing in the Battles, Skirmishes and Engagements of the War for the Years 1861 and 1862.

CONFEDERATE VICTORIES.

Battles, Skirmishes and Engagements.	Date.	Confederates Killed.	Confederates wounded.	Confederates captured.	Federals Killed.	Fed's wounded.	Federals captured.
	1861.						
Evacuation of San Antonio	February ..18	....	....	....	....	....	250
Surrender of Fort Brown.	March 12	....	....	....	....	....	160
Fort Sumter	April.......13	....	....	....	....	....	....
Surrender of Fort Bliss...	April.....15	....	....	....	....	....	100
Surrender at Indianola...	April.....20	....	....	....	....	....	600
Sewell Point....	May.......19	....	....	....	6	10	....
Fairfax Court House.....	May.......31	1	2	....	6	4	6
Acquia Creek.............	June 1	....	....	....	....	....	....
Pig's Point....	June 5	....	....	....	....	....	....
Great Bethel.............	June 10	1	7	....	150	250	....
Vienna...................	June 18	....	....	....	50	100	....
Kansas City.............	June 17	15	30	....	5	150	150
New Creek .....:.......	June 19	....	....	....	3	6	....
Romney.................	June 26	2	3	....	15	....	....
Mathias Point..........	June 27	....	1	....	6	10	....
Hainesville............	July 4	2	12	....	16	45	53
Carthage..............	July 5	70	200	....	300	200	....
Scary Creek..........	July 17	3	1	....	50	100	....
Bull Run..............	July 18	55	95	5	197	200	....
Manassas.............	July 21	309	1483	....	1000	2200	1000
Mesilla...............	July 25	....	....	....	32	....	500
Fort Stanton....	July 28	....	....	....	....	....	750
Oak Hill..............	August ...10	265	800	30	800	1000	300
Mathias Point........	August ...15	1	....	....	....	5	....
Hawks' Nest..........	August ...20	....	....	....	29	30	....
Charleston...........	August ...21	3	7	....	9	13	....
Bailey's Cross Roads.....	August ...26	....	....	....	35	....	72
Big Creek, Va...........	September.. 3	....	2	....	3	3	....
Fort Scott.............	September.. 7	....	6	....	7	18	....
Gauley, or Carnifax Ferry.	September 10	....	20	....	150	250	....
Lewinsville	September 11	....	....	....	5	9	....
Toney's Creek..........	September 11	....	....	....	20	30	50
Blue Mills, Mo.........	September 17	5	20	....	60	230	....
Barboursville.........	September 19	2	....	....	50	....	2
Lexington.............	Sept 19-20-21	25	72	....	39	120	3500
Alamosa...............	September 25	2	....	....	80	....	17
Steamer Fanny.........	October 1	....	....	....	....	....	45
Greenbrier River.......	October 3	7	33	10	100	150	....
Chicamahcomico	October 5	....	....	....	....	....	32

CONFEDERATE VICTORIES—(Continued.)

Battles, Skirmishes and Engagements.	Date.	Confederates killed.	Confederates Wounded.	Confederates captured.	Feder's killed	Federals wounded.	Federals captured.
Santa Rosa	October ..8-9	20	42	32	50	70	50
Mississippi Passes	October ...12	....	....	....	....	....	....
Boliver	October ...16	1	10	....	15	40	12
Leesburg	October ...21	36	118	2	475	835	710
Rock Castle Ford	October ...21	11	30	....	20	47	....
Belmont	November . 7	105	419	117	473	627	227
Piketon	November 8, 9	11	20	7	220	97	....
Guyandotte	November 19	5	9	....	43	57	118
Upton Hill	November 16	....	....	....	6	....	30
Fall's Church	November 18	1	2	....	10	....	23
Pensacola	November 22	13	7	....	11	23	....
Near Vienna	November 26	....	....	....	10	....	26
Annandale	December . 2	2	....	2	4	....	15
Alleghany	December .13	20	96	28	95	178	8
Woodsonville	December .17	7	11	....	20	42	....
Gen. Price's Retreat	Dec. 17-18-19	5	19	200	15	60	....
Chustenahlah	December .26	.18	32	....	250	170	209
Skirmish on Green River	December .28	2	3	....	15	20	15
	1862.						
Port Royal River	January.... 1	8	15	....	17	9	....
Middle Creek	January ...10	10	14	....	200	230	....
Near Boston, Ky	January ...22	...	3	....	8	5	....
James Island	January ...27	5	8	....	45	15	35
New Concord	February .14	....	....	....	5	9	....
Near Galveston	February .18	....	....	....	3	....	....
Near Savannah, Tenn River	March...... 1	7	14	....	22	45	....
Near New Madrid	March...... 1	....	....	....	15	....	20
New Creek, Va	March...... 6	3	....	....	....	....	40
Hampton Roads	March ... 8-9	9	18	....	250	....	....
Near Nashville	March ... 8-9	....	....	....	....	....	60
Charleston	March 8	....	....	....	....	....	17
St. Mary's River	March 25	....	....	....	40	16	....
Warrenton, Va	March 15	6	108	....	40	....	100
Point Pleasant	March 18	....	....	....	....	....	....
Valverde	March 21	86	156	....	230	200	500
Mosquito Inlet	March 22	....	....	....	9	15	....
Winchester	March 23	93	163	230	275	460	24
Near Jefferson City	March 27	3	....	78	130	200	....
Edisto Island	March 29	....	....	....	1	3	24
Rappahannock River	March 29	....	....	3	....	....	29
Jacksonville	March 31	4	1	....	4	....	3
Shiloh	April 6-7	1728	8012	959	2535	7082	4044
Near Shiloh	April 8	4	6	....	50	200	48
East Tennessee	April ... 6-7	....	....	....	30	10	17
Skirmishing on Peninsula	April ..12-13	5	13	16	17	28	....
Whitemarsh Island	April.....16	5	4	....	8	12	....
Lee's Farm	April 16	30	55	....	100	280	....

CONFEDERATE VICTORIES—(Continued.)

Battles, Skirmishes and Engagements.	Date.	Confederates Killed.	Confederates Wounded.	Confederates Captured.	Federals Killed.	Federals Wounded.	Federals Captured.
	1862.						
South Mills...............	April 19	18	50	....	43	150	....
Peninsula, Va............	April 18	16	52	....	49	78	....
Logan County............	April 23	13	40	....	15	39	....
Pittsburg Landing.......	April 28	....	....	....	5	16	....
Cumberland Gap........	April ..28–29	27	61	....	100	284	....
Barhamsville...........	May 7	....	....	....	174	255	....
Williamsburg..........	May 5	520	1100	....	1000	2700	....
McDowell's...........	May 8	100	250	....	175	255	....
Farmington...........	May 9	19	109	....	35	100	....
Parisburg............	May ...10–11	5	17	....	20	100	100
Pollocksville	May 11	3	....	4	10	....	....
Drury's Bluff........	May 15	7	8	....	13	11	....
City Point...........	May 18	....	....	....	8	....	9
Near Corinth........	May 18–19–20	25	65	....	32	120	....
Near Warrenton	May 19	2	....	....	4	....	....
Searcy	May ...18–19	5	11	....	10	30	....
St. Marks...........	May 20	....	....	....	17	....	....
Front Royal.........	May ...23–24	....	....	....	....	....	1470
Lewisburg..........	May ...23–24	70	160	....	91	270	....
Garnett's Farm......	May ...23–24	25	80	....	37	85	....
Winchester	May 25	41	83	....	50	200	800
Hanover Court House...	May ..26–27	90	232	....	63	279	....
Seven Pines.........	May 31, June 1	1037	2760	....	2070	4800	550
Washington........	June 2–5	3	4	....	9	17	....
James Island........	June 3	2	8	....	....	....	20
Sweeden's Cave......	June 4	15	....	....	....	....	....
Harrisburg.........	June 5	40	100	....	72	97	....
Port Republic........	June ...8–9	130	330	....	200	800	700
Cross Keys..........	June ...11	43	160	....	160	640	....
Secessionville.......	June ...16	40	100	....	74	226	....
Williamsburg Road.....	June ...25	40	165	....	79	194	....
Battles of the Chickahom'y	June 26, July 1	1850	6920	....	1985	8800	6000
Near Murfreesboro.....	July 13	....	....	....	60	140	1900
"Arkansas," near Vicksb'g	July 15	9	4	....	63	84	....
Seige at Vicksburg.....	May 26, July 24	7	18	....	....	....	....
Courtland	July. 25	....	....	....	....	....	133
Gen. Morgan's raids.....	June and July	23	47	....	130	300	1200
Stevenson	July ...27–30	17	40	....	16	88	....
Near Malvern Hill.......	August...5–6	5	9	....	9	31	....
Tazewell............	August.... 5	21	35	....	31	64	....
Baton Rouge.........	August.... 5	42	173	....	140	480	....
Near Decatur........	August.... 7	2	7	....	....	....	123
Culpepper Court House ..	August.... 8	....	....	....	5	19	21
South West Mountain.....	August... 8–9	220	670	....	300	900	....
Lone Jack	August 15–16	25	48	....	69	240	....
London..............	August ...17	3	....	....	12	17	111

CONFEDERATE VICTORIES—(Continued.)

Battles, Skirmishes and Engagements.	Date.	Confederates Killed.	Confederates Wounded.	Confederates Captured.	Federals Killed.	Federal Wounded.	Federals Captured.
	1862.						
Gallatin	August. 20–21	27	39	....	40	102	.....
Catlett's Station	August 22	2	5	....	....	....	350
Near Bridgeport	August 27	9	37	....	16	50	213
Richmond, Ky	August. 29–30	125	300	....	178	450	.....
Second Battle of Manassas	August. 29–30	1800	4000	....	2000	7800	7000
Near Centreville	September ..1	45	135	....	55	190	.....
Near Williamsburg	September ..9	10	17	....	15	....	70
Cotton Hill	Sept.13–14–15	9	15	....	90	300	.....
Harper's Ferry	September .14	31	43	60	40	90	11583
Boonsboro' Gap	September 13	600	1800	....	1000	3500	.....
Newtonia	September 13	22	76	....	30	120	100
Ponchatoula	September 17	5	....	....	5	6	.....
Munfordsville	September 17	....	....	....	....	....	4800
Sharpsburg	September 17	1900	6915	800	2010	9416	1044
Sheppardstown	September 20	50	200	....	500	2000	.....
Franklin	October ... 3	3	15	....	20	18	40
Perryville	October ... 8	700	2000	300	1000	3000	2000
Pocotaligo	October ..22	22	50	....	100	287	.....
In various Skirmishes during the last ten months		400	1000	900	600	1000	1500

FEDERAL VICTORIES.

Battles, Skirmishes and Engagements.	Date.	Confederates Killed.	Confederates Wounded.	Confederates Captured.	Federals Killed.	Federals Wounded.	Federals Captured.
	1861.						
Phillippa	June. 3	9	20	....	....	15	....
Boonville	June 17	7	29	73	24	65	....
Carrock's Ford	July.. 12	45	57	....	20	50	....
St. George	July.... ..13	17	....	500	4	11	....
Hatteras	August....28	12	....	691	....		
Osceola	September .21	....	7	....	30	10	....
Chapmansville	September .25	8	4	....	10	33	....
Frederickton	October 21						
Port Royal	November ..7	11	48	7	8	23	....
McCoy's Mill	November. 14	7	9	....	4	13	....
Capture of Col. Magoffin	December..19	....	....	960	....		
Drainsville	December..20	60	139	8	85	110	....
Surrender of Fort Smith	April.....23	....	....		....	....	150
Surrender at Neosho	July..... 5	....	....		....	....	80
Frederickstown	....	15	35	....	23	52	....
	1862.						
Hanging Rock	January 5	5	....	7	....	....	
Fishing Creek	January ...19	114	102	45	92	194	....
Near Occoquan	January ...29	9	1	....	....	....	
Bloomery	February ...1	....	....	35	3	12	....
Fort Henry	February .5-6	10	13	57	45	66	....
Roanoke	February .7-8	23	58	2437	175	300	....
Cobb's Point	February.. 10	6	3	....	11	4	
Fort Donelson	Feb.... 14-15	231	1007	5079	1200	2000	....
Winton	February.. 20	7	5	....			
Newbern	March......4	45	55	202	150	500	....
Elkhorn	March....7-8	125	400	200	300	900	350
Cumberland Gap	March....11	2	1	....	....	....	40
New Madrid	March....13	16	29	....	25	47	....
Near Cumberland Gap	March....14	2	5	....			
Near Cumberland Gap	March....22	2	5	....			
Polk County	March....26	6	9	....	....	17	....
Union City	March....30	2	3	30	2	....	
Fort Pulaski	April....11	....	4	....			
Island 10	April 7	3	3	2000	150	300	....
Fort Jackson	April....24	38	125	....	300	900	....
Fort Macon	April....25	7	18	....			
Cassville	April..27-28	30	....	62	....		
Near Lebanon	May.....5	20	35	45	....		
Lewisburg	May.. 23-24	46	184	....	53	179	....
Garnetts Farm	May.. 23-24	28	72	....	30	74	....
Naval battle near Memphis	June.......6	80	....	75	....		
Fayetteville	July.....15	....	....				
Mt. Sterling	July.....29	13	20	....	....	3	7
Near Bolivar	July.....27	5	11	....			

FEDERAL VICTORIES—(Continued.)

Battles, Skirmishes and Engagements.	Date.	Confederates Killed.	Confederates Wounded.	Confederates Captured.	Federals Killed.	Federals Wounded.	Federals Captured.
	1862.						
Orange Court House......	August......2	2	10	....	....	....	....
Fort Craig............	September. 14	65	275	....	18	30	....
Near Opelousas.........	Sept....13–14	15	30	50	10	....	150
Iuka................	Sept....19–20	265	687	....	188	582	....
Corinth	Oct.... 3–4–5	1200	2300	2000	450	1820	320
Albemarle............	Oct........27	17	15	203	....	....	....
Williamston	November ..4	4	32	....	7	28	....
In various skirmishes during the last ten months..		800	2500	2000	500	1200	800

TOTAL LOSSES.

Confederates killed.......16,536		Federals killed.........29,440	
Confederates wounded....48,769		Federals wounded.......74,472	
Confederates captured....20,793		Federals captured.......57,479	

RECAPITULATION.

Total number of Confederates killed, wounded and prisoners..... 86,098
Total number of Abolitionists killed, wounded and prisoners....161,350

Number of Confederate victories....... 152
Number of Abolition victories..........................' 53

Number of Engagements.............................205

The probable number of Confederates who have died from sickness, disease, and from wounds received in battle, from the commencement of the war to the present time, 110,000.

The probable number of Abolitionists who have died from sickness, disease, and from wounds received in battle, from the commencement of the war to the present time, 200,000.

8

NARRATIVE OF THE BATTLE OF SHILOH.

BY ALEX. WALKER, OF THE N. O. DELTA.

To describe the battle of Shiloh with anything like fullness and distinctness, would be a task involving weeks of examination, study and investigation of facts and reports. There has rarely been fought such a battle in modern times, regarding the extent of the fighting, the character of the combat, its duration, obstinacy and the disregard of the customary rules of modern and scientific warfare. Though admirably planned, and arranged on scientific principles, circumstances converted the battle into a hand-to-hand combat of 38,000 men against 65,000, in which for more than twelve hours every individual of that 38,000 was engaged. Such a battle will have to be described as it was fought in detail, and it can only be done by one who has the time and industry to collect the reports of reliable person who witnessed all the various details. I can only hope to give you from my own observations some general and vague idea of the main contest.

For some time past the enemy had been collecting a large force on the Tennessee river, near Pittsburg, twenty-two miles from Corinth. There he had established an immense encampment, extending for miles along the river, between two creeks, Owl Creek on the north and Lick Creek on the south. These camps fronted from the river, and rested the right on Owl Creek and the left on Lick Creek. The country in which this encampment was established is a high, rolling land, heavily wooded. The camps were about a mile from the river. Pittsburg was the landing place for their boats, and several gunboats protected their camps on the river side. From Pittsburg run two main roads, one to the north-west to Purdy, a small town some five or six miles from the Mobile and Ohio Railroad, and the other to the south-west, to Corinth, twenty miles. About half way on

this latter road is a place called Monterey, where several
roads unite. The enemy had already been established on
the Tennessee river, and had augmented his force to most
formidable proportions before our army began to concentrate at Corinth. The march of Buell from Columbia in
the same direction indicated a purpose to seize Corinth, the
possession of which would have given him control of our
lines of communication from Memphis and the South with
Virginia and Charleston. He had already begun to feel his
way towards Corinth, by sending large reconnoitering parties, which advanced as far as Monterey, about twelve miles
from Corinth. The enthusiasm with which our volunteers
responded to the call of Beauregard soon enabled our generals to collect quite a formidable force at Corinth, which it
was determined to defend at all hazards. Bragg brought a
fine body of troops from Alabama; Polk moved a large
portion of his force to the same point; Johnston advanced
several of his divisions in the direction, and several new
and hastily raised regiments, including some eight or ten
from Louisiana, were sent forward to this general rendez-
vous. In a few days, Gen. Johnston, on repairing to
Corinth, found himself at the head of a fine army, tolerably
disciplined, and full of ardor and zeal. In the meantime,
the enemy, discovering our movements, became more cau-
tious and hesitating, and the roads being impassible, quietly
settled down in his camp, determined to wait for the arrival
of Buell and for better roads to advance. It was under
these circumstances that our generals—Beauregard having
joined Johnston at Corinth—determined in council to make
an attack on the enemy before Buell came up. The army
was divided into three corps—the first corps commanded
by Polk, the second by Bragg; the third by Hardee—John
ston Commander-in-Chief, Beauregard second in command,
and Bragg Chief of Staff. The troops were ordered to
cook five days' rations, and, without baggage, to move
forward by the various roads that converge just beyond
Monterey and attack the enemy in his camp, in the follow-

ing order: Hardee, with a division of his own corps and two brigades of Bragg, was to make the main attack, covering the whole front of the enemy. Ruggles's division and the other brigades of Bragg were to support this attack, whilst Breckinridge was to march up from Burnsville, and take position on our right, preventing the enemy from flanking in that direction; whilst Clark's division, of Polk's corps, should cover our left flank. The other division of Polk, Cheatham's was to move from Purdy, so as to clear that direction of any troops of the enemy which might threaten us from that quarter and take up a position on our left flank. It had been reported that Wallace's division of the enemy still occupied some position on the road.

This was the general order of the battle. An eloquent and inspiriting order was issued by Gen. Johnston, which was read at the head of the various commands.

On Thursday the various divisions took up their line of march. No vehicles but ambulances and a few forage wagons, were allowed in the column. The roads were execrable and the advance of the army was very slow. The great deficiency of our engineering department was seriously felt. The streams were poorly bridged, and the various vehicles found it very difficult to make their way over the deep ruts in the road. Thus two days were consumed in the march, the nights being cold and rainy, and the troops having to bivouac in the woods, with a very insufficient supply of food, for few had had time or the material to cook their five days' rations, and many, to lighten their loads, threw away that which they had. These untoward circumstances, however, produced not the slightest effect upon the spirits of the army. Indeed, the enthusiasm of our gallant troops grew warmer and stronger with every discomfort and obstacle. On Friday the ears of our soldiers were delighted with the sound of a rattling fire in front. It was evidently a prolonged skirmish, and everybody was eager to know what was going on.

It was not long before the news flew down our column

that the enemy was only a few miles in front, and that our cavalry had had a brisk skirmish with them, and had killed several and taken some prisoners. The truth of this was presently confirmed by the appearance of one of our mounted men leading rapidly down the road up which Ruggles's column was struggling, a fine looking young officer in the Federal uniform, without a hat. He had been slightly contused on the forehead, and as he galloped along our columns, he gave our men a very bold, defiant look. He proved to be Lieut. Geyer, an Aid of Gen. Buchner, of the Federal army, who had been captured whilst reconnoitering by Clanton's Cavalry. Our men treated the brave looking fellow with proper respect. Shortly afterwards another officer, of still higher grade, was led by on horseback. This was Major Crockett, of Illinois. Immediately behind him came two Texan horsemen, with their Sharpe rifles directed to the unfortunate captive, a most unnecessary precaution, considering that the captives were in the midst of a great army of their enemy. This officer was a smiling, pleasant looking gentleman, and as he passed our several regimental commanders he saluted and was saluted by them. Halting near the head of the Crescent Regiment, he saluted Col. Smith, remarking, as he surveyed our Crescent boys: "A fine set of fellows you have, Colonel; if they were in blue, I should take them for my own boys." Following these officers were some eighteen or twenty other prisoners, who rode behind their captors, members of Clanton's Cavalry. This little circumstance produced considerable vivacity along our lines.

Friday night found our troops bivouacked a few miles beyond Monterey. It was a most uncomfortable night, cold, dark and rainy—and our troops greatly wearied by the day's march, lay down to sleep supperless. Early the next day, Saturday, the troops were all in motion, towards the road leading to Michie's house, which was the converging point of all the divisions. The various divisions had reached the vicinity of this point by different roads, and were all reported to be in position, or near at hand, for immediate action. Bragg's corps had come up by the Farmington road. Polk's by the straight road from Corinth to Pittsburg. Cheatham was advancing by the Purdy road, and Breckinridge was defiling into the Monterey road, to bring up the rear of the army. The firing of two guns during the night had signaled the advance of Hardee's position near the enemy's outposts. The various columns being drawn up in the road, Gen. Johnston and Staff, and Gen. Beauregard and Staff, rode by and were greeted with loud cheers.

After breakfast on Saturday morning the various divisions began to move forward on the Pittsburg road from Michie's house, to take up position in front of the enemy, preparatory to the attack the next day. The camp of the enemy was six miles off, and the plan contemplated the occupying his whole front between the two creeks, with one or two divisions, with strong flanking columns on the right and left.

All Saturday was consumed in the marching of the columns. Hardee's division was already in front; next came Bragg's Corps, which being the strongest, occupied several hours in passing. A gallanter body of men, more spirited, resolved and enthusiastic, never marched forth to battle. Gladden had, with his usual promptitude, already passed before we reached the spot where we could command a view of the column. Next came the brigade of Mississippians, under that heroic and indefatigable officer, whom I had met a few days before on his way homeward to recover his broken health, Gen. Chalmers. He had heard that there was to be a fight and had hurried back to lead his brigade. Though very pale and feeble his dark eye was lit up by martial fire, and his diminutive and frail form appeared full of vigor and vitality. The Mississippians marched forward at a quick step in their usual rollicking bold style, overflowing with impatient and long pent up ardor for the fight, the promise of which had reconciled them to their long and tedious camp service at Pensacola. Each corps had its separate battle-flag. That of Hardee was a blue ground with a white globe or circle, that of Bragg was our ordinary battle-flag, with yellow trimmings. that of Polk was a tasteful banner of light blue with white stars on a red ground. They were distinct and easily recognizable at a distance. Ruggles's division followed Chalmer's brigade, which brought up the rear of Wither's division. Of course I surveyed this fine body of troops with special interest, as it contained our gallant boys. Our regiments all appeared in the best condition. The boys were full of life and joy, and never marched better nor seemed in better condition. They could be easily distinguished from the other regiments by their neater dress, their more soldierly bearing, and their more orderly marching. The Crescents and Orleans Guards could scarcely restrain their buoyancy, but double quicked it across the field in the gayest style. The Washington Artillery boys brought up the rear of one of the brigades, and though with two horses less to their guns than the other batteries, they moved with ease and rapidity over the rough roads. Pond's and Anderson's brigades, of Ruggles's division, passed. Gibson's brigade brought up the rear, and a splendid brigade it was, composed of those noble regiments, the 4th and 13th Louisiana, an Arkansas and a Tennessee regiment, and a battery. As the large and splendid 4th Louisiana marched by, the gallant Col. H. W. Allen leading it. the brass band of the regiment struck up a lively air. but the Colonel shouted "Stop that music," and then turning to the band he said, "Wait, boys, until this fight is over. and then you may play either the Dead March or the Bonnie Blue Flag."

All the Louisiana troops had filed by except one regiment. So large a body of the gallant youth of our State. embracing the sons of our best citizens, the very soul and life of our rising generation, the rose and expectancy of our fair estate, going forth to battle against a hireling host of invaders, who had come to desolate our homes, so many of them mere boys, raised to comfort, ease and luxury, all unaccustomed to deadly strife, unused to war's dread realities, could not but suggest melancholy reflections. But there is no time now for such reflections. Honor and duty call them forth. Terrible as is the sacrifice, it can not be denied to our country, our honor and our homes.

Ruggles's division was followed by Gen. Polk's two divisions of nine regiments each, the first led by Gen. Charles Clark, of Mississippi, and the other by the gallant and elegant Cheatham. These divisions were composed chiefly of Tennessee troops, and appeared to be well drilled and in fine condition for the fight. In one of them we noticed the splendid battery of Capt. Smith P. Bankhead, which has already earned such high distinction for efficiency and drill. There was an interval of half an hour after the march of Polk's column before the splendid division of Breckinridge appeared in the road. It consisted of Crittenden's division and Breckinridge's brigade, and was as noble a body of men as ever marched forth to battle.

The Kentucky regiments, especially, were composed of stalwart men who, in their appearance and bearing, showed high state of military drill and efficiency. Their gallant chief looked every inch the General—self-possessed, calm and earnest—his tall figure, resolute air, and noble countenance, inspired all beholders with admiration, confidence and respect. And this closed the column of our army, which was followed by a long train of wagons and ambulances. On summing up the totals of the various divisions and brigades which made up the column, including several regiments and squadrons of horse which had been sent forward by various routes, we made the effective force of the army thirty-eight thousand men and about fifty pieces of artillery—most of them small guns. But few of the batteries had ever been under fire. This number, too, included about four thousand cavalry, which, from the nature of the ground, could hardly be made available; and, as the events of the battle proved, added but little to the effective force of the army. The principal of these cavalry corps were Wirt Adams', Clanton's and Terry's Regiments, the Alabama Horse, Bennett's Mounted Riflemen, Morgan's squadron, and several other troops—all admirable light cavalry, well mounted and well armed. The Jefferson Horse, Captain Dreux, had been detailed as an escort for Gen. Beauregard.

That night the army bivouacked near the enemy's out posts. It was the only pleasant night since we had left Corinth, and though the ground was damp and the atmosphere raw, there was no rain, and for once we found a bed of leaves in the woods not disagreeable. Our brave soldiers went to sleep without suppers or camp fires, and dreamed of their happy homes and dear friends, in the very face of a vindictive and hostile enemy, within distinct hearing of their drums, and even of the call of their sentinels. The quiet and silence that reigned through the dark forests were solemnly impressive, and suggested many painful reflections and anxieties, which, despite fatigue and exhaustion, long banished sleep from our eyelids and filled even our few hours of slumber with disquieting visions and ghastly dreams.

THE BATTLE OF THE SIXTH OF APRIL.

Providence seemed to interpose in behalf of our army, in affording them one pleasant, dry night since their departure from Corinth, on the eve of the great battle, the anticipation of which had sustained our soldiers under the terrible fatigue, discomforts and deprivations of their three days' tedious march. The men had slept soundly in the deep, dark recesses of the unbroken forest between Owl and Lick Creeks. With the first streak of daylight visible through the light mist that ascended from the woods, they sprang from their lairs to arms, and every man took his position in line, and prepared for the onset. The greatest vivacity and enthusiasm prevailed throughout the whole army. Already a rattling fire some two miles in front proclaimed that Hardee had opened the ball. First, a few scattering shots were heard. Quickly volleys of platoons succeeded, and soon the fire extended and increased, until the rolling reports of long lines of musketry could be distinctly recognized. This continued for nearly an hour, and was followed by a lull and pause of some minutes. The order then came along the lines of all the divisions to forward at quick step. The whole army was now in motion. The woods were alive with troops, and the various lines were well preserved, and moved forward as if on parade. The word came from the front, "Hardee is at it, hot and heavy; press forward the other divisions to support him." The day began now to brighten, and the troops moved forward with alacrity. Proceeding from the rear, we passed through the lines of Breckinridge and Cheatham, the latter fronting towards Owl Creek, as if to cover our left flank, and the former skirting Lick Creek and keeping a sharp look on that flank; whilst between these two columns Withers, with several brigades, and Ruggles, with his heavy division, and Clark, with Polk's first division, covered the whole front between the flanking divisions. It was cheering and inspiriting, indeed, to observe their calm, determined air, and the unbounded enthusiasm and confidence with which the men followed them— Cheatham, sitting on his horse with a lounging air, smoking his cigar, smiling and shouting to his aids, as if on a holiday hunt—Breckinridge, erect and precise in his carriage, towering in height above his staff, calm as a summer morn, circumspect, wary and observant. In this order the army moved quickly forward. And now the volume of the firing in front began to swell and extend over the whole area. Soon the big guns began to join in the horrid concert, at first as slowly as the notes of the basso in an opera rise above the softer tone of the barrytone and tenor, at first slowly and regularly, but soon in rapid succession as if whole batteries had got to work. "That is Robinson's battery; there goes Ketchum's," exclaimed scores of anxious listeners. On foot, through the dark woods, over gently rolling mills—now and then through small open fields, we pushed forward, with the purpose of reaching the rear of Ruggles' line. To this we were impelled partly by curiosity, to see how our boys would bear themselves in the perilous drama, so actively opened, but still more, by the strongest of all human motives, to be near a youth of sixteen, in whose fate we had a special interest. For some distance, as we advanced, we could see no signs of the crash and conflict which had preceded us, yet we knew we were following the course of Hardee's division. Suddenly, however, while stepping over a small stream, we stumbled over the first reminder of the skirmish which had opened the ball. It was the body of one of our soldiers, a stalwart Tennessean, in the brown jean uniform usually worn by our troops. He had been shot through the head and his tin cup was full of blood and brains, evidently a victim of the enemy's sharp-shooters, the woods in front being admirably adapted for this sort of fighting. As we passed along, we observed other dead bodies in the woods. From the uniform they were evidently our own men. This was not encouraging, but we could easily understand that, in driving in the enemy's scouts, Hardee's skirmishers had labored under great disadvantage in fighting men who had selected their positions and fired from ambuscades and from behind trees. Arriving in sight of Ruggles' line, we concluded that as there were already two lines in front, we should still be some distance from the scene of conflict. Still the firing seemed to be very near, perilously so, it appeared to an unarmed spectator and non-combatant. Yet our fatigued condition in the effort to catch up with the line, gave warning that what we regarded a reserve would soon be precipited into the action. We halted and were resting upon a fence, in view of one of Ruggles' brigades. We could recognize it from the light uniforms of the Confederate Battalion occupying the center. It was the brigade of J. Patton Anderson.

The line had halted and were resting, many of the men

lying down—taking it easily and listening to the heavy firing off to the right. Suddenly, however, we and they were aroused from this state of imagined security, by a tremendous discharge of artillery, accompanied by a prolonged rattle of musketry. It appeared to come from the very front of the brigade—and through the field enclosed by this fence, on which we sat, there swept a tempest of canister, and Minie, while small shell exploded in every direction. This was more than we had bargained for. We had made the common mistake, of every body in that battle, of imagining that it would be fought by the successive conflict of advancing lines with reserves to be called into action after the exhaustion of the front or main lines. It was now hardly breakfast time, and our armies were already in the midst of the fight. At first we sought the shelter of a large tree, thinking that it was a safe cover, but the cruel Minies with their devilish screech seemed to come from every direction, and we could hear them and the grape shot cutting through the branches of the trees.. There was no shelter short of an old cotton shed, about two hundred yards to the rear. To this we hastened across the field, over which the balls and shells still swept. Gaining the shed, we found that it had already been occupied by several stragglers and wounded men from Anderson's brigade. We could perceive the effect which the sudden opening of a masked battery and of a large force of musketry had produced upon Anderson's line. The men who, a minute before, were lying on the ground in a state of perfect security, were now all on their feet, and not a few of them were breaking to the rear. The effect of so sudden and terrible a fire from an invisible foe was very startling and disheartening. A great many, too, had been killed and wounded by this fire. No wonder the simple-minded Floridians were broken and many of them hurried to the rear. Soon we saw an aid galloping to the rear, and as he passed he hallooed out, " Where is the Washington Artillery ?" We pointed to the rear, where we had seen our battery struggling over a very bad road. Meantime the gallant Anderson was galloping down the front of his lines, cheering and assuring his men and restoring order. Still we could see many stragglers, and many of them availed themselves of the cotton shed which we had occupied. It was a source of proud satisfaction to observe that, though Anderson's brigade was composed chiefly of Louisiana troops, there were no Louisianians among the stragglers. But now, hurrah! Here come the Washington Artillerists, tearing through the woods like madmen—the strong voice of Hodgson ringing above the rattle of the wheels, and the gallant form of the intrepid Slocomb, conspicuous on his noble charger, urging them forward. With terrible speed the battery rushed forward, and reaching the position assigned to it, wheeled into battery, and with wonderful celerity all six guns opened. The fire was terrific. The enemy opened in response from his masked battery.

The lookers on were breathless with anxiety for the issue of this artillery duel. This curiosity, however, was soon relieved by the grateful and familiar yells of our men, which, with the receding fire of the enemy, we had no difficulty in interpreting. The enemy had been uncovered: they could not stand the fire of our famous battery, and were rapidly retiring. The stragglers from Anderson's brigade could now be seen stealing back to their lines. But, alas! a great many are left behind, poor fellows— torn, bleeding, limping. And here the horrors of war began to glare upon us. The roads were full of the wounded seeking surgeons, and inquiring for hospitals. And these were only the wounded of a small brigade, and of an incident of a battle which was now raging all over the field. Anderson's brigade having pressed forward in the direction of very heavy firing, we concluded to take another course, and accordingly passed further to the right, in the hope of catching up with Pond's brigade, which included our own Crescent and Orlean's Guards. But, we soon became confused in the dense forest and lost our bearing. The woods were full of men, some in regiments, some in detachments, all pressing forward with ardor and eagerness. There was an equal number, slowly wending their way to the rear, singly, sometimes in small parties. and frequently in threes and couples. These were the wounded, hurrying to the hospital. This was the most distressing sight of all. The dead bodies of the slain soon became familiar, and excited little interest or attention. But the poor, limping, bleeding boys—supported by companions, or frequently making their way alone—some borne in blankets and on litters, and others riding horses led by comrades, aroused the warmest sympathy and pity, and subdued the excitement and enthusiasm of conflict to despondency and sorrowfulness. But this is no time for these feelings : such is the fortune of war. It is consoling to see how bravely our boys bear up under their misfortunes and the agony of dreadful wounds ; many of them are smiling and happy as if returning from a pleasure party. "Well, they have popped me this time," exclaimed one poor fellow with a ball through his face, "but I will be at them again." "Hallo, Bill," shouted in a faint voice, a half-grown country boy from an ambulance, to a friend on foot who was holding up his shattered arm, "they have broke my thigh, but it is in a glorious cause." Many with slight wounds are hurrying rapidly to the hospitals to have their wounds dressed, so that they may get back in time to have a chance to "get even" with the Yankees. But few, indeed, exhibited any great despondency, and all bore up with wonderful fortitude under their afflictions. And now we could perceive that we had reached the neighborhood of the main attack by Hardee. The battle still raged in front with uninterrupted and augmenting fury. Rumors came that we were driving the enemy back, and had gained his camp. Our whole army was pressing forward. Lines which I had passed hours ago were now hurrying by. I could see Polk's blue banner far away to the left, and a dark line to the right double-quicking it forward. I concluded it was Breckinridge moving forward to relieve Hardee's exhausted and shattered column. And well it might be torn and exhausted, for that division had had the first and hardest part of the work to do, and nobly it had done it. Rushing to their arms, as soon as they could see ten paces ahead of them in the scarcely perceptible dawn, Hardee had pushed speedily forward with his skirmishers, and soon became engaged with the enemy. The enemy skirmished well and vigorously. His men could select their position. Our men had to advance in open and exposed order. The Yankees, availing themselves of the trees and every convenient cover, kept up a constant galling fire. But Hardee had no time for this trifling, and pushed forward his line, driving the cloud of skirmishes before him, and thus advanced about a mile. Here he perceived the enemy drawn up in line in excellent order, with batteries strongly posted, and in great force. This was what the cool, skillful and scientific Hardee wanted. He had never had his opportunity in this war. Always assigned to posts where large bodies of troops had to be disciplined and drilled, performing, perhaps, a greater amount of military labor than any Major General or Brigadier General in our army, he had been denied all the chances enjoyed by other commanders of displaying his talents for command in the field. Now was his opportunity. The self-possession and coolness with which he formed his line, under a fire from the enemy's skirmishers, who filled the woods in every direction, was in the highest degree inspiriting. No man could do this better than Hardee. There was the brigade of the intrepid Hindman, composed chiefly of the hardy men of Arkansas, and there the soldierly Claybourne, also of Arkansas, but commanding chiefly Tennesseeans and Mississippians—all armed with the new English Minies, part of the cargo of the Gladiator, which had recently reached Corinth from the Atlantic coast. Two fine batteries completed this division, which was further prolonged by the addition of Chalmer's Mississippi brigade, and

Gladden's three Alabama regiments, and the famous fighting Louisiana Regulars, with Robinson's and Ketchum's batteries, including, in all, a little over seven thousand effective men. It was now about eight o'clock, when Hardee ordered this line forward to the charge. The order was obeyed with a terrible yell and shout. The enemy met it bravely and vigorously for a while. Their line opened a terrific fire of musketry, which mowed down Hardee's men by the hundreds, whilst the powerful batteries on the flanks and from intervals belched forth a tornado of shot, shell and schrapnell. Our men, after delivering their volleys, did not pause to re-load, but the order "Charge bayonets," ringing along the lines, was quickly responded to, and with desperate onset, the whole line rushed upon the enemy, the Louisiana Infantry and Dea's Alabamians making their charge against the formidable battery. The enemy's infantry gave way, and Col. Daniel W. Adams, bearing the flag of the Louisiana Infantry, called out to his boys to follow him, whilst the veteran Gladden, in stentorian tones, urged them onward. Those gallant fellows, a large number of whom had several days before served out their term of service, and had volunteered to remain and fight out this battle, needed not such incentives. They followed quickly their Colonel and their idolized General—their old Colonel—and soon cleared away the infantry support of the battery, and bayonetting some of the gunners, and capturing the rest, and hurling the men from the caissons and carriages, wheeled them around and opened his own guns upon the retreating foe. But the field was not cleared, for the great force of the Yankees, seeing the comparative small body of the assailants, fell back on another battery further up the camp. "You have only begun the job, there is more to be done," exclaimed Gladden, "pitch into them again, my boys," and again, with a terrible rush, the old Pensacola brigade, supported by Hindman and Cleybourne, now badly cut up, charged the larger battery and the strong, heavy lines of infantry.

The enemy poured into them a cruel, crushing fire, but in vain. Their onset could not be checked, the second and strongest battery was carried, though at a fearful sacrifice, and the enemy now rushed back pell mell, in great terror and confusion, and did not stop until they had fled beyond view to a distant camp, "Bravo! bravo!" exclaimed Hardee, in an ecstacy of admiration and delight. "Trot the pieces to the rear," ordered Gladden, and then was exhibited the strange and somewhat ludicrous spectacle of the Louisiana Infantry leading the large brass pieces and caissons to the rear, with the Yankee gunners sitting on the boxes, looking as frightened as trapped partridges. The formality of demanding their surrender and requiring them to dismount, was dispensed with, and the captors were allowed the rare privilege and honor of riding to the rear, with their gallant captors leading their horses.

These brilliant results, alas! had been achieved at fearful cost. Hardee's division had been cut to pieces—not half the force with which he had commenced the charge remained in line. The others were either left on the field bloody corpses, or mangled and bleeding, were dragging themselves to the rear. Twenty of the company officers and over two hundred men of the Louisiana Infantry had been placed *hors du combat*. The heroic and commanding Capt. Jack Wheat had fallen among the first. Capt. Bond followed him, and others of the youthful officers of this noble regiment were cut down with severe wounds. Among them the fate of that delicate, rosy-cheeked youth, so gentle and boyish in his appearance and manners, that we could not but shudder at the bare thought of one so young going to battle in a conflict of full-grown men—the young son of our patriotic citizen, J. L. Levy, excited special interest. He was killed at the first fire. Marvelously the gigantic colonel had passed scatheless through the thick tempest, but his noble gray charger had not been so fortunate. Riddled with balls, he only lived to bear forward his master until he had planted the battle flag of

9

the Confederacy in the very centre of the enemy's camp. The lithe and delicate figure of Hindman, too, had escaped the thick bullets of the enemy. Terrible and trying as was the scene presented by his torn and reduced regiments, this heroic officer, pale with sickness, his long hair streaming over his haggard face, sat his wounded charger, the very picture of a chevalier *sans peur et sans reproche*, unawed and unshaken by the surrounding terrors and disasters, and still eager for the conflict. So, too, his brother-invaliid, the bright-eyed, boyish Chalmers, calm and self-poised, galloped along his now feeble lines of Mississippians, and emboldened them to further efforts by cheering appeals and grateful praise. It was now about 11 o'clock, and Hardee's division had borne more than its share of the toil and suffering of the day. But they could not rest here. Forward they must move. It was at this point that a great calamity fell upon our army. That noble old chief Gladden had at last attained the summit of his aspirations. He had led his brigade in just such a charge as for many months past he had so earnestly panted for the opportunity of making. He had won a splendid success. His brigade had justified his confidence and his pledge. He was justly proud and exultant at the splendid display of courage and heroism which had been made by troops whom he had drilled, and in whose organization and welfare he had centered all his care and ambition. There were other charges to make, and other batteries to be carried, "So forward—let us go," were the words which he had just exultingly uttered, when his faithful friend and aid, Capt. Scott, from Mobile, observed a sudden shock and thrill of his body, as a crushing fire of shot and shell came tearing through the camp. His bridle arm fell helpless, and raising his right hand to his brow he said, "Scott, I am struck, but let's go on." His wounded and exhausted charger, as if in conscious sympathy with his master, moved but a few steps, when the General said, "It is a serious hurt; help me down, Scott." His aid quickly assisted him to alight, and applying his hand to the wounded limb of his General, found that the left arm, near the shoulder, was crushed to a jelly. An ambulance was called, and he was placed in it and bonre to the rear, Captain Scott driving. That gallant officer himself had just made a narrow escape. A grape shot had struck him directly in the eye. It was fortunately spent, and left only a contused wound.

We were then but a short distance from the scene, and meeting the ambulance driven by Scott, galloping towards the rear, we apprehended the very casualty that had occurred; for Scott would never leave the side of his beloved General. He waived his hand mournfully towards us. We ran forward, and looking within the ambulance, there saw our gallant friend stretched out in intense agony—pale, faint, but still smiling with the exultation of his great victory. We followed the ambulance until it halted before Beauregard's headquarters. Dr. Choppin was on hand, busy in his terrible avocation of amputating limbs and dressing wounds. He paused from all other labors to attend the case of our gallant General. The necessity of immediate amputation was quickly perceived, and the operation was performed with masterly skill and celerity. The mutilated limb still presented a dangerous aspect. It had been dreadfully contused, and the shock of such a blow must have been excessively violent. The wounded hero remained at Beauregard,s headquarters. On our return to the battle field we overtook a sergeant in the uniform of the Louisiana Infantry. He was a powerful-looking fellow, and the horse he rode was bleeding from several wounds. It was a small but noble-looking black Ranger. "Is not that Gen. Gladden's horse?" we asked. "Yes," mournfully answered the sergeant, "it is the charger of as brave a man as ever drew a sword. I was in the Crimean and Indian wars, and saw the best fighting in those campaigns, but I never saw such fighting as the 'Old Bengal' got out of our boys to-day—two hundred of whom he persuaded to continue for the battle, though their time was out. I never

saw any General bear himself like that little man. God
grant he may get well," and the tears stealing down his
swarthy cheeks attested the sincerity of the rude and honest
soldier. Alas! alas! an all-wise Providence had decreed
that this, the prayer of so many thousands of others in the
army and throughout his beloved South should not be
heeded, and after a few days of agony the heroic Gladden
departed from the scene of his glory and triumphs amid a
circle of mourning friends. The President of the Southern
Rights Association of Louisiana had attested the sincerity
of his devotion to the cause, of which he had been one of
the first champions. Among the noble martyrs of our
great struggle, no name will shine with a brighter and a
fairer lustre than that of A. H. Gladden, the gallant leader
of the renowned Palmetto Regiment in the Valley of
Mexico, and the idolised commander of the fighting
brigade of Pensacola.

THE BATTLE AND THE VICTORY.

The death of Gladden devolved the command of the
Pensacola Brigade on Colonel Daniel W. Adams, who still
moved forward on the right, with Claybourne, Hindman
and Chalmers' brigades, cut down to mere regiments,
carrying other batteries and sweeping from their camps
large bodies of infantry, who kept up, however, even in
their retreat, a cruel fire of Minies. Finally, driven to their
fifth camp, the enemy gained a position on a ridge from
which the ground sloped into a hollow, where our men
were collected in a crowded mass. Then they had us at
great advantage, their flanks being covered by undergrowth
which swarmed with sharpshooters, and their batteries
admirably posted to play upon our advancing lines. The
eagle eye of Hindman saw the desperate nature of our
position. He could only recover himself by charging their
batteries at every risk. Adam's brigade was pressing their
left, but it would be in vain, if Hindman did not clear the

large mass that still clung to the bridges with their frowning batteries. Resting his men for a few minutes, filling down their ranks and addressing to them words of cheer and encouragement, he formed them and ordered the charge.

It was done with a rush and yell; but the terrific fire of the batteries and of their infantry supports swept the men down in such numbers as to cause them to recoil. Again resting his men in the undergrowth and collecting all the stragglers from the other commands, he ordered another charge, with the same disastrous results and recoiling effect. It was now evident that Hindman's force was too weak to carry this position. Looking around for help, he perceived several bodies of our men advancing on his left. He rode towards them and soon met the fine brigade of Col. Gibson, of Louisiana, of Ruggle's division, composed of the 4th and 13th Louisiana, 1st Texas, and a Tennessee regiment with a strong battery. Uniting these forces, and advancing the battery of the Jefferson Mississippi Artillery, the whole line rushed upon the enemy's strong position, delivering their fire and charging with a terrible whoop. This onset was irresistible, but fearful was the loss it produced in our ranks. Our two regiments, the 4th and 13th, were shivered as if by thunderbolts. At least one-fifth of each of them were cut down, killed or wounded. The gallant and accomplished acting Brigadier had his horse shot under him; the clothes of the intrepid and chivalric Col. Allen were riddled with balls, one of which struck him in the face, inflicting a painful but slight wound; the youthful Major Avegno, of the 13th, had his horse shot under him; and that gallant son of Erin, Capt. Stephen O'Leary of the 13th, received two bullets in his body, while scores of the officers and men strewed the ground or dragged themselves to the rear. But the point was gained, the batteries of the enemy were in our possession, and the ridge afforded a fine position for our cannon to play with much destruction upon their retreating masses.

It was as the batteries were thus playing upon the affrightened enemy that the undaunted Hindman, ever in in the front, and whose escape thus far had been one of the marvels of the day, was seen on the crest of the hill waving his cap in triumph. Almost at the same moment his charger was observed to leap high into the air, and falling with great violence, rolled over and over, apparently crushing the rider beneath his huge corpse. A large shell had struck him in the breast and torn his whole forequarters into shreds. The soldiers, to whom their commander had so endeared himself by his splendid valor, held their breaths with deep anxiety, and men who had faced the enemy's batteries so many times unmoved and unblanched, grew pale with terror at the fearful spectacle of the fall of their beloved chief. Inexpressible was the relief, unbounded the joy of the brave men of Arkansas, Texas and Tennessee, as they saw the frail body of their gallant leader disentangled from the crushed remains of his charger, and standing erect, feebly cheering and waving his hat. Then uprose from our whole line the loudest cheer of the day. No victory yet won caused such joy and enthusiasm. Still, the noble General had been terribly contused. This, and his great exhaustion, had placed him • *hors du combat*, and his friends bore him to the rear.

These brilliant and substantial results we have described, were all witnessed by the Commander-in-chief of our army, who, from the beginning of the fight, had occupied a position near all the critical points. His cool sagacity comprehended every movement and its consequences, and with infinite self-possession amid a continual shower of shot, shell and Minie balls, he issued his orders to the various corps and divisions to move to the several positions where they were most needed. After the storming of the fifth camp he discovered the shattered condition of Hardee's division, and consulting with Gen. Bragg, the Chief of the Staff, the order was quickly determined on to bring up the reserves—Polk on the left and Breckinridge on the right, while Ruggles, with his several brigades, was to move against the centre. "This thing must be done with the bayonet," he shouted along the lines. "Every man must be brought into the fight." Bragg galloped towards the centre to direct these movements. This gallant and energetic officer had also, from the beginning, been in the midst of the fiercest of the fight. Two horses had been killed under him. Never were orders more quickly executed than those for the advance of our reserves. They had already pressed forward to the front, and were near at hand to fill the gaps created by the incessant combat of the morning. Breckinridge's strong column came up compactly and steadily, taking the place of Hardee's division, the fragments of which, however, still unsated and unexhausted, marched with the Kentuckians, in a noble rivalry to share in every triumph of the day. Polk, too, as ardent and enthusiastic as a young soldier in his first skirmish, pushed forward his brave Tennesseeans, with his splendid batteries, Bankhead's. Smith's and Polk's leading. A nobly appearing chief, so full of vigor and life, he dashed along the lines, inspiring his men by his brave and self-possessed bearing. Clark led the First Division, the chivalric Planter-General of Mississippi, among the first to abandon the ease and comfort of a luxurious home, to engage in the perilous conflict for Southern independence. Conspicuous on his staff we observed the noble form and dauntless front of that gallant champion of Southern rights on another field, Maj. W. H. McCardle, of Vicksburg. Clark's fine division needs no appeals or incentive. It overflows with ardor and impatience for the conflict. The Tennesseeans burning to avenge the wrongs and insults of their State—the Mississippians shouting "Donaldson" as their new battle-cry—the "bloody Louisiana," Eleventh, with the cold and intrepid veteran Marks to lead them, as he led them to victory and glory at Belmont, responded with a shout to the command to forward.

Meantime, the Chief of the Staff, Bragg, having explained to Ruggles, in the centre, the order of the advance—galloping in front of the several brigades, and delivering to each a few words of encouragement, next proceeded to the right, and held a brief consultation with Breckinridge. And now the whole army advanced, Cheatham's, the last division, forming close on Clark's, ready to leap into the first opening in the front lines. The fight now became universal. Each line poured forward, and encountering every hundred yards or so a battery strongly supported by infantry, with the same unvarying result. Often our lines would recoil and falter under the iron tempests from these terrible batteries, but their indomitable chiefs would re-collect and re-form the men and return to the charge. It was in one of these charges that the noble and patriotic Commander-in-chief received the wound which produced his death. The enemy maintained his position with unusual firmness. Three several times did our brave fellows throw themselves upon it, and were hurled back, as if by a resist-less and superhuman power. The brigade and regimental officers galloped along the lines calling loudly for another charge. The lines halted—the men seemed transfixed with horror or stupefied with dismay—they neither advanced nor receded, but glaring at the frightful row of big-mouthed cannon which appeared to cover their whole front, and then at the ground before them, covered with their killed and wounded comrades, they paused, faltered, and seemed to be fast verging towards dismay and panic. It was a critical point in the drama. Unless that battery was forced and its supports driven in, the enemy would have us at great dis-advantage. Johnston perceived this—Johnston whose actions throughout the day had so changed the ideas of those who had so falsely interpreted his wise and masterly retreat from Bowling Green into proofs of over-caution and lack of daring and energy—who, in his plan and execution of this battle, had evinced a boldness approaching to au-dacity—an audacity that proved to be the highest wisdom and skill. The sagacious Kentuckian saw and appreciated the imminence of this peril to the army, if the strong po-

sition now held by the enemy was retained. He determined
to throw himself into the breach—not in a spirit of bravado,
of a mere vain-glorious desire of parading his heroism—
least of all, from any such petty and ignoble weakness, as
that imagined by small minds—a feeling of chagrin and
conscious injustice on account of the criticisms and censure
that had been so heedlessly indulged towards him by the
thoughtless and uninformed—but from a high and lofty
spirit of patriotism and self-sacrifice, that looked only at
the danger to his country and his cause, which confronted
him. Seeing the inability of the other commanders to
reform the broken and dismayed line, he rode forward,
with the ever cool and undaunted Breckinridge, and,
seizing a musket, presented it at a charge bayonet, and
called on the men to follow. The grand figure of the
Commander-in-chief, mounted on a large bay horse, looming
up from the foreground, (so conspicuous a target for the
enemy's sharp shooters,) seemed to expand to gigantic proportions, as he beckoned his men on to the charge. The
gallant Kentuckians were the first to follow—Tennesseeans,
Mississippians and Arkansians caught the heroic contagion,
and now the line moved steadily forward at double-quick,
and then, with a wild rush, receiving the deadly iron blast
as it swept along the slopes, and pouring over the batteries,
they scattered the heavy masses of the infantry in the wildest confusion. This was perhaps the mightiest effort of
physical force and courage of the day, and when it was
performed, the tall figure of Breckinridge could be seen on
the crest of the hill, waving his cap in triumph, whilst the
shouts of his men echoed far off like the roar of many
waters. As soon as Gen. Johnston perceived the success
of his appeal, and that his men had caught the spirit which
he sought to infuse into them, and were moving forward
with the requisite vigor and resolution, he rode from the
front, and returned to his original commanding position, a
little in the rear and on the right, and waited the result of
the assault. It was only when its success was evident and

the enemy was in retreat, that one of his aids, perceiving blood on his clothes, anxiously asked if he was not wounded. He replied, " Only a scratch!" adding in entire unconsciousness of self, " Was not that splendidly done : glorious fellows ; we have got them now." There was a pause and a few minutes of observation and consultation, when evident symptoms of weakness manifesting themselves, the aids of the General insisted that he should dismount and have his wound examined. He did so in a careless and unconcerned manner. His boot being pulled off, it was discovered to be full of blood, and that the purple current was still flowing rapidly from a small wound under the knee. It proved, on examination, to be what Dr. Choppin pronounced the smallest wound that he ever knew to produce death in a hale and vigorous man. But an artery had been severed. Though much blood had been lost, the presence of a surgeon, or the application of a proper ligature by any one familiar with the location of the artery, would have saved his precious life. But the humanity and generosity of Johnston had deprived him of the aid of his accomplished surgeon. He was the victim of his own philanthropy. In passing through the enemy's camp, he had observed some of the wounded of the enemy suffering grievously from their wounds and crying aloud for help. " Stop, Doctor, and help these poor fellows," he said to Dr. Yandell of his staff, who promptly dismounted and was engaged in dressing their wounds, when Johnston and his staff were riding forward to engage in the active scene of the terrible struggle in front. The surgeon was therefore absent when the wounded General dismounted and fell exhausted on the ground, surrounded by his grief stricken staff. He grew rapidly fainter. It was obvious to all that he was sinking fast. A few words of kindness to his friends, and of joyful exultation at the victory 'already' won, only escaped him, when in fifteen minutes after he received the wound he departed this life gently and with a smile irradiating his grave and serious countenance. So sudden and

mournful an incident in the very midst of victory seemed
to palsy the gallant gentlemen of his staff. Personally
devoted to him by ties and sympathies of the strongest nature, by his pure and unselfish traits, his entire freedom
from all petty jealousy, his lofty moral courage and fearless
personal bearing, they were unnerved by the great calamity
which had fallen upon them, the army and the country.
Mournfully they bore his remains to the rear, where they
were placed in an ambulance, and sent to Corinth.

Thus fell Albert Sydney Johnston, the second General
in the Confederate army. A native of Kentucky, a cadet
from Louisiana, a long resident of Texas, these States may
claim to share the honor of contributing so noble and
brave a patriot and soldier to the cause of Southern Independence. A soldier of the Texan war of independence—
a successful and brilliant chief in the Mexican war, he had
appropriately closed his noble career in a great battle for
the rights and independence of the South. His name and
virtues, and his heroic sacrifice, will ever be held in warm
recollection and affection by his grateful countrymen. The
melancholy intelligence of Johnston's death was quickly
communicated to Gen. Beauregard, who occupied a prominent position near the centre of the army, where he was
actively engaged in superintending the formation and advancing of troops. "This is sad news, indeed," he exclaimed
to his aids with a deep sigh. "Gentlemen, to your horses,
we must go to the front;" and quickly the staff were all
mounted, and escorted by the fine troop of the Louisiana
Jefferson Mounted Guard, Capt. Guy Dreux, the General-
in-Chief now proceeded rapidly towards the front. Meantime the whole army had been set in motion, chiefly under
the direction of the ubiquitous and indomitable Bragg.
Every division, every brigade, every regiment was brought
into requisition, and in turn was hurled against the enemy's
lines and batteries. Clark, on the left, had led his division
far into their camps, making many desperate charges. In
one of these, Russell's brigade, in which was our fighting

"Louisiana," Col. F. Marks, was brought suddenly under a terribly destructive fire. The brigade faltered at first, in some confusion. More than a hundred of the 11th had been cut down. But again they came back, and were again shivered like a wave against a rocky shore. Finally, however, their indomitable fortitude conquered, and the enemy were routed and fell back under a terrible fire from Bankhead's, Polk's and Smith's batteries. The casualties of these assaults were terrible. The gallant Marks had been badly shot, and his youthful Major cut down with a severe wound, and now the Lieutenant-Colonel, Barrow, and the heroic Captain, Ed. Austin, of the Cannon Guards, set to work vigorously to restore order and confidence to the mutilated remnant of that once strong regiment. Stewart's brigade, of the same division, shared a like fortune and like triumphs. The gallant Polk, of the Polk battery, in bringing his guns into position, fell severely wounded. Many others, officers and men, of these brigades, were in like manner placed *hors du combat.* A shade of grief and distress darkened the calm and serene countenance of the gallant General of the corps, the patriotic Polk, as riding down the lines he observed the fearful gap which had been made in his corps.

Cheatham's division had got fairly in on the extreme left and was actively at work. Our whole line began now to assume a firm order and continuity which it had not before had. Bragg took charge of the right and centre, and Polk of the left, and both pressed the enemy with unbroken steadiness and vigor. The enemy gave way slowly, retiring towards his camp, fighting whenever the ground afforded a favorable position for a battery, and for their legion of sharp-shooters. Ruggles, near the centre, had held his division chiefly in reserve, throwing forward his brigades to support and aid those engaged in assailing the batteries. Anderson had already stormed and carried several of them. Gibson's had performed like service near our right, and Pond's Third Brigade was ordered on like duty, but by some mistake the brigade was not held well together, and when ordered to charge, Col. Mouton, of the gallant and steady 18th, found the whole burden of the charge thrown upon his small regiment, which gallantly obeyed, but was fearfully cut up. In all that army there was no gallanter or abler regimental commander than our Creole Colonel, not one who bore himself so like a veteran. Wounded in the face, his clothes riddled with balls, he maintained his position in front, keeping his men well together, and driving them ahead with resistless might. The confusion incident to so extensive a formation, under such a terrible fire, with so many inexperienced officers, led to sad mistakes, by which several of our regiments suffered at the hands of their own friends. The Orleans Guards, wearing a uniform resembling that of the enemy, were frequently fired upon by our own troops. The gallant Creoles, however, never faltered or shrunk, but though embarrassed by their isolated position, cut off from the rest of the brigade, they marched forward, charging and routing several bodies of the enemy. This battalion, and our noble Crescent Regiment were left pretty much as orphans, to take care of themselves. They groped their way through the forest, hunting for the enemy, and throwing themselves on every side where they were needed. The Crescent, after marching through the enemy's camp, proceeded in the direction of the river, to dislodge a strong force of the enemy, which was firing with great effect from the cover of some cotton bales and a hedge in an old field. Col. Smith, leading his boys gallantly into the field, gave the order to charge, and as it was done with steadiness and vigor, the enemy flying from their cover through the hedge, which the Crescent occupied, and from an old log house opened upon the enemy, who had halted a short distance off. This drew a heavy fire of musketry upon the Crescents, from which they suffered some casualties. In the meantime the enemy having established a battery to sweep the field, Col. Smith, with great sagacity, moved his regiment off under cover of the woods. There he fell in with a strong force, which had been formed by Gen. Polk, to surround a large encampment of the enemy.

The Crescents arrived in time to participate in this, one of the most glorious events of the day. The troops were quickly formed, the most dangerous and prominent position being assigned to the Crescent. The order was to encompass the camp on all sides, and open upon it a heavy fire. A force of cavalry were ordered up to cut off the retreat. Unfortunately it did not arrive in time, but the infantry regiments quickly gained their position, the Crescent leading. It was a large encampment, evidently of two or more brigades. A short resistance was made, a few volleys fired, but the Crescent and several other regiments poured a heavy fire into the camp from across a ravine, and then filing around were about to charge, when the enemy ceased firing, and several white handkerchiefs were seen waving from muskets. The troops ceased firing, and an officer of the enemy, who turned out to be Adj. Gen. Morton, came forward to Col. Smith and offered to surrender the whole force. Gen. Polk now rode up, and presently Gen. Prentiss, commanding one of the divisions of the enemy, came out of a tent, stepped forward and surrendered. The officers of the command generally remained clustered around the General, and the men collected in groups through the camp, having stacked their arms. The absence of the cavalry, however, enabled a large number of the prisoners to escape towards the Tennessee river, and we only succeeded in capturing about 2700, including three Colonels, four Lieutenant-Colonels and about forty Captains. They were all of the division of Gen. Prentiss, and belonged to Missouri, Illinois, Ohio and Iowa regiments. They had arrived but a few days before, and declared that they were completely surprised, and had no idea we were near when the attack was commenced. The prisoners were sent to

the rear, and Gen. Prentiss and staff were escorted to
Beauregard's headquarters, which were now established
near the centre of the enemy's camp.

The whole army had now passed through and beyond the
enemy's camps. What remained of his force had been
driven now three quarters of a mile beyond, and was heavily
massed towards the river, under the cover of several large
batteries in position, and of a plunging and vertical fire of
shells from the gunboats, the commanders of which, knowing the relative positions of the two armies, could now throw
their dangerous and destructive projectiles so as to inflict
no damage upon their own men, and to produce great confusion in our ranks. In this they achieved no little success. Our regiments were frequently thrown into confusion
by the bursting of shells in their midst and around them.
The Crescent, which had moved very near the river, came
in for a large share of these terrifying missiles. The more
dangerous Minie balls produced no such terror. The
enemy being unseen added to the nervousness of our men.

Our infantry was now utterly worn out. The men fell
down in the ranks from sheer exhaustion. They had
fought for twelve hours, an incessant and unparalleled
fight, routing and pursuing large bodies of infantry, and
performing such prodigies of valor as, if fully related, would
fill a large volume. The infantry are now no longer
available, even if the enemy were within reach, save to
hold him in his present exposed position until the cannon
can all be brought to play upon him. Our regiments are
severely cut up, many of them disorganized, broken into
detachments that wander around seeking their commanders.
There is no demoralization, no fear—not all the horrors
and dangers of the terrible and uninterrupted conflict have
affected their unconquerable spirits. The woods for miles
are full of the wounded, and the hospitals are crowded.
Every species of vehicle is employed to conduct them to
the rear. Hundreds are borne on litters or on blankets.
The surgeons are now busy in their terrible labors. Large

details, too, to attend the wounded, have further reduced the army. And now the whole army is collected in advance of the enemy's camps, with the fragments of brigades and regiments consolidated with little reference to their original formation. But Breckinridge, now some distance in advance, holds what remains of his division well together, and Cheatham is not far off defending our left. Both these officers have performed wonderful exploits of gallantry, endurance and fortitude. The high soldierly qualities of Breckinridge filled all beholders with amazement. The oldest regular officers of the army bestowed the warmest eulogies upon him. Not alone his personal heroism, but his amazing self-possession—his infinite patience and tact, his quick sagacity and unerring judgment—were themes of universal admiration. Wisely now was he assigned the position of guarding the enemy, and holding the advance of the army.

It was in the last assaults, as the enemy fell back through his camps, now stretching along an open country—on his large parade grounds—on one of which a spacious square had been carefully cleared and leveled, where Grant intended to hold a grand review on Monday, the 7th April—it was here that his greatest losses had been incurred. His dead lay in heaps and thickly strewn in every direction.

The artillery were all hurried forward to complete the work. Thirty-six of our best guns were now brought into position on a ridge at a distance of three-fourths of a mile from the enemy's main body. There was the Watson heavy battery, of Breckinridge's Division, among the first to take its place, under the fearless and skilful Beltzhoover, who had already performed several brilliant feats in aid of Cheatham's movement. In this battery the liberal and patriotic gentleman after whom it was named, who had been instrumental in putting it into the field with his own means, worked at the guns as an artillerist. There, too, was the battery of the still unwearied Robinson, of Mobile, whose guns were the handiwork of one of our own foundries, Leeds & Co—and splendid guns they were—which had been incessantly engaged all day, performing among other notable exploits, that of silencing and capturing a large battery of the enemy without the necessity of an infantry support. There were Bankhead's powerful pieces, which had been hard at work during the day; Polk's, Smith's, the Jefferson county (Miss.) battery, and Girardey's Washington Artillery, of Augusta, the only representatives of Georgia on the field; and last, though far from least, our own Washington Artillery, which, too, had had no pause during the day in its gigantic labors and constant progress over all obstacles, utterly reckless of the enemy's stronger batteries or of his swarms of sharpshooters. These guns took up position and opened their fire. They had filled their exhausted caissons from the enemy's magazines; vigorously they set to work to finish off the victory of the day. Such firing was never perhaps before heard on this continent. The gunners emulated each other in the celerity of their loading and priming. For two hours were these incessant volleys continued, mingling in one horrid roar that shook the earth for miles around, and filled the heavens with sulphurous vapor and odor. Every description of projectile was called into use. Shell, cannister, round shot, percussion shells, James' shells, were poured upon the enemy with relentless fury. He replied from some of his remaining batteries, and from some field works, established near the river to protect his retreat, whilst the gunboats unceasingly threw their large shells in every direction over the camps and fields occupied by our troops. These shells, thrown with reckless uncertainty and wide range were excessively annoying, and inflicted much damage, wounding and killing many of our men. But the other practice of the enemy produced little effect upon our batteries or our troops. A vast amount of ammunition was consumed in the prolonged exchange of fires between the batteries; but from the position of the enemy, selected in an exposed and open locality, crowding towards the river, our fire must have inflicted a heavy loss. But the shades of evening began to darken over the scene. The curtain of night was about to fall on the bloodiest tragedy ever enacted on this continent. As long as there was a streak of light by which a gun could be aimed, our indefatigable artillerists would make use of it. But now the darkness comes to the relief of the distracted and persecuted foe—with undeserved mercy, draws over him a shield, and affords him the respite and security for which, throughout that long day, he had doubtless so fervently prayed. What relief must have been this kindly interposition of nature! Nothing more can now be done. Our batteries are limbered up; some remain in their position; others return to the camp, that the men and horses may be refreshed and the caissons refilled. One of these was our Fifth Company. In the highest joy and exultation over their triumph and their gallant deeds, those chivalric young men merrily returned to the camp of the enemy. And then occurred a scene which gave a suitable and appropriate conclusion to the services of the day. The men formed in line, the Captain thanked them for their gallant and efficient conduct, and then Mr. F. N. Thayer, a well known and greatly esteemed citizen, in the name of his comrades, proposed that they should all kneel and offer up a prayer to Almighty God for their safety and their triumph. A prayer was read by Mr. Thayer, in his peculiarly impressive style, from the Common Prayer Book. Sergeant Bakewell added a few words of eloquent thankfulness, and the whole company uttered a solemn "Amen." Rarely has there been exhibited so sublime a display of natural piety as that of those gallant young men, who had been all day engaged in the wildest scenes of mortal destruction and reckless daring—who had not had a moment for reflection or thought, for any gentle or tender emotion, now kneeling in the midst of an enemy's camp, surrounded by the dead and dying, and all the desolating consequences of a deadly and remorseless conflict, and offering up fervent prayers to

Almighty God for his care, protection and aid in the hour of danger and trial.

THE BATTLE OF SHILOH.

A NIGHT OF ANXIETY.

The rest and refreshment in the inglorious camps of the enemy, so greatly needed and so fondly anticipated, by our exhausted troops on the night of the 6th April, were rudely interrupted. Early in the night that invariable effect of a severe battle and great cannonading followed the prolonged struggle of the day. A heavy shower came up and continued the greater part of the night. The heavens had been clear and cloudless, the air warm and balmy during that day, but now, at night, dark clouds hung heavily in the sky, and the rain fell in torrents, and the atmosphere became suddenly chilly. Our men huddled in the enemy's tents without blankets, or any other covering but their ordinary uniforms. There was another source of trouble and anxiety. The enemy's gunboats continued firing all night, throwing conical shells into the camps, which exploded with destructive effects, scattering small fragments of iron in every direction, and frequently wounding men and horses. Under these depressing circumstances, our army passed the night. To our Generals it was a night of special anxiety. Gen. Beauregard and staff had established their headquarters in the midst of their Yankee camps near the old log and boarded church or rather meeting house, which had given a name to the battle-field. Long and anxious consultations were held at these head quarters. Gen. Polk, in apprehension of the enemy making an effort to get in on our left flank, had established his quarters some distance in the rear and on the left. Here he and staff passed the night in the midst of what was intended as the amputating hospital, but which had soon become a general hospital. This hospital quickly became overcrowded with the wounded. To the kind-hearted and sympathetic General, that must have proved a terrible, sleepless night, which was passed amid such harrowing scenes—the constant groans of agony, the throat-rattle, the pitiful moans, and heroic utterances, and last gentle words, for home and friends, of the dying.

Before seeking a place of retirement and rest for the night, we made the rounds of several of our largest hospitals. We have no heart to revise the harrowing scenes they presented. We had already during the prolonged conflict of the day witnessed enough of suffering to have left impressions which a life-time could not efface. The unbroken processions of those mournful ambulances—the continual current of poor, bleeding, mutilated, but still heroic soldiers, making their way to the rear, had banished from our mind all pride, exultation and enthusiasm for our brilliant success. The most agreeable emotions that ever thrilled our heart were those we experienced in affording many of these wounded the grateful relief of a drink from our canteen. The earnest thankfulness with which they received this little comfort was indescribably eloquent and touching. But even these harrowing scenes were somewhat relieved and lightened by the heroic bearing, cheerful resignation, the wonderful fortitude with which our wounded bore up under their afflictions. This was especially conspicuous in the younger soldiers. Mere striplings, who were badly wounded—many of them mutilated or mortally hurt—seemed to have as little heed of their pains and danger as if returning from the play ground. Every where it was apparent that the older class of the wounded manifested far more gravity and solicitude, more sensibility to pain, and more anxiety as to the character of their wounds, than the younger soldiers, many of them boys from our high schools.

All the hospitals were soon crowded. There were few buildings near the battle-field. These had been appropriated as hospitals, but were quite inadequate, and all the tents that had been brought by our army were devoted to hospital purposes. Still there were hundreds who had no shelter. Many remained in the wagons; many, alas! were left in the air, exposed to the cold rain. All that could be done for them was done. The surgeons were diligent and indefatigable. Their labors were incessant. By dim lights, and in the open air, they were compelled to perform the most delicate surgical operations. It was cheering, indeed, to observe the universal spirit of brotherly love, the earnest humanity, the entire absence of selfishness which were displayed by all classes in attendance on the wounded.

The constant shelling of the Yankee camps by the gunboats early in the night, induced us to shift our quarters, and creeping into a wagon (already pretty well filled with sleepers) near one of the hospitals, we sought a few hours of sleep. But, exhausted as we were, we could only snatch a few minutes of broken and unsatisfying slumber. The groans of the suffering, the cries of those undergoing operations, and, more than all, the awful gurgling sound made by a poor fellow who had been shot through the lungs, and had been laid out to die under the wagon in which we lay, was terribly trying to our nerves and sensibilities.

Thus the night passed—a night of continual rain. We were aroused before daylight by a rapid and irregular fire, extending along the whole line and over the whole area occupied by our troops. We soon learned that this was the firing of our own men, whose guns had become wet and foul from exposure during the rain. We now proceeded to the front, to learn what was to be the order of the day. Repairing to the headquarters of Gen. Beauregard, we found that ever cool and vigilant chief sitting in front of one of the enemy's tents with his aids, Col. Jacob Thompson, Col. Jordan, Col. Chisolm and several of his staff. The General was receiving reports from couriers and scouts. It was obvious that he intended to renew the fight. It was cheering and inspiring to observe his calm self-possession and thoughtful precision and alertness. There came to him every minute the most conflicting accounts of the enemy's movements. First, it was reported the enemy was flanking our right. The General quickly gave an order to send a brigade in that direction. The order had hardly issued before another courier contradicted this report, and stated that no enemy was visible in that direction. The General, smiling, remarked to one of his aids : "This is one of Morph's blind games. I wish I had him here to help me play it out." Presently rode up Col. Beard, of Florida, an acting aid of Gen. B., holding his left arm, which was bleeding. Dismounting, he reported the reconnoisance he had been ordered to make that the enemy's outposts were not nearer than three-quarters of a mile from our lines— that from the strength of his advance parties it was obvious that he intended to renew the battle. In making this reconnoisance, the Colonel had been fired at by about fifty skirmishers, and one of the balls had struck his left arm.

The General now issued a number of orders, which were rapidly carried off by his couriers and aids. One order, which was found the most difficult to enforce, directed several of his aids to proceed to the rear, and with such of our cavalry as could be found to occupy all the roads and prevent straggling parties from leaving the field, and to capture and drive back to their posts those who were leaving. In this way a good many stragglers were reclaimed. Many were induced to return by the appeals of officers, but a great number excused themselves by the plea of utter exhaustion, by wounds and sickness; others set up the still weaker excuse of having lost their officers, and not knowing where to find their regiments. These reductions and the casualties of the day before had greatly thinned our army. But the spirit of those who remained to fight was unbroken. Regiments and brigades were now made up of all the fragments that could be marched to the front. In many cases the commanders of these newly organized corps were extemporized, the authority of any gallantly bearing officer being cheerfully recognized by subordinates and privates. It was now light. The heavens were still hung with murky clouds, and the air was cold. We were sitting in the enemy's camp, near the staff of Gen. Beauregard. when the familiar but never to us agreeable whistle of Minie balls began to strike unpleasantly upon the ear. "The enemy must be near," coolly remarked the General. "We will mount, gentlemen, and go to the front."

The General arrived in front in time to witness the advance of the enemy. Here the indefatigable Bragg had already busied himself. in making the best formation that could be made to meet the advancing foe. Hardee, with the remnant of his corps, with Wood's, Hindman's, Chalmer's and Gladden's brigades—the latter no longer led by the gallant Col. Adams, of Louisiana, who had been severely wounded on Sunday—still held the right. Breckinridge with what remained. of his division, with Trabue's, Statham's and Bowen's brigades, stood as firm as Gibraltar on the left of Hardee, while Bragg and Ruggles held the extreme left of our line with the remainder of their fine division, eked out by a portion of Cheatham's and Clark's divisions of Polk's corps; while Gen. Polk, with the remainder of his corps, brought up a strong reserve to support either division in the front that might need aid. The several batteries were placed in the most favorable positions, with little regard to brigades.

Gen. Beauregard riding to the right, was everywhere received with huzzas. A few words of cheer and encouragement were uttered by him to the several commanders as he passed. It was no time now for speeches or cheers. The enemy was bearing down on our greatly weakened line with a confidence and boldness which satisfied every body who observed them that they had been reinforced. It was apprehended that Buell's whole army had reached the Tennessee. This conclusion was confirmed by previous intelligence of the advance of his army from Columbia. We have no reliable information even now that such rein

forcements had reached him. It was regarded more probable that he should be reinforced by Wallace's division, which
had abundant time to come up from Crump's Landing,
where it had arrived from a scout towards Purdy. Even
this division of eight or ten thousand men would have
been a most valuable reinforcement, competent to turn the
scale of battle between two armies which had already been
engaged in the exhausting and prolonged conflict of the
day before. A much smaller reinforcement of fresh troops
for our army would have enabled us to complete the work
of the day before—indeed, would have made one day's job
of it. Many thought it the best strategy to have pushed
the fight to a conclusion on the first day, and that our army
might easily have been induced to advance under the fire
of the enemy's batteries and gunboats, and thus have accomplished the end much more efficiently than by the long
and furious bombardment of the artillery. It was pretty
evident that that bombardment had not produced the effects
anticipated from it. From the quantity of shot and shell
fired by our thirty-six pieces, we concluded that the enemy
was annihilated. But we had not learned what a great
quantity of ammunition may be wasted in a battle. We
did learn on this occasion how little effective the best artillery is without being followed up by that weapon which
determines the results of battles, the invincible musket.
The enemy did not give Hardee, the ever reliable, observant
and careful Hardee, long to complete and strengthen his
division. They began the attack near the river, with a
large force of infantry and several batteries. The vigor,
spirit and resolution of this assault surpassed any of their
efforts of the day before. Hardee met them with unbroken
energy and unexhausted valor. The batteries opened terribly, and the whole lines, on both sides, seemed to be
wrapped in a bright flame, from the constant fire of the
musketry. This was one of the severest conflicts of the
two days. It was maintained with great obstinacy by both
parties. The two opposing lines oscillated with the varying

results of the conflict. Now the enemy—and now our lines would be pressed backward. Some of the batteries changed hands several times. At one time the enemy would over-power and drive back the infantry support of a battery and obtain possession of it, and then by a like advance of our infantry would be despoiled of his trophies and routed. Thus our own 5th company, Washington Artillery, was twice rescued from them—once by the 1st Missouri, under Col. Rich, who was himself badly wounded. At the same time fell that gallant young officer, so well known and so much beloved in this community, Capt. Sprague. On the second occasion the Washington Artillery, which was always getting into dangerous places, and often too near the covers of the enemy's sharp shooters, who seemed to take a special grudge against our gallant boys, was saved by a timely charge of the Crescents, who, pouring a heavy volley into the enemy, enabled the artillerists to limber up and haul off their pieces to the rear. The losses of both the 5th company and the Crescents, on this occasion, were heavier than on the day before. It was in this conflict that noble officer and gentleman, Capt. Graham, of the Louisi-ana Guards, Co. C, of the Crescent Regiment, fell at the head of his company. By his side fell young Arthur R. Clark, son of Dr. Clark, of this city, one of the most inter-esting and noble youths we ever knew. He was just seven-teen, a delicate, graceful, gentle but brave and manly youth as ever bore a musket. Even now, we cannot recall our last interview with this noble boy without an inexpressible feeling of anguish. He was an only son, the idol of his family and of all who knew him. He said to us, as gaily marching to the field of combat, " I want you to tell my father how I fight to-day; and if I am killed take my body back to him." " I have no better man in my company than that boy," remarked Capt. Graham. Alas! that such a man, and such a youth could not have been spared as ex-amples and models for our volunteer soldiers. In this same conflict fell that tall and martial-looking officer, Captain

Campbell, of the Sumter Rifles—a most promising commander, who had left a sick bed to take his post in the march and battles. So, too, fell young Todd—the brother of the "Lady of the White House," who holds high revelry after the recent decease of her own son, and while her own brothers are pouring out the blood they derived from a common parent in the defense of the soil of her and their ancestors, against the hired mercenaries of her husband. Then, too, fell, either killed or wounded, others of the best blood of our city—young men, who had left homes of ease and wealth, and doting relatives and friends, in response to the call of our gallant Louisiana chief. Among the wounded there was not one which excited greater anxiety and alarm than that heroic and dashing officer, Lieut. Slocomb, of the 5th company Washington Artillery. His bearing during the two days had drawn upon him the admiration of the whole army. He had shown something even more valuable than the most brilliant courage and daring. That was no rare virtue in our army. But with it Slocomb united the most careful attention to every detail of duty—a perfect knowledge of all the appliances and rules for the efficient use of artillery, and wonderful quickness in seizing every advantage and in controlling his men and even his horses. Struck by a ball in the breast, it was believed that the wound was mortal. But he would not leave the field until his guns were all limbered up and borne safely out of the reach of the enemy's infantry. He then galloped to a hospital. His faithful horse, pierced by a half dozen bullets, bore him some distance—indeed to the very hospital tent; and when he was lifted from the saddle, the noble animal lay quietly down and breathed his last.

But these incidents have carried us ahead of the regular order of our narrative. After sustaining, with various fortunes, the vigorous onset of the enemy on our right, Hardee perceived the enemy moving a large force towards his left, as if to force back that point of his lines. Brookinridge was as quick to perceive the movement, and bringing his men up handsomely, gave the order to charge. Most effectually was this charge made. The enemy reeled and fell back, broken and disordered. Meantime, Hardee's batteries opened upon them with great vigor. But still, in large bodies, the enemy continued to press forward on other points, and now the whole line became engaged, and the battle raged with great fury. Through the clouds of smoke and the storms of bullets and balls, the erect and dauntless figures of Bragg and Beauregard could be seen galloping from point to point, reforming and reorganizing corps, filling up lines, and urging the men forward. Thenceforward the battle became the severest and most hardly contested of any ever fought on this continent. We had but 15,000 to contend with 30,000 or 40,000. Everybody was now engaged in the contest. Every corps was now brought into the thickest. It was, in fact, a series of battles. Ruggle's division, from its original position of reserve, was thrown forward into the centre of the battle—all the regiments engaging briskly in the conflict. It would be vain in our limited space to attempt a description of the operations of all the various corps.

Full justice cannot be done until all the reports have been made and a large book might be made up, of even brief descriptions of these exploits. Suffice it for us here to say Louisiana had a large share in the combat, and that no soldiers could have borne themselves more nobly in this terrible conflict than those of our several regiments. We cannot mention any particular corps without being regarded as invidious; but in spite of this danger, we must bear special testimony to the ever soldierly and dauntless bearing of Col. Monton, of the 18th, who received his second or third wound in the conflict; to the self-possessed air with which Reichard led that fine regiment the 20th Louisiana, whose Lieutenant-Colonel, the true and brave Sam Boyd, was ever in the thickest of the fight. So, too, the "bloody 11th," still without the veteran Colonel and their dashing

Major, but in good hands when led by the chivalric Lieutenant-Colonel, Robert M. Barrow, aided by the young and intrepid Capt. Austin, as second in command. All these regiments had suffered dreadfully in the fight of the day before, but with the remnants of other Louisiana regiments they still mustered their thinned ranks in front. Whilst the battle was thus raging all along the centre and right, Cheatham never relishing the position of reserve, had stolen around on the left, and encountering a large force of the enemy, which was pressing forward in that direction, made one of the most splendid charges that had yet been made by our troops. This was done with Stephen's, Douglas's, Vaughan's and Preston Smith's Tennessee Regiments. Gen. Beauregard seeing this charge, clapped his hands with joy, and declared that it was the grandest charge he had ever witnessed. Driving the enemy back three hundred yards, Cheatham now occupied a hill from which the foe had been driven, and establishing his batteries here, opened upon the enemy one of the most destructive fires he had yet suffered. It was on this occasion that Cheatham, seeing how few artillerists were left to man his guns, dismounted and set to work vigorously as a gunner. With such an example, no wonder that those batteries were worked with such power and effect.

Though the Kentucky regiments had been terribly cut up in the desperate charge so opportunely made by Breckinridge there remained enough of them to execute the order to charge a large body of the enemy stationed on a hill. The 3d and 4th Regiments leaped forward at the command, and rushing forward found themselves contending with several thousand of the enemy. The shots were showered on them from the right and the left, and the front. Their attack and position were in many respects like those of the Light Brigade at Balaklava. Here the Kentuckians lost in a few minutes more than in the whole previous day's fight. It was here that Lieut. Col. Hines and Capt. Knuckles, and Capt. Ben. Monroe, were wounded ; and here it was while gallantly leading his men to the desperate charge that the gallant Major Monroe received the shot that terminated his useful life. In justice to the memory of the noble dead, and as an incentive to the aspiring young men of our country, we propose to dwell for a moment upon the history of this youthful hero.

Descended from a family that gave a President to the United States, the grandson of that Gen. Adair who, as Governor of Kentucky, Senator, and military chieftain, has left an immortal name, he inherited blood that has not been disgraced in his veins. At the age of twenty-one he was elected Mayor of Lexington, though he was a prominent Democrat, and the town being in the heart of the Ashland District, was almost unanimously Whig. His ability soon attracted attention, and he was selected by the stock holders of the Lexington Statesman to edit that paper. This he did for several years ably and fearlessly. In 1860 he was made Secretary of State, though but 26 years old. On the election of Lincoln, himself and his aged father, who had been appointed U. S. Judge by Gen. Jackson, immediately took position with the South. Day after day the Lexington Statesman issued from the press filled with fearless and powerfully written articles in favor of our cause, and it is a well known fact that so long as young Monroe remained the adviser of Gov. Magoffin, that weak man favored the Southern cause. It was only when he lost the powerful support of this youthful adviser that he went to the side of the enemy. At length the Monroes, the gray-haired father and two sons, were driven from their homes. Young T. B. Monroe, on the recommendation of Gen. Buckner, was immediately appointed Major, and thenceforth devoted himself, day and night, to preparing his regiment for duty. At Bowling Green he shared to so large a degree Johnston's confidence, in Breckinridge's Brigade, that his regiment was placed fifteen miles in advance of all the rest of the army, except Hindman's Arkansas Brigade.

Major Monroe fought all day Sunday at the head of his regiment, part of the time commanding. His horse was twice wounded. On Monday, at about 1 o'clock, a ball passed through his body. He was removed to the hospital, where he lived two hours. He said he could not complain at his fate—it was what a soldier should be always ready to expect, and then sending messages to his family, he laid himself in the arms of his wounded brother at his side, and his spirit passed away. He leaves a wife (a daughter of Judge Grier, of the U. S. Supreme Court) and two infant children. He was born in Frankfort, Ky., and died at the age of 28. The army being compelled to fall back, and there being an insufficiency of ambulances, his body was left in one of the tents; but a flag of truce sent by Gen. Breckinridge brings the intelligence that his body was with his former friends, and would be decently interred.

The loss of the Kentucky Brigade exceeded 58 per cent. and was larger than that of any other brigade in the army.

But we cannot mention all the charges, all the valorous efforts of our gallant army. They were uniformly successful; but again the enemy would return with increased numbers and renovated vigor. We could always whip them back, but it was always at fearful sacrifice. Rarely did the men hesitate or falter in obeying the order to charge. Whenever they did, some of our chiefs would seize the flag and bear it ahead, and then with a yell the men would rush after him. On more than one occasion did Gen. Beauregard seize the opportunity of a momentary hesitation to lead on the charge. On one of these occasions, when passing the battalion of Garde d'Orleans, now reduced to little over a company, he grasped their beautiful standard, and shouting "Allons mes braves Louisianois en avant," he galloped forward, the whole line following with an irresistible impulse. This little corps of Garde d'Orleans had suffered heavily. It had been treated as a regiment and left to perform the work of a regiment, regardless of its numerical weakness. But the brave Creoles never shrink from any peril, especially when led by the gallant Querouz; and, when he was wounded, they were directed by that splendid soldier, a volunteer for this occasion, Major Dumonteil, who had served in the French army, and had been engaged in some of the severest battles on the continent. On Sunday, when the battalion had been inconsiderately ordered with the 18th and 16th Louisiana Regiments to attack a power-ful battery of the enemy, supported by a large force of infantry, Major D. volunteered to pioneer them, and, at great personal risk, approached within a short distance of the enemy's position through a tremendous storm of bullets. This charge of the Gardes d'Orleans was one of the most desperate of the day. Nearly half of the battalion were struck down by the enemy's big guns and musketry. In justice to Gen. Pond we should here state that though he made this order, it was given him by a superior officer, and he protested against it. During the fighting of this bat-talion on both days, the bravest man perhaps in the whole corps was that meek and pious, but fearless priest, the Rev. Mr. Turgis, who throughout these bloody days never left his position near the colors of the regiment, save to render aid to the wounded, to administer religious conso-lation to the dying, and to secure the bodies of the dead. In the discharge of these duties he was ever the last man to leave the field, and even when it was occupied by the enemy, he remained behind to look after some of the wounded. Whilst supporting one of the wounded men of the Gardes d'Orleans, several of the enemy's balls passed through his clothes, and one between two of his fingers as they were pressing the breast of the wounded man.

The conflict had now continued from 8 o'clock A. M. till 3 P. M. The enemy had been repeatedly driven from his position, but this game seemed to be to exhaust and wear out our men. Thus far he had had some success in this strategy. Our losses had been very heavy. Our ranks were growing perceptibly weaker—the men still indomita-ble. In proportion to the numbers engaged the casualties were much greater than in the battle of the day-before. It was now after three o'clock, when Gen. Beauregard determined to withdraw the army. This was admirably done. Bragg, with Ketchum's and other batteries, and several regiments of infantry, engaged the attention of the enemy on the left, whilst Breckinridge held him securely on the right. Among the regiments still kept together by Bragg, were the remnants of several from Louisiana. They were now reduced to companies, but were still at their posts. There were what was left of Pond's brigade—the 16th, his own regiment, the 17th, under Lieut. Col. Jones, a regiment which went into the fight very weak, and had now been further reduced by the constant conflicts through which it had passed—the 19th, Col. Hodges, another fragmentary regiment, but brave and true, what was left of it. Pond, on the left, was stoutly maintaining his ground, and had brought up two guns of Barns' battery, which, in conjunction with Ketchum's battery, directed personally by Bragg, played with effect upon the on pressing enemy. These small bodies, preserving a bold front, kept the enemy back whilst the remainder of the army withdrew to the rear, taking up the march to Corinth. This was done with little confusion, and without panic or alarm.

When the main body of the army had thus retired, and were safely started en route for Corinth, Bragg and Breckinridge, supported by several batteries, and covered by Clanton's, Wirt Adams's and Terry's cavalry, slowly retired in good order, Bragg himself being the last man to leave the field. Now and then the line would be halted to receive the enemy, who slowly and languidly followed. A few volleys from our musketry and our batteries would quickly check his progress. In the meantime the broken fragments of the rest of the army took the various roads back to Monterey. A few of the wounded, who could not be removed without endangering their lives, remained behind in the hospitals. Some of our surgeons remained with them. Among them was Dr. Breedlove, the faithful, brave

and efficient surgeon of the 20th Louisiana. In this order
our whole army fell back to Monterey, about six miles from
the field of battle, and here Breckinridge and Bragg halted
and encamped. The enemy halted near Michies, about
three miles from the field of battle. Both sides seemed to
be utterly exhausted by the terrible conflicts of the two
days. A large force of cavalry was thrown in front of our
positions, which kept a close watch and greatly harassed
the enemy, capturing many stragglers. Thus closed the
battle of the 7th of April, the most bloody, determined and
stubbornly contested conflict ever fought on this continent,
in which less than 15,000 Southern volunteers proved the
equals of a splendidly appointed army of 50,000 of the
best soldiers of the great Northwest.

——:–o–:——

THE BATTLE OF ANTIETAM.

THE FIGHT ON THE LEFT.

With the first break of daylight the heavy pounding of
the enemy's guns on their right announced the battle begun,
and for one hour the sullen booming was uninterrupted by
aught save their own echoes. McClellan had initiated the
attack. Jackson and Lawton (commanding Ewell's division,)—always in time—had come rapidly forward during
the night, and were in position on our extreme left. What
a strange strength and confidence we all felt in the presence
the man, "Stonewall" Jackson. Between six and seven
o'clock the Federals advanced a large body of skirmishers,
and shortly after the main body of the enemy was hurled
against the division of Gen. Lawton.

The fire now became fearful and incessant. What were
at first distinct notes, clear and consecutive, merged into a
tumultuous chorus, that made the earth tremble. The
discharge of musketry sounded upon the ear like the rolling of a thousand distinct drums, and ever and anon the
peculiar yells of our boys told n of some advantage gained

11

We who were upon the centre could see little or nothing of this portion of the battle, but from the dense pall of smoke that hung above the scene, we knew too well that bloody work was going on.

The Federals outnumbered us three to one. Their best troops were concentrated upon this single effort to turn our left, and for two hours and a half the tide of battle ebbed and flowed alternately for and against us. Still our boys fought desperately, perhaps as they never fought before. Whole brigades were swept away before the iron storm, the ground was covered with the wounded and the dead. Ewell's old division, overpowered by superior numbers, gave back. Hood, with his Texans, the Eighteenth Georgia and the Hampton Legion, rushed into the Gap and retrieved the loss. Ewell's men, rallying on this support, returned to the fight, and adding their weight to that of the fresh enthusiastic troops, the enemy in turn were driven back. Reinforced, they made another desperate effort on the extreme left, and here again was a repetition of the scenes I have described. For a time they flanked us, and our men retired slowly, fighting over every inch of ground. It was a trying hour. The Federals saw their advantage, and pressed it with vigor. Eight batteries were in full play upon us, and the din of heavy guns, whistling and bursting of shells, and the roar of musketry, was almost deafening.

At this juncture Lee ordered to the support of Jackson the division of Gen. McLaws, which had been held in reserve. And blessing never came more opportunely. Our men had fought until not only they but their ammunition were well nigh exhausted, and discomfiture stared them in the face. But, thus encouraged, every man rallied, and the fight was redoubled in its intensity. Splendidly handled, the reinforcements swept on like a wave, its blows falling thick and fast on the audacious column that had so stubbornly forced their way to the position on which we originally commenced the battle. Half an hour later and the enemy were retreating. At one point we pursued for nearly a mile, and last night a portion of our troops on the left slept on Yankee ground. The success, though not decisive as compared with our usual results, was complete as it was possible to make, it in view of the peculiar circumstances of the battle and the topography of the country. Certain it is, that after the cessation of the fight at 10½ o'clock, the Yankees did not renew it again at this point during the day. They had been defeated, and all they could do thereafter was to prevent us from repeating in turn the experiment which they had attempted on our line. It was, beyond all doubt, the most hotly contested field on which a battle has taken place during the war.

THE FIGHT UPON THE CENTRE.

Soon after the cessation of the fight on the left, the enemy made a strong demonstration upon our centre, in front of the division of Gen. D. H. Hill. Here, for awhile, the contest was carried on mainly by artillery, with which both the enemy and ourselves were abundantly supplied. The only difference between the two, if any at all, was in the superiority of their metal and positions, and on our part, the lack of sufficient ammunition. Battery after battery was sent to the rear exhausted, and our ordnance wagons, until late in the day, were on the opposite side of the Potomac, blocked up by the long commissary trains, which had been ordered forward from Martinsburg and Shepherdstown to relieve the necessities of the army.

As indicated in the former part of this letter, our artillery, was posted on the summits of the line of hills which ran from right to left in front of the town. That of the enemy, with one exception, was on the ground at the base of the Blue Ridge, and upon the various eminences this side. A single Federal battery was boldly thrown over the Stone Bridge on the turnpike, nine hundred or a thousand yards in our front, and held its position until disabled with a hardihood worthy of a better cause. I cannot now name all the positions of the different batteries—only those which

I saw. Altogether we may have had playing at this time one hundred guns. The enemy having at least an equal number, you may imagine what a horrid concert filled the air, and how unremitting was the hail of heavy balls and shell, now tearing their way through the trees, now bursting and throwing their murderous fragments on every side, and again burying themselves amid a cloud of dust in the earth, always where they were least expected.

The exchange of iron compliments has been kept up from early morning, but at 11 o'clock the fire began to concentrate and increase in severity. Columns of the enemy could be distinctly seen across the Antietam, on the open ground beyond, moving as if in preparation to advance. Others were so far in the distance that you could recognise them as troops only by the sunlight that gleamed upon their arms, while considerable numbers were within cannon-shot defiantly flaunting their flags in our faces. At 12 o'clock the scene from that apex of the turnpike was truly magnificent, and the eye embraced a picture such as falls to the lot of few men to look upon in this age.

From twenty different stand points, great volumes of smoke were every instant leaping from the muzzles of angry guns. The air was filled with the white fantastic shapes that floated away from bursting shells. Men were leaping to and fro, loading, firing and handling the artillery, and now and then a hearty yell would reach the ear amid the tumult that spoke of death or disaster from some well aimed ball. Before us was the enemy. A regiment or two had crossed the river, and running in squads from the woods along its banks, were trying to form a line. Suddenly a shell falls among them, and another and another, until the thousands scatter like a swarm of flies, and disappear in the woods. A second time the effort is made, and there is a second failure. Then there is a diversion. The batteries of the Federals open afresh; their infantry try another point, and finally they succeed in effecting a lodgment on this side.

Our troops, under D. H. Hill, meet them, and a fierce battle ensues in the center. Backwards, forwards, surging and swaying like a ship in a storm, the various columns are seen in motion. It is a hot place for us, but it is a hotter still for the enemy. They are directly under our guns, and we mow them down like grass. The raw levies, sustained by the veterans behind, come up to the work well, and fight for a short time with an excitement incident to their novel experiences of a battle; but soon a portion of their line gave way in confusion. Their reserves come up, and endeavor to retrieve the fortunes of the day. Our centre, however, stands as firm as adamant, and they fall back. Pursuit on our part is useless, for if we drove the enemy at all on the other side of the river, it would be against the side of the mountain, where one man fighting for his life and liberty, disciplined or undisciplined, would be equal to a dozen.

Meanwhile deadly work has been going on among our artillery. Whatever they have made others suffer, nearly all the companies have suffered severely themselves. The great balls and shells of the enemy have been thrown with wonderful accuracy, and dead and wounded men, horses and disabled caissons are visible in every battery. The instructions from General Lee are that there shall be no more artillery duels. Instead, therefore, of endeavoring to silence the enemy's guns, Col. Watson directs his artillery to receive the fire of their antagonists quietly, and deliver their own against the Federal infantry. The wisdom of the order is apparent in every shot, for with the overwhelming numbers of the enemy, they might have defeated us at the onset, but for the powerful and well directed adjuncts we possessed in our heavy guns.

Time and again did the Federals perseveringly press close up to our ranks, so near, indeed, that their supporting batteries were obliged to cease firing lest they should kill their own men, but just as often were they driven back by the combined elements of destruction which we brought to bear upon them. It was an hour when every man was wanted. The sharpshooters of the enemy were picking off our principal officers continually, and especially those who made themselves conspicuous in the batteries. In this manner the company of Captain Miller, of the Washington Artillery, was nearly disabled, only two out of his four guns being fully manned. As it occupied a position directly under the eye of Gen. Longstreet, and he saw the valuable part it was performing in defending the centre, that officer dismounted himself from his horse, and, assisted by his Adjutant-General, Major Sorrell, Major Fairfax and Gen. Drayton, worked one of the guns until the crisis was passed. To see a general officer wielding the destinies of a great fight, with its care and responsibilities upon his shoulders, performing the duty of a common soldier, in the thickest of the conflict, is a picture worthy of the pencil of an artist.

The result of this battle, though at one time doubtful, was finally decisive. The enemy were driven across the river with a slaughter that was terrible. A Federal officer who was wounded, and afterward taken prisoner, observed to one of our officers that he could count almost the whole of his regiment on the ground around him. I did not go over the field, but a gentleman who did, and who has been an actor in our battles, informed me that he never, even upon the bloody field of Manassas, saw so many dead men before. The ground was black with them, and according to his estimate, the Federals had lost eight to our one. Happily, though our casualties are very considerable, most of them are in wounds.

There now ensued a silence of two hours, broken only by the occasional discharges of artillery. It was a sort of breathing time, when the panting combatants, exhausted by the battle, stood silently, eyeing each other, and making ready, the one to strike, and the other to ward off another staggering blow.

THE FIGHT ON THE RIGHT.

It was now about 3 o'clock in the afternoon, but notwithstanding the strange lull in the storm, no one believed it would not be renewed before night. Intelligence had come from the rear that Gen. A. P. Hill was advancing from Harper's Ferry with the force which Jackson had left behind, and every eye was turned anxiously in that direction. In a little while we saw some of his troops moving cautiously, under cover of the woods and hill, to the front, and an hour more he was in position on the right. Here, about 4 o'clock, the enemy had made another bold demonstration. Fifteen thousand of their troops in one mass had charged our lines, and after vainly resisting them we were slowly giving back before superior numbers.

Our total force here was less than six thousand men, and had it not been for the admirably planted artillery, under command of Major Garnett, nothing, until the arrival of reinforcements, could have prevented an irretrievable defeat. I know less of this position of the field than any other, but from those who were engaged, heard glowing accounts of the excellent behavior of Jenkins' Brigade, and the Second and Twentieth Georgia, the latter under the command of Col. Cummings. The last two regiments have been especial subjects of comment, because of the splendid manner in which they successively met and defeated seven regiments of the enemy, who advanced across a bridge, and were endeavoring to secure a position on this side of the river. They fought until they were nearly cut to pieces, and then retreated only because they had fired their last round. It was at this juncture that the immense Yankee force crossed the river, and made the dash against our line which well nigh proved a success. The timely arrival of Gen. A. P. Hill, however, with fresh troops, entirely changed the fortune of the day, and after an obstinate contest, which lasted from six o'clock until dark, the enemy were driven into and across the river with great loss. During this fight, the Federals had succeeded in flanking and capturing a battery belonging, as I learn, to the brigade of Gen. Toombs. Instantly dismounting from his horse and placing himself at the head of his command, the General, in his effective way, briefly told them that the battery must be re-taken, if it cost the life of every man in his brigade, and then ordered them to follow him. Follow him they did into what seemed the very jaws of destruction, and after a short but fierce struggle they had the satisfaction of capturing the prize and restoring it to the original possessors.

A HISTORICAL FACT ABOUT BOMBARDMENTS.
THE CALIBRE OF A FLEET.

The following named steamers, under the chief command of Flag Officer David G. Farragut, made the attack on Forts St. Phillip and Jackson and the Confederate gunboats, at 3 A. M., 24th April, 1862:

Hartford, Richmond, Pensacola and Brooklyn, each carrying twenty-six 9 inch guns, two 80-pounder rifles, two 12-pounder howitzers, in their tops, which were protected by a bulkhead of boiler iron; Mississippi, nineteen 8-inch guns, two 12-pounder howitzers, in the tops; Varuna, eight 8-inch guns, four 32-pounders, (57 cwt.) two 80-pounder rifles, one 12-pounder howitzer; Oneida and Iroquois, each two 11-inch pivots, six 32-pounders, one 80-pounder rifle, one 12-pounder howitzer. The Pensacola and Brooklyn had each one 11-inch gun in addition to their other guns. The Westfield, Miami and Katahdin, each six guns, of which one was an 11-inch pivot, one 80-pounder rifle, four 32-pounders. Harriet Lane, six guns; Kittaning, nine guns; sailing sloop Portsmouth, sixteen 8-inch guns; two 80-pounder rifles, fourteen 8-inch guns; and four hundred men from the Colorado, unable to get over the bar, were divided amongst the squadron. The steam gun-boats

Pinola, Clifton, Cayuga, Itasca, Kennebec, Sciota, Kanawha, Owasko, Winona, Wissahickon, (widow Higgins.) Kinso, each carried one 11-inch pivot, one 20-pounder rifle, one 12-pounder howitzer, two 24-pounder howitzers. In addition was Porter's mortar fleet, numbering twenty-one vessels, each carrying one 13-inch mortar, two 32-pounders— 33 cwt. Total number of vessels, forty-eight. Total number of guns and mortars, 356, of which there were twenty 11-inch, one hundred and four 9-inch, forty-nine 8-inch, seventeen 30-pounder rifles, eleven 20-pounder rifles, eighty-four 32-pounder: the remainder being howitzers. These ships were manned by about six thousand men. Only thirteen vessels passed the forts during the battle; the remainder were driven back. Forts Jackson and St. Phillip mounted about two hundred guns, of which number nineteen twentieths were 32-pounders and 24-pounders. The Confederate gunboats numbered fourteen only, and carried forty-six guns. When the enemy's vessels passed the forts they were met by the gunboats, but the superiority of the enemy was so great that it was impossible to contend against them. The Louisiana, iron-clad, lay between the forts; so did the Manassas and McRae, leaving only a few little steamers to fight this immensely superior force. The U. S. steam sloop Verona was the only one of the enemy attacked and sunk.

THE BATTLE OF SHARPSBURG—APPEARANCE OF THE BATTLE FIELD—SAD PICTURES.

An army correspondent who visited the battle field of Sharpsburg after two days of bloody fighting, writes of the ghastly scene presented:

The horrid scene defied description. Like cords of wood the black, swollen bodies of the dead lie piled up one upon the other. The smell is perfectly unbearable and overpowering. Between the fences of a road to-day, in the space of one hundred yards long, I counted more than two hundred soldiers dead, lying where they fell. Over acres and acres they are strewn, singly, in groups, and sometimes in masses, piled up almost like cord-wood. They lie—some with the human form indistinguishable, others with no outward indication of where the life went out—in all the strange positions of violent death. All have blackened faces. There are forms with every rigid muscle strained in fierce agony, and those with hands folded peacefully upon the bosom, some still clutching their guns, others with arm upraised, and single open finger pointing to heaven. Several remained hanging over a fence which they were climbing when the fatal shot struck them. I saw the body of a soldier who was shot in the act of climbing a fence. It remained hanging where he was killed. Four balls had entered his back and one the side of his head.

It is strange what a difference there is in the composition of human bodies, with reference to the rapidity that change goes on after death. Several bodies of soldiers strewed the ground on the bank, in the vicinity of the bridge. They fought behind trees and fence-rail and stone-heap barricades, as many a bullet-mark in all these defences amply attested; but all that availed not to avert death from these poor creatures. They had been dead at least forty-eight hours when I looked at them. Almost all of them had become discolored in the face and much swollen; but there was one young man with his face as life-like, and even his eye so bright, it seemed almost impossible that he could be dead. It was the loveliest-looking corpse I ever beheld. He was a young man not 25, the soft, unshaved, brown beard hardly asserting yet the fullness of its owner's manhood. The features were too small, and the character of the face of too small and delicate an order to answer the requirements of masculine beauty. In death his eye was the clearest blue, and would not part with its surpassingly gentle, amiable, good and charming expression. The face was like a piece of wax, only that it surpassed any piece of wax-work.

One other young man, beardless but of brawnier type, furnished another example of slow decomposition. His face was not quite as life-like, still one could easily fancy him alive to see him any where else than on the field of carnage; and strange, his face wore an expression of mirth, as if he had just witnessed something amusing. A painful sight especially was the body of a soldier who had evidently died of his wounds, after lingering long enough at least to apply a handkerchief to his thigh himself, as a tourniquet to stop the bleeding. His comrades were obliged to leave him, and our surgeons and men had so much to do that they could not attend to him in time. Perhaps nothing would have saved him; but perhaps, again, a little surgical aid was all he needed. How long he dragged out his lessening pulse in pain no one can tell.

NOTES OF THE BATTLE OF CORINTH, MISS.

DARING OF GEN. W. L. CABELL.

On Saturday morning Cabell's brigade, of Maury's division, was ordered to charge the formidable fort on College Hill. They advanced unhesitatingly at a charge bayonets to within thirty yards of the position before they were fired upon, when they were awfully slaughtered. Still onward they went, after returning the fire, with their daring General at the head. When they reached the entrenchments Gen. Cabell boldly mounted the enemy's parapet, closely followed by his command. The first man he encountered was a Federal Colonel, who gave the command to kill that d—d rebel officer. Cabell replied by making a right cut with his sabre and placing the Yankee officer *hors du combat*. Although the brave brigade had gained the threshold of the enemy, a fire at a few yards, which nothing could withstand, compelled them to fall back with but a handful remaining of their courageous brigade, which came out of the three engagements with not more than 400 left uninjured. Gen. Cabell was afterwards injured by a fall from his horse. Major Jones, the former commandant of the post at Tupelo, was killed in the first charge on the entrenchments, while daringly leading his men to the charge. He was an officer young in years, and known for his ability and courage, and is lamented by the whole command.

GEN. GREEN BELIEVES HE WAS SHOT AT.

Brig. Gen. Green, of Missouri, commanding the second division, was one of the most prominent men upon the field. His own brigade was the first to enter Corinth, and penetrated as far as the Tishomingo Hotel. This was the critical moment of the day. This brigade, forming Price's centre, had surmounted all obstacles in their way, carrying entrenchment after entrenchment, until they found themselves in the centre of the enemy's position. Lovell was to have encountered the enemy on the left, and thus to have compelled a withdrawal of a portion of his forces from the centre, while Green continued to force their centre back. For some reason •which is not deemed altogether satisfactory, Lovell failed to do this, and the Federals threw their whole centre upon Green and compelled him to retire, after having at such enormous sacrifices gained the position. Prior to his forcing the enemy from their position, he sent an aid to Gen. Price, saying that there were heavy seige guns in front of him, which disputed his further progress. Price replied, "Then tell Gen. Green to take them:" and take them he did—there being thirty in number—but being forced to retire after gaining possession of them, he was obliged to relinquish this heavy armament to its original owners. One of Price's staff riding by, observed Gen. Green covered with gore from head to heels, and asked him if he had sustained any injury. He replied, that his horse had been shot in the neck, and dismounted to stop the flow of blood, when another bullet pierced the animal again, but without fatal effect. The General was attempting to staunch the wound, when still another ball struck his steed in the forehead, and which after a few convulsive plunges, caused his death. The bullets continued to pour hot and heavy, cutting of twigs and branches, and one scraped the skin off of Gen. Green's hip. He turned around to a bystander, and quietly remarked: "I believe those d—d scoundrels are trying to hit me!" If such was their intention, they certainly came as close to this brave officer as they possibly could without injuring him.

ACKNOWLEDGMENT OF CONFEDERATE BRAVERY.

It is the concurrent testimony of all who witnessed it, that the charge made by the head of the rebel column on our breastworks, on Saturday, has no parallel in this war for intrepid, obstinate courage, and none to excel it in history. I have conversed with many officers of all grades, who express this opinion, and make no attempt to conceal their admiration for the men and discipline that could face the murderous leaden storm of our forts and batteries; sweep across the field with closed ranks, despite the yawning gaps made by every discharge of our guns; and actually mount our works and plant their banners there, in the agonies of the death-struggle. The 2d Texas infantry, under Col. Rogers, lead the charge, and the Colonel himself fell on our breastworks, with the colors of his regiment in his hand. A piece of paper was found under his clothing, giving his name, age, rank, command, and the address of friends. After the battle but four of his entire regiment were left alive, and three of these were wounded and all taken prisoners. An officer who witnessed it declared he scarcely knew which to admire most: the daring bravery of the rebel troops, or the steady valor that repulsed and scattered them despite their determined and obstinate attack.

Instances of reckless and utter disregard of life were common in every quarter, in both armies, and it was literally a tug of war, in which each confessedly met a foeman worthy of his steel.

A HERO.

Gen. Van Dorn, while riding along the line on Friday, encountered a Missouri private with his face covered with blood and his hand pressed against his jaw. The General inquired if he was wounded and where he was going. He removed his hand, disclosing to sight a broken jaw, which he commenced working with his hand, and replied as distinctly as he could, in broken sentences, "Only got my jaw broke—they're giving 'em hell back there—be back again soon as can get face fixed up—just go down there and see what hell these Yanks are catching," and in half an hour afterwards, with bandaged face, he returned to his company to go with them through the balance of the bloody struggle.

THE MOST EXTRAORDINARY MARCHES ON RECORD.

The late marches of Gen. Stuart and of Gen. Pleasanton, as reported from Harrisburg (the first ninety-six miles in twenty-four hours and the last seventy-eight miles in the same time,) surpasses anything of military record. It is stated in Gen. Halleck's work on Military Art and Science that Cæsar marched the legions from Rome to the Sierra Morena, in Spain, at the rate of twenty leagues a day. In the campaign of 1800, Macdonald, wishing to prevent the escape of an enemy, in a single day marched forty miles crossing rivers and climbing mountains. Clausel, after the battle of Salamanca, retreated forty miles in twelve hours. In 1814, Napoleon, wishing to form a junction with other troops for the succor of Paris, marched his army the distance of seventy-five miles in thirty-six hours. On the day of the battle of Talavara, in Spain, Gen. Crawford, fearing that Wellington was hard pressed, made a forced march with three thousand men the distance of sixty-two miles in twenty-six hours. In 1803, Wellington's cavalry in India marched the distance of sixty miles in twenty-two hours.

It is said that the English cavalry under Lord Lake marched seventy miles in twenty-four hours.

The Kirby Smith brigade of cavalry during the late advance into Kentucky marched one hundred and sixty-five miles in seventy-four hours.

As a general rule, troops marching for many days in succession, will move at the rate of from fifteen to twenty miles per day. In forced marches, or in pursuit of a flying enemy, they will average from twenty to twenty-five miles a day. Only for two or three days in succession, with favorable roads, thirty miles a day may be calculated on. Where marches beyond this occur, they are the result of extraordinary circumstances.

A GRAPHIC SKETCH OF THE BATTLE OF MANASSAS——(FIRST BATTLE.)

Gen. Johnston had arrived the preceding day with about half of the force he had, detailed from Winchester, and was the senior officer in command. He magnanimously insisted, however, that Gen. Beauregard's previous plan should be carried out, and he was guided entirely by the judgment and superior local knowledge of the latter. While, therefore, Gen. Johnston was nominally in command, Beauregard was really the officer and hero of the day. You will be glad to learn that he was this day advanced from a Brigadier to the rank of a full General. But to the battle.

At half past six in the morning, the enemy opened fire from a battery planted on a hill beyond Bull Run, and nearly opposite the centre of our lines. The battery was intended merely to "beat the bush," and to occupy our attention, while he moved a heavy column towards the Stone Bridge, over the same creek, upon our left. At 10 o'clock, another battery was pushed forward, and opened fire a short distance to the left of the other, and near the road leading north to Centreville. This was a battery of rifled guns, and the object of its fire was the same as that of the other. They fired promiscuously into the woods and gorges on this, the southern, side of Bull Run, seeking to create the impression thereby that our centre would be attacked, and thus prevent us from sending reinforcements to our left, where the real attack was to be made. Beauregard was not deceived by the manœuvre.

It might not be amiss to say that Bull Run, or creek, is north of this place, and runs nearly due east, slightly curving around the Junction, the nearest part of which is about 2½ miles. The Stone Bridge is some seven miles distant, in a northwesterly direction, upon which our left wing rested. Mitchel's Ford is directly north, and distant four miles, by the road leading to Centreville, which is seven miles from the Junction. On our right is Marion Mills, on the same stream, where the Alexandria and Manassas Railroad crosses the Run, and distant four miles. Proceeding from Fairfax Court House, by Centreville, to Stone Bridge, the enemy passed in front of our entire line, but at a distance ranging from five to two miles.

At 9 o'clock, I reached an eminence nearly opposite the two batteries mentioned above, and which commanded a full view of the country for miles around, except on the right. From this point I could trace the movements of the approaching hosts by the clouds of dust that rose high above the surrounding hills. Our left, under Brigadier Generals Evans, Jackson and Cocke, and Col. Bartow, with the Georgia Brigade, composed of the 7th and 8th Regiments, had been put in motion, and was advancing upon the enemy with a force of about 15,000, while the enemy himself was advancing upon our left with a compact column of at least 50,000. His entire force on this side of the Potomac is estimated at 75,000. These approaching columns encountered each other at 11 o'clock.

Meanwhile, the two batteries in front kept up their fire

upon the wooded hill where they supposed our centre lay. They sent occasional balls from their rifled cannon to the eminence where your correspondent stood. Gens. Beauregard, Johnston and Bonham reached this point at 12 o'clock, and one of these balls passed directly over and very near them, and plunged into the ground a few paces from where I stood. I have the ball now, and hope to be able to show it to you at some future day. It is an eighteen pound ball, about 6 inches long. By the way, this thing of taking notes amidst a shower of shells and balls is more exciting than pleasant. At a quarter past 12 o'clock, Johnston and Beauregard galloped rapidly forward in the direction of Stone Bridge, where the ball had now fully opened. Your correspondent followed their example, and soon reached a position in front of the battle-field.

The artillery were the first to open fire, precisely at 11 o'clock. By 11½ the infantry had engaged, and there it was that the battle began to rage. The dusky columns which had thus far marked the approach of the two armies, now mingled with great clouds of smoke, as it rose from the flashing guns below, and the two shot up together like a huge pyramid of red and blue. The shock was as tremendous as were the odds between the two forces. With what anxious hearts did we watch that pyramid of smoke and dust. When it moved to the right we knew that the enemy were giving way; and when it moved to the left we knew that our friends were receding.

Twice the pyramid moved to the right, and as often returned. At last, about 2 o'clock, it began to move slowly to the left, and thus it continued to move for two mortal hours. The enemy was seeking to turn our left flank, and to reach the railroad leading hence in the direction of Winchester. To this, he extended his lines, which he was enabled to do by reason of his great numbers. This was unfortunate for us, as it required a corresponding extension of our own lines to prevent his extreme right from out flanking us—a movement on our part which weakened the

12

force of our resistance along the whole line of battle, which finally extended over a space of two miles. It also rendered it the more difficult to bring up reinforcements, as the further the enemy extended his right, the greater the distance our reserve forces had to travel to counteract the movement.

This effort to turn our flank was pressed with great determination for five long, weary hours, during which the tide of battle ebbed and flowed along the entire line with alternate fortunes. The enemy's column continued to stretch away to the left like a huge anaconda, seeking to envelope us within its mighty folds and crush us to death; and at one time it really looked as if he would succeed. But here let me pause to explain why it was our reinforcements were so late in arriving, and why a certain other important movement miscarried.

The moment he discovered the enemy's order of battle, Gen. Beauregard, it is said, dispatched orders to Gen. Ewell, on our extreme right, to move forward and turn his left or rear. At the same time he ordered Generals Jones, Longstreet and Bonham, occupying the centre of our lines, to co-operate in the movement, but not to move until Gen. Ewell had made the attack. The order to Gen. Ewell unfortunately miscarried. The others were delivered, but as the movements of the centre were to be regulated entirely by those on the right, nothing was done at all. Had the orders to Gen. Ewell been received and carried out, and our entire force brought upon the field, we should have destroyed the enemy's army almost literally. Attacked in front, on the flank and in the rear, he could not possibly have escaped, except at the loss of thousands of prisoners and all his batteries, while the field would have been strewed with his dead.

Finding that his orders had in some way failed to be executed, Gen. Beauregard at last ordered up a portion of the forces which were intended to co-operate with Gen. Ewell. It was late, however, before these reinforcements came up. Only one brigade reached the field before the battle was won. This was led by Gen. E. K. Smith, of Florida, formerly of the United States army, and was a part of Gen. Johnston's column from Winchester. They should have reached here the day before, but were prevented by an accident on the railroad. They dashed on the charge with loud shouts, and in the most gallant style. About the same time, Maj. Elzey, (formerly of the Augusta Arsenal, I may have his title wrong,) coming down the railroad from Winchester with the last of Johnston's brigades, and hearing the firing, immediately quit the train and struck across the country, and as a gracious fortune would have it, he encountered the extreme right of the enemy as he was feeling his way around our flank, and with his brigade struck him like a thunderbolt, full in the face. Finding he was about to be outflanked himself, the enemy gave way after the second fire. Meanwhile Beauregard rallied the centre and dashed into the very thickest of the fight, and after him rushed our own brave boys with a shout that seemed to shake the very earth. The result of this movement, from three distinct points, was to force back the enemy, who began to retreat, first in good order, and finally in much confusion. At this point the cavalry were ordered upon the pursuit. The retreat now became a perfect rout, and it is reported that the flying legions rushed past Centreville, in the direction of Fairfax, as if the earth had been opening behind them. It was when Gen. Beauregard led the final charge, that his horse was killed by a shell.

A STORY OF SHILOH.

"Brigadier General Gladden, of South Carolina, who was in Gen. Bragg's command, had his left arm shattered by a ball on the first day of the fight. Amputation was performed hastily by his staff surgeon on the field; and that instead of being taken to the rear for quiet and nursing, he mounted his horse, against the most earnest remonstrances of all his staff, and continued to command. On Monday he was again in the saddle, and kept it during the day; on Tuesday he rode on horseback to Corinth, twenty miles from the scene of action, and continued to discharge the duties of an officer. On Wednesday a second amputation near the shoulder was necessary, when Gen. Bragg sent an aid to ask if he would not be relieved of his command, to which he replied : " Give Gen. Bragg my compliments, and say that Gen. Gladden will only give up his command to go into his coffin." Against the remonstrances of his personal friends, and against the positive injunctions of the surgeons, he persisted in sitting up in his chair, receiving dispatches and giving directions, until Wednesday afternoon, when lockjaw seized him, and he died in a few moments.

NORAH McCARTEY.

A REMINISCENCE OF THE MISSOURI CAMPAIGN.

Thus far, Missouri has the better of other seats of hostility for the real romance of war. Most assuredly the fight there has been waged with fiercer earnest than almost anywhere else. The remote geography of the country, the rough, unhewn character of the people, the intensity and ferocity of the passions excited, and the general nature of the complicity reduced to a warfare essentially partizan and frontier, gave to its progress a wild aspect, peculiarly susceptible to deeds, and suggestive of thoughts, of romantic interest. None of these struck us more forcibly than the story of NORAH McCARTEY, the *Jeanie Deans* of the West.

She lived in the interior of Missouri—a little, pretty, black-eyed girl, with a soul as huge as a mountain, and a form as frail as a fairy's, and the courage and pluck of a buccaneer into the bargain. Her father was an old man—a secessionist. She had but a single brother, just growing from boyhood to youthhood, but sickly and lamed. The family had lived in Kansas during the troubles of '57, when Norah was a mere girl of fourteen, or thereabouts. But even then her beauty, wit and devil-may-care spirit were known far and wide; and many were the stories told along the border of her sayings and doings. Among other charges laid to her door, it is said she broke all the hearts of the young bloods far and wide, and tradition does even go so far as to assert that, like Bob Acres, she killed a man once a week, keeping a private church-yard for the purpose of decently burying her dead. Be this as it may, she was then, and is now, a dashing, fine looking, lively girl, and a prettier heroine than will be found in a novel, as will be seen if the good natured reader has a mind to follow us down to the bottom of this column.

Not long after the Federals came into her neighborhood, and, after they had forced her father to take the oath, which he did partly because he was a very old man, unable to take the field, and hoped thereby to save the security of his household, and partly because he could not help himself; not long after these two important events in the history of our heroine, a body of men marched up one evening, whilst she was on a visit to a neighbor's and arrested her sickly, weak brother, bearing him off to Leavenworth City, where he was lodged in the military guard-house.

It was nearly night before Norah reached home. When she did so, and discovered the outrage which had been perpetrated and the grief of her old father, her rage knew no bounds. Although the mists were falling and the night was closing in, dark and dreary, she ordered her horse to be re-saddled, put on a thick *surtout*, belted a sash round her waist, and sticking a pair of ivory-handled pistols in her bosom, started off after the soldiers. The post was many miles distant. But that she did not regard. Over hill, through marsh, under cover of the darkness, she galloped on to the headquarters of the enemy. At last the call of a sentry brought her to a stand, with a hoarse—

"Who goes there?"

"No matter," she replied, "I wish to see Col. Prince, your commanding officer, and instantly, too."

Somewhat awed by the presence of a young female on horseback at that late hour, and perhaps struck by her imperious tone of command, the Yankee guard, without hesitation, conducted her into the fortifications, and thence to the quarters of the Colonel commanding, with whom she was left alone.

"Well, madam," quoth the Yankee officer, with bland politeness, "to what have I the honor of this visit?"

"Is this Col. Prince?" replied the brave girl, quietly.

"It is, and yourself?"

"No matter. I have come here to inquire whether you have a lad by the name of McCartey a prisoner?"

"There is such a prisoner."

"May I ask, for why?"

"Certainly; for being suspected of treasonable connection with the enemy."

"*Treasonable* connection with the enemy! Why, the boy is sick and lame. He is besides my brother; and I have come to ask his immediate release."

The Yankee officer opened his eyes; was sorry he could not comply with the request of so winning a supplicant; and must really beg her to desist and leave the fortress."

"I *demand* his release," cried she, in reply.

"That you cannot have," returned he; "the boy is a rebel and a traitor, and unless you retire Madam, I shall be forced to arrest you on a similar suspicion."

"Suspicion! I *am* a rebel and a traitor too, if you wish. Young McCartey is my brother, and I don't leave this tent until he goes with me. Order his instant release, or," here she drew one of the aforesaid ivory-handles out of her bosom and levelled the muzzle of it directly at him, "I will put an ounce of lead in your brain. before you can call a single sentry to your relief."

A picture that!

There stood the heroic girl; eyes flashing fire. cheek glowing with earnest will, lips firmly set with resolution, and hand out-stretched with a loaded pistol ready to send the contents through the now thoroughly frightened, startled, aghast soldier, who cowered, like blank paper before flames, under her burning stare.

"Quick!" she repeated, "order his release, or you die."

It was too much. Prince could not stand it. He bade her lower her infernal weapon for God's sake, and the boy should be forthwith liberated.

"Give the order first," she replied, unmoved.

And the order was given: the lad was brought out; and drawing his arm in hers, the gallant sister marched out of the place, with one hand grasping one of his, and the other hold of her trusty ivory-handle. She mounted her horse, bade him get up behind, and rode off, reaching home without accident before midnight.

Now that is a fact stranger than fiction. which shows what sort of metal is in our women of the much abused and traduced nineteenth century.

AN INSTANCE OF INTREPIDITY.

A correspondent communicates the following incident of the battle at Gaines' Mill:

James Harrison, a brave and stalwart private of Company D, 4th Alabama regiment, whilst charging the enemy's battery at Gaines' Mill, discovering that his officers had, by some inexplicable means become separated from their con-mand, rushed forward in advance of his regiment, shouting to his comrades to follow him. Encountering a deep ditch, whose bottom was overgrown with tall weeds, he sprang across it. The earth on the opposite side gave way beneath him, and he landed upright amidst what seemed, to his astonished gaze, a host of live Yankees. One, more alive or less panic-stricken than the rest, clambered up the side of the ditch, and had reached the level ground, when a ball from Harrison's trusty musket, laid him a bleeding, mangled corpse at his captor's feet. Drawing his revolver, and demanding instant surrender, a thrilling cry for mercy burst from a score of the trembling miscreants. Mounting the bank, he commanded them to follow him. Again, with ashy lips and pallid cheeks, they begged permission to remain in their hiding place. Regardless of their craven supplications, he marched them toward the rear, and surrendering them to the first officer he met, again dashed into the thickest of the fray, and aided in driving the enemy with ignominy from the intrenchments, which, if defended by strong hands and stout hearts, were almost impregnable.

BATTLE OF CEDAR RUN, VA.

A participant in the engagement gives a lively description of a hand-to-hand conflict between one of the Confederate and one of the Federal regiments. The former advanced rapidly upon the latter; neither fired a gun, though each had an equal advantage to pour a destructive volley into one another's ranks before they closed. In a few moments their bayonets were crossed, and the struggle commenced. Each man seemed to have his match, and here and there, amid the clash of arms, one man would fall, pierced through the heart. Around them the battle was raging. Volley after volley of musketry, and boom after boom of artillery, echoed amid the hills. Yet they fought on with cold steel, as if determined only to crimson their bayonets in one another's blood. But scarcely fifteen minutes had elapsed before the Federal front began to waver, and our men taking advantage of the indication, redoubled their energies, and rushed amid them with unparalleled impetuosity. The enemy broke and fell into confusion, and the Confederates, now uncontrollable, dashed upon them, and left scarcely one in the entire Federal regiment "to tell the tale."

INDEX.

APPENDIX.

(*Diary of the War, Continued from Page* 107.)

November 16th. Fight at Bolivar Point, Texas. A party of Yankees attempted to land and were fired on, and driven back with a loss of five killed and wounded.

November 27-28. Battle of Cave Hill or Prairie Grove, Benton county, Ark. The Confederates under Gen. Hindman, repulsed the enemy, winning a decided victory after two days hard fighting. Confederate loss 850 killed, wounded and missing. Federal loss, 985 killed and wounded and 300 taken prisoners.

November 28, 29. Skirmishing at Holly Springs, Miss. Confederates forced to retreat, with a loss of 5 killed. Enemy's loss, 18 killed.

Nov. 29–Dec. 1 Fighting near Abbeville, Miss The Confederates compelled to fall back before an overwhelming force of the enemy. Considerable loss on both sides. The Confederates fall back beyond the Tallahatchie River.

December 1st. Great bombardment at Galveston, Texas. Several citizens killed and wounded.

December 1st. Fight at Snickersville Gap, Va. The Abolitionists routed after a severe contest, and 9 killed. Confederate loss 7 killed and 18 taken prisoners.

December 2. A party of Confederate cavalry made a dash into a Yankee camp in Westmoreland county, Va., and captured 48 prisoners, and destroyed their camps and stores.

The Democrats carried the late election in New York by 12,000 majority Republicanism rebuked.

December 3. The Yankees entered Winchester, Va., and retired before the Confederate forces sent to give them battle.

December 3. Fight at mouth of San Bernard River, Texas. A large force of Abolitionists were surprised and routed with considerable loss on the part of the enemy.....Skirmish at Bird's Mill, Tenn......48 Yankees captured on the Rappahannock.

December 3-4. Skirmishing near Oxford, Miss. Abolitionists repulsed in several brisk engagements. Confederate loss, 3 killed.

December 4. Bombardment of Port Royal, Va The enemy repulsed.

their gunboats damaged by our batteries.....Attack on St. Marks, Fla. The enemy repulsed.

December 3--4. Fighting at Walter Valley, Miss. Confederates defeated with considerable loss. A large amount of Confederate stores and money captured by the enemy. Federal loss 20 killed and wounded.

December 4. Skirmish near Tuscumbia, Ala. Confederates taken by surprise and 70 captured as prisoners. Federal loss 9 killed and 22 wounded.

December 5--6. Battle of Coffeeville, Miss. A desperate fight took place, in which the Abolition army were completely defeated and checked in their invasion of Mississippi. Confederate loss 19 killed and 40 wounded, and 100 taken prisoners. Federal loss, 25 killed, 82 wounded and 10 taken prisoners.

December 7. Skirmish near Oakland, Miss. The Abolition army commanded by Gens. Navey and Steele, is repulsed by Whitfield's cavalry, and driven back.

Dec. 7. Claiborne F. Jackson, Governor of Missouri, died near Little Rock, Arkansas.

December 7. The Yankee transport Lake City captured at Carson's Landing, Mississippi river.

December 7. Battle of Hartsville, Tenn. Gen. Morgan accomplishes a most brilliant victory over the Abolitionists, defeating them and taking the entire garrison. Federal loss, 100 killed, 300 wounded and 2,104 taken prisoners. Confederate loss 130 killed and wounded.

December 7. Fight at Prestonburg, Ky. Abolitionists defeated and put to rout by Col. Clarkson, 100 taken prisoners, 90 killed and wounded, and large quantities of stores taken. Confederate loss, 4 killed and 9 wounded.

December 8th. Gen. Floyd surprises the enemy at Piketon, Ky, and captures the place; over 100 Yankees killed; large amount of stores captured.

December 10. Battle of Plymouth, Va. The Federals defeated and driven from the town, 25 taken prisoners. Confederate loss, 7 wounded.

December 12. The Federal iron-clad ram Cairo, the flag-boat of the Yankee fleet, was blown up by torpedoes, in the Yazoo river, Mississippi. Over 100 lives lost.

December 11. The Yankees repulsed in their first attempt to cross the Rappahannock.

December 12. Skirmish near Kingston, N. C. Confederates defeated.

December 12. Fight at Joyner's Ford, Washington river, Va. Confederate cavalry surprised and 35 captured prisoners.

December 13. Skirmish at Ellis' Ferry, Va. Abolitionists routed with heavy loss.

December 11. Skirmish near Tuscumbia, Ala. Confederates repulsed, and 20 killed and wounded. Federal loss, 30 killed and wounded.

December 13--14. Battle of Fredericksburg, Va. In this, the most bloody battle of the war, the Federal army under Gen. Burnside, was most signally repulsed and defeated by Gen. Lee. Federal loss, 10,000 killed, 8,500 wounded, and 1,626 taken prisoners. Confederate loss, 400 killed, 2,500 wounded, and 476 missing. Generals Cobb and Gregg killed, of the Confederates.

The Yankee attempts to capture Richmond, now numbering four, have cost them at least 125,000 men. Beginning with the first Manassas battle, and going through McClellan's fatal campaign in the Peninsula, Jackson's week of fighting in the Valley, Lee's hurling back of the Pope expedition, including the second battle of Manassas, and now the slaughter on the Rappahannock, we have an amount of carnage that ought to satisfy even Black Republicans.

December 13--14. Battle of Kingston, N C. Confederates repulsed, and fell back before an overwhelming force.

December 16. Battle of Whitehall, N C, Confederates defeated. After occupying Kingston for a short time, the Federals evacuated the place, which was again taken possession of by the Confederates. Federal loss, 845 killed and wounded. Total Confederate loss in the several battles was 71 killed, 286 wounded, and 400 missing.

December 12- 16. President Davis visits Tennessee and Mississippi.

December 17. Battle near Goldsboro, N C. The Federals repulsed, and driven back after a severe engagement.

December 18. General Lovel is removed from the Army of the West, and sent to Virginia. Gen Loring takes his place. Gen Van Dorn is appointed to take command of the cavalry forces in the West.

December 18--19. General Grant's Abolition Army falls back from Mississippi.

December 15--16. Gen Burnside recrosses the Rappahannock river, Va., under cover of night, after the desperate battle of Fredericksburg.

December 16. Gen. Banks, with 8,000 men, arrives at New Orleans, La, and supercedes the ' Brute Butler," who is sent North.

December 18. Brigadier General J K Duncan died in Knoxville, Tenn.

December 17--18. Gen Forrest annoys the Federals in West Tennessee, destroys railroad bridges and Federal property, and captures several towns in his successful raids.

December 18. Skirmish at Lexington, Tenn. Gen. Forest surprised the Yankees ; a sharp fight took place in which 400 of the enemy were killed and wounded. Confederate loss 120 killed and wounded.

December —. Van Buren, Arkansas, captured by the Federals. Large amounts of Confederate property destroyed.

December 20 The Thirty-Eighth Georgia Regiment numbered 1100 men when they left home for the War in Virginia. They lost in killed and wounded 564 men (not counting those having died from sickness and disease) in the various battles in which they have been engaged.

December 20. Yankee transports fired on near Newbern, N C. fifty killed and wounded. General Wheeler drives in the Yankee pickets at Newbern. •

December 20. A large force of Abolitionists, under General Millroy, are devastating the country in the Virginia valley. Confederate property stolen. People maltreated.

December 20. Great trouble in the Lincoln Cabinet at Washington Seward threatens to resign. The Yankee papers admit the slaughter of their men at Fredericksburg to be unparalleled.

December 20. Gen. Van Dorn surprises the Yankee garrison at Holly Springs, and captures the place after a brisk fight. 1,950 Yankees taken prisoners: $6,000,000 worth of Federal stores and property destroyed by the Confederates. Federal loss 250 killed and wounded Confederate loss 15 killed and wounded.

December 21. Fight on the Franklin Pike, Tennessee Federals routed with considerable loss. Confederate loss 2 killed and 4 wounded

December 21. Skirmish at Davis Mills, Mississippi, Gen Van Dorn s cavalry engages the Yankees; after a severe fight, the Confederates were defeated with a loss of 65 killed and wounded. Federal loss 83 killed and wounded.

December 22. An Abolition election going on at Isle of Wight Court House, was broken up by the Confederates. Several killed on both sides. President Davis issues his proclamation proscribing Butler as a felon

December 23. General Buckner takes command at Mobile, Ala.

December 24. Fighting at Glasgow, Ky. General Morgan routes the enemy, killing a large number. 3 Confederates killed.

December 24--25. Gen Rosecranz with 35,000 men advances from Nashville. Severe skirmishing continues near Lavergne, Tennessee The Confederates fall back, A great battle imminent.

* December 24--25 A party of Yankees make a successful raid into Louisiana, on the line of the Shreveport and Vicksburg Railroad; they burn bridges and commit depredations in several towns on the Road.

December 26. General J E B Stuart accomplishes another successful raid in the rear of the Federal army, destroys large amounts of Federal property, and captures 180 prisoners.

December 26--27. Heavy skirmishing near Triune and Lavergne, Tenn.

December 26. The Federals land a large force at Baton Rouge, La. Gen. Banks establishes his headquarters there. The Yankees burn the State House and destroy all Confederate property. Skirmishing on the Yazoo River, Miss. Yankees repulsed and driven to their gunboats.

December 28--29--30. Battle of Chickasaw Bayou, near Vicksburg, Miss. The Yankees most signally defeated and put to route after three days' hard fighting. Enemy's loss 1,000 killed and wounded, and 400 taken prisoners. Confederate loss 170 killed and wounded.

December 29 A large force of Yankee cavalry make a successful raid into East Tennessee, destroy several bridges. Fight at Watauga Bridge, Tenn. Confederates surprised, and 112 men captured by the enemy; several killed and wounded on both sides.

December 30. The great Federal gunboat Monitor foundered at sea.

Several of the Yankee fleet of gunboats sunk.

December 28.. High prices. At an auction sale in Mississippi, flour was sold at $102 per barrel. Gold is selling at 300 per cent. premium. Cotton sold in New York city at 70 cents per pound. Sugar in Richmond, Va., is worth 70 cents per pound; Coffee $3.95 per pound. Cotton Cards, $25 per pair.

December 29. Skirmish at Baton Rouge, La. Confederates repulsed.

December 31—January 1-2, 1863. Battle of Murfreesboro, Tenn, Skirmishing as a prelude to the great battle commenced on December 26. The Confederate force under command of Gen. Bragg, numbered 30,000 men. The Federal force under Gen Rosecranz numbered 50,000 men. The hardest fight took place on the 31st. The Federals were repulsed and retired from the field with terrible loss. On the 1st of January the Federals were largely reinforced, and the battle renewed, and continued until the evening of the 2d. The Confederates being greatly outnumbered, fell back to secure a better position. The enemy were unable to follow. The Confederates captured 4,000 prisoners, a large number of cannon, stores, &c., taken from the enemy. Confederate loss, 9,000 killed and wounded; Federal loss, 15,000 killed and wounded, 4,000 taken prisoners.

January 1st, 1863. Engagement in Galveston Bay, Texas. The Yankees defeated, the steamer "Harriet Lane" captured. Several Yankee gunboats blown up to prevent their capture. Several killed on both sides. 600 Yankees taken prisoners.

January 1, 1863. An estimate of the killed, wounded and missing from the commencement of the war to the present time:

Federals Killed	43,874	Confederates Killed.	20,893
Federals Wounded	97,029	Confederates Wounded	59,615
Federal Prisoners	68,213	Confederate Prisoners	22,169
Total	209,116	Total	102,677
Died from sickness, disease and wounds	250,000	Died from sickness, disease and wounds	120,000